MW01436918

At Risk of Being a FOOL

At Risk of Being a FOOL

Jeanette Cottrell

Five Star • Waterville, Maine

Copyright © 2005 by Jeanette Cottrell

All rights reserved.

This novel is a work of fiction. Names, characters, places and incidents are either the product of the author's imagination, or, if real, used fictitiously.

No part of this book may be reproduced or transmitted in any form or by any electronic or mechanical means, including photocopying, recording or by any information storage and retrieval system, without the express written permission of the publisher, except where permitted by law.

First Edition
First Printing: July 2005

Published in 2005 in conjunction with
Tekno Books and Ed Gorman.

Set in 11 pt. Plantin.

Printed in the United States on permanent paper.

Library of Congress Cataloging-in-Publication Data

Cottrell, Jeanette.
    At risk of being a fool / by Jeanette Cottrell.—1st ed.
      p. cm.
    ISBN 1-59414-292-0 (hc : alk. paper)
    1. Women teachers—Fiction.   2. Retired teachers—Fiction.   3. Tutors and tutoring—Fiction.   4. Memory disorders in old age—Fiction.   5. Juvenile delinquents—Fiction.   6. Salem (Or.)—Fiction.   I. Title.
    PS3603.O87A94 2005
     813'.6—dc22   2005006642

With love to my sisters:

Susan Katie O'Brien, whose lively correspondence has been an anchor in my life for decades;

and Jennie Lynn Cottrell, whose loving care for our father has earned her a permanent place on the family's Angel List.

Acknowledgments

This book has many roots. In particular, I treasured my year of teaching in Youth Development, Inc.'s GED Program, of Albuquerque, New Mexico. Thanks also to Mary Ann Caldwell for her kindly shepherding. Mary Ann: I borrowed your initials for Mackie Sandoval's name.

I offer my sincere gratitude to the Nightingale Lane Memory Loss Facility of Arvada, Colorado, and Channel Point Village of Hoquiam, Washington. You gave my father's final years the safety and dignity he sorely needed.

Last but not least, I greatly appreciate the time and efforts of three people in the writing world who gave me the benefit of their knowledgeable eyes and willing hearts: C. J. Hannah, Monty Montee, and the late Fay Robinson. It's difficult to believe I never met any of you except online, but I sure know those critiques! Ouch! And thank you!

ONE

A human tornado barreled across the parking lot. Jeanie McCoy, sitting behind her steering wheel, enjoyed the spectacle. Sorrel Quintana, the tornado, looked like a model for an arcade game heroine, with a lush figure, smoldering eyes, her every motion a symphony of controlled mayhem. Jeanie's young grandson was enamored of such games. She wondered what Andy would make of Sorrel Quintana. Probably, he'd drool at a safe distance, peering around the edge of a dumpster. Andy was a child of great good sense. Sorrel, on the other hand—

The car door flew open, and Sorrel landed on the seat with a thud, yanking the door closed an instant later. Jeanie noted the flushed cheeks and the quick rise and fall of her chest, and mentally backed off a pace.

"Good," she said. "I'm glad you found me."

"Can we get the hell out of here?" Sorrel set her electric-green vinyl purse against her thigh and snapped the safety belt in one smooth motion. She glared at the industrial gray building hulking in front of the car. "God, he's a bastard." Randy Firman, Sorrel's parole officer, had an office tucked into gray stone anonymity scarcely a mile from the Oregon Capitol building.

"Hmmm," said Jeanie. "Sorry you had a rough time." The newspaper crumpled under Sorrel's shifting feet. "Let me get that out of your way."

Sorrel snatched the paper. "I've got it." She shrugged herself into the corner against the door, half-facing Jeanie.

The newspaper rustled, trapped under Sorrel's lap belt. "Can we just go?" She caught Jeanie's glance at the newspaper, and yanked it loose. "I'm folding it, all right? You happy?"

"Yes, thank you." Jeanie drove out of the parking lot, heading north. She glanced at Sorrel, wondering how much classwork she'd manage to get out of the girl today. Not much, likely.

"What are you staring at?"

"I was admiring your fingernails." Thirty years of teaching had taught Jeanie McCoy a thing or two. Indirection and small surprises worked better than confrontation. And they were nice nails, perfectly shaped, probably glued on yesterday: Revlon's finest, coated with poisonous green. Sorrel's blouse, artfully decorated with large green sequins, spilled open in front, displaying an impressive cleavage. Darker green shadowed her eyes, shining with something indefinable, picking up the gloss of her raven-black hair. The earrings twirled lightly, a lacquered fantasia in green and bronze. How did she manage the artful effects under the rigors of life at Bright Futures Transition Facility for Girls? She must stash makeup everywhere: at school, in the van, and at work. Certainly, the buttons came undone in the step from the Bright Futures' van to the sidewalk.

Jeanie ruffled her own short white hair, still spattered with its original brown. "Your sense of style is better than mine ever was." Sorrel's face softened. The two bright spots in her cheeks faded. Mentally, Jeanie gave herself a point for defusing tension. Kherra had been right. Coaching students through their General Equivalency Diplomas, or GEDs, was infinitely preferable to sitting around the house, fretting about Edward. "Just toss the paper in the back. Sorrel?"

Sorrel's eyes were riveted on the paper.

At Risk of Being a Fool

"Sorrel, is there a problem?"

"No," Sorrel said, a small strangled sound. Her reddened cheeks flushed deeply, then went sheet-white. She threw the paper into the back seat, flipped down the visor, and groped through her purse for lipstick.

Jeanie turned into a narrow parking lot behind the pink stucco building. The administrative offices that housed the GED school were a conglomerate of public services and cheaply rented professional offices. The two-story building, painted an incongruous pink with white trim, always reminded Jeanie of a petrified birthday cake.

"Sorrel, are you all right? You look ill."

"I'm fine." Sorrel scrabbled her makeup together. She jumped out the door while the car was still rolling, and fled to the doorway.

Jeanie slammed on the brakes. She'd probably run to the bathroom, to rebuild her armor in front of a larger mirror. Sorrel's rages were legendary, but she hadn't looked mad just now. She'd looked scared. Jeanie retrieved the newspaper, trying to steel her heart against her protective instinct. She'd fought the same battle on a daily basis for thirty years. She nearly always failed.

Jeanie scanned the paper, still opened to the third page. After skimming interviews with legislators explaining a third round of social service budget cuts, she found the small article.

EXPLOSION ON CONSTRUCTION SITE

Salem, Oregon. An explosion at a north central Salem construction site critically wounded one man as a homemade explosive device exploded at five forty-five p.m. last evening. The blast severely injured Bryce Wogan and partially destroyed a truck owned by

Delancey Brothers Contractors.

The victim was found by Daniel Rivera, assistant foreman, and rushed to the Salem Hospital, where he is reported to be in critical condition. Police are conducting investigations. The work crew includes at least one minor presently engaged in a work-release program through Youth Authority. Delancey Brothers Contractors has offered a reward for information leading to the conviction of the person or persons responsible.

Jeanie's eyes flew open wide. Delancey Brothers was one of the school's business partners. And the "minor engaged in a work-release program" was Quinto, her spray-paint king. Ever since Mackie landed the job for him, all he could talk about was the construction site, and the "way cool" Mr. Rivera. And naturally, the newspaper jumped right onto him, prating about Oregon Youth Authority. Wouldn't you know they'd pinpoint any teenager they could lay hands on, however vaguely connected? They always did it, and rarely trumpeted the teen's innocence once proved.

She grimaced at her leap of faith, denying logic. Teachers resisted thinking evil of their students. Sometimes, their apparent blindness made them look like hens fluttering sheltering wings over a nest full of buzzards. It was only natural for the media to jump on the connection, and of course the police would do the same. But she hated the instant assumption that an adolescent in trouble was the automatic suspect in the next crime occurring nearby. She understood it, but she hated it.

Poor Quinto. He'd be devastated. Even if he knew nothing, he'd be running scared. But why was Sorrel afraid, too? The article really threw her for a loop.

At Risk of Being a Fool

An engine rumbled to a stop parallel to the street curb. Mr. Matthews, the usual driver for the Dandridge House Residential Transition Facility for Boys, saw her when he was halfway out of the van's driver's seat. He raised a hand and heaved his perspiring bulk back into the seat, growling warnings to the three heads in the back seats.

The van's side door opened and slammed shut. Quinto walked towards the building, his head hanging. Galvanized, she stepped fast to catch up with him.

Twenty minutes later, she meditated her approach while watching Quinto from the corner of her eye. He'd given her a hunted look, sidled into the room, and found a chair with its back to the wall. By the time she engaged her other students in some semblance of study, he'd covered his paper with frantic sketches and flipped the paper to the other side. She'd give him another five minutes, she decided, before trying to get any work out of him. Thirty years of experience had honed her reflexes, keeping students engaged and relatively contented. Now, however, those reflexes tripped her constantly. She'd had less than a month to unlearn thirty years of habits. She felt like a first-year teacher again. This batch of kids certainly kept her hopping.

The problem must be my nose, Jeanie McCoy reflected.

First, her uneducated nose had stumbled over Brynna. At nineteen, Brynna looked like a lost waif, a deceiving appearance for a girl with a razor-like tongue and the soul of a vampire. Biding her time, waiting for a chance to build rapport, Jeanie had seized on a perfect opportunity. Brynna had walked in smelling of sweet musk. Jeanie McCoy chirped, "New perfume, huh, Brynna? Interesting, what's the brand?"

How on earth, in all those years, had she missed the

marijuana-recognition courses? Why hadn't any of the trainers at the in-services brought marijuana for all the goody-two-shoes to sniff? Books on eye dilation and behavioral changes only went so far. Now *there* was a thought. Scratch-and-sniff books for educators: *The Dummy's Guide to Marijuana, Hashish, and Aerosols.*

Jeanie followed this performance by tripping over a drug dealer down the street and wishing him an expansive good morning. Later she mistook a small sack of leaves in the office for tea leaves and audibly mourned the lack of hot water.

About then, the kids decided she was putting them on. No one could be that naïve. She'd wound up with a backhanded reputation for a jaded sort of street smarts. Quinto, in fact, had been admiring.

"That Jeanie, she's some wicked joker."

After that, "tea leaves" no longer appeared in the office and tricks died to a minimum. Nowadays, three weeks into class, she only contended with daily pandemonium.

Jeanie McCoy, the wicked joker, aged fifty-eight, twisted her wedding ring and looked over her tiny kingdom with resigned frustration. There were six students, all between seventeen and twenty-one. Sorrel Quintana, Dillon Henley, Rosalie Perea, Tonio Valenzuela, Brynna Gallagher, and Joaquin a.k.a. Quinto Cervantes. All of them had criminal records for drugs, vandalism, and in two cases assault with intent. They worked in the mornings at various jobs, laboriously lined up by the inexhaustible Miss Mackie Sandoval. In the afternoons, they attended class with Jeanie, studying for the GED exams.

Silently, she recited her mental tags: Sorrel, the Amazon; Dillon, the wolf; Rosalie, the random; Tonio, the still waters; Brynna, the vampire; Quinto, the artist.

At Risk of Being a Fool

"Dillon, how's it going?" she said to the "timber wolf" at the corner desk. Dillon had perfectly-waved brown hair and a Dick Tracy jaw on a face that stopped showing expression years before.

"Percentages are a load of crap," muttered Dillon.

"A startling number of people agree with you," she said, settling next to him. She demonstrated the technique again. Dillon tolerated education in five-minute spurts and no more. If she stayed near him beyond that, he jumped out of his seat to pace the floor. Like a wolf, he had a predatory look, rippling and hypnotic. She'd met hundreds of braggarts and show-offs, mouthy teenagers with heavy crusts and custard-cream fillings. Dillon, she knew instinctively, was for real.

A swish of color caught her eye. Rosalie flitted through the room. Like an exotic hummingbird, she chose to light on whatever object took her fancy. "Rosalie, back to your seat."

"Sure." Rosalie wandered in the general direction of her chair. "Hey, Quinto, that's pretty." Rosalie's fingers brushed his paper lightly.

"Yeah," Quinto said. Under his hands, a rose bloomed in exquisite perfection. Usually, he drew faces. Rosalie's thin, haggard beauty peered from many corners of his papers. Dillon's face graced others, unmistakable threat clear in the angle of his head, the tension in his jaw. Quinto's eye was far faster than his brain. The toe of his shoe tapped restlessly. Only his hand moved quickly and surely.

A phone rang. Dillon pulled the tiny phone out of his coat pocket and flipped it open. "It's me," he said, as he'd said countless times in the last few weeks, sometimes several times in an afternoon. His eyes still on the math book, he held out the phone. Jeanie took it.

"Hi, Randy, it's Jeanie McCoy. He's here." Her eyes traveled to the clock over the door. "Yes, on the dot. He's working just fine. What? Oh. Yes, I got Sorrel, no problem." She switched off the phone, and set it on the desk. It was handy having Randy Firman as parole officer to both Dillon and Sorrel, though she doubted they'd agree. "Sorrel, put the mirror away."

Sorrel threw her an open-mouthed look of contempt. "In a minute, woman."

"It's 'Jeanie,' not 'woman.' "

"All right, all right, girl. Jeanie."

Brynna snickered. Without looking, Jeanie knew Brynna wore the look of sly pleasure that ate at Sorrel like water torture. Drip, drip, drip. *Brynna, you'll be the death of me,* Jeanie thought. Envy was part of the equation. Sorrel's colorful extravagance suited her. Brynna's surreptitious attempts along the same line only made her look like a hooker on the prowl.

She sidestepped, shielding Sorrel from Brynna's vulture act. Sorrel's eyes dropped. Jeanie didn't rush her. Slowly, I-was-about-to-do-this-anyway, you're-not-pushing-me, Sorrel put away the mirror. She stood and stretched elaborately, sank back down, crossed her legs, and pulled her book closer.

"So Brynna," said Jeanie, "can I snitch a pretzel from you?"

Startled, Brynna shoved the bag over. Jeanie slipped out a broken pretzel and slapped the bag shut, as though trapping a mouse. "Have to move fast," she whispered, "so the calories don't get out."

Brynna's wide-eyed look faded perceptibly. The ghost of a chuckle escaped. Jeanie winked as she left, drawn by Quinto's unnatural silence. She drew up a chair next to him. If she'd been in her high school classroom, with a student obviously upset, she'd have opened with a casual punch on the shoulder. Not here, though. Mackie had drilled her on that during those first watchful days. *Never touch. Not ever.*

"Hey, Quinto. I heard there was some trouble at your work site. Are you doing okay?"

His hand jerked. Seeming to move by itself, his hand shaded a rose petal. "Hmm." A thorn sprouted from the rose's stem, sharp and deadly.

"Mackie said you were doing really well there. She's proud of you."

Quinto's face lightened. "Yeah, I done real good, Mr. Rivera said. Even the boss, the big guy." Earnestly, Quinto's eyes sought hers. "Only now, I can't go for a while, 'cause the boss, Mr. Wogan, he got hurt real bad."

"Yes, I read about that in the paper. An explosion?"

His voice dropped. "Pipe bomb, cops said. He's hurt bad. One of his eyes got ripped out, and his hands are all—well, you know."

"I'm so sorry, Quinto. It must have been a terrible shock. Were you there when it happened?"

"No. It was right after I left. See, Mr. Matthews, he comes for me every day, to take me back to the House." The rose sprouted thorns, dark and savage. Drops of blood dripped from them. "Pipe bombs, they're really bad, 'cause they stick nails and stuff in them and they all go flying." From the side of the rose, a nail shot out. Another arched higher. A third spiked into an unidentifiable mass, possibly human.

Quinto's face twisted. He threw the pencil across the room and sent the wadded paper after it. He buried his face in his arms. "Some of the guys thought he was mean, but he

17

wasn't so bad," he said, voice muffled and cracked. "He was getting to like me, said I done good. It really means something, you know, when a guy like that says it. I was so happy when I left work, told Mr. Matthews all about it. And then, later on, the cops come."

"Quinto." Jeanie's hand edged out to touch him on the arm. She snatched it back. *Never touch.* "Quinto, I'm so sorry. Do you want to make a card for him or something? Send one of your drawings to the hospital, so he knows how you feel?"

"The cops think I done it."

"They do not! Quinto, don't you even *say* such a thing."

"I worked there, I'm in a gang. I mean, I was in a gang."

"Quinto, you're in the House now. You're under someone's eye all day long. The police know that. How could you possibly build a pipe bomb?"

Quinto raised his head. The tear-streaked face looked oddly wise. "Shit, Jeanie, it don't take nothing but a phone call to get a pipe bomb. There's phones everywhere. I could of done it. Two minutes, that's all."

"I guess I'm out of touch."

Quinto snorted softly. His half-smile pulled at her. "Hey, like that's news? They think somebody brung it over, and I hid it by the truck. But I didn't. Nobody touches that truck but Mr. Wogan. I did once, the first day, see, and he had a fit. Damn, I thought he was gonna hit me, or something, but it was just, you know, Mr. Rivera, he said Mr. Wogan really liked that truck a lot."

"Quinto, you're a graffiti artist, a shoplifter, but you're not violent. The police know that."

"Yeah. I couldn't hurt nobody. I don't got the balls for that."

"It's not a matter of balls, Quinto."

At Risk of Being a Fool

The aged eyes in the childish face studied her pityingly. "Yeah, well. Mr. Maldonado, you know, the supervisor at Dandridge? He told the cops that, they looked up my record. Mr. Rivera, he talked for me too, said how Mr. Wogan was okay with me. I ain't got no *reason* to do that stuff. I mean, I got me a *job* there, when I get out the House, you know? Like I'm going to throw that away?"

"Of course not, Quinto."

"Of course not, Quinto," mimicked Brynna. "Like Quinto gives a shit about that son-of-a-bitch."

Quinto shied back, edging his chair another foot or two from Brynna. He clamped his mouth shut, snatched up another sheet of paper, and sketched a battered truck as if his life depended on it.

"Brynna, hush. This is a private conversation."

Brynna rolled her eyes. "Jeanie, get real, would you? Wogan was a first-class bastard, sticking his damned nose into everything, a real prick. Ask Dillon, he worked there last summer, until Wogan—"

"Shut up," said Dillon, his voice flat.

Brynna cut her eyes at Dillon, and took another tack. "Quinto don't care nothing about no job. Nine to five, work your guts out—"

Sorrel's voice stabbed the air. "Leave Quinto alone, bitch."

Oh no, they were back on the merry-go-round again. Jeanie jumped out of her seat. She should have seen it coming. Consciously or not, Sorrel had decided to drown her fears in rage.

"Who you calling a bitch, bitch?"

"Stop it," Jeanie yelled over the screams. She waved her arms. She'd broken up fights in the high school by walking between the combatants, putting an arm around one and

19

literally walking him away. Try it here? Fat chance. Sorrel or Brynna, either one, would view it as an assault or a deep insult.

Sorrel slapped the desk and threw out one hand, middle finger rigidly extended. "Fuck you, whore. If I had me a knife—Bitchmeat!" She writhed in her seat, but stayed in it, as though riveted into place. Fear of the State Detention Facility fueled the restraint. Sorrel was maddening, but she wasn't stupid. Not at all.

"Yeah, like you did that one guy?" spat Brynna. "You fucking bitch, need a knife to get tough, huh? Or a pipe bomb, maybe, like your boyfriend? Well tough shit, slut. All you got is your hands. Come at me, why don't you?" Brynna also remained plastered to her chair.

Jeanie grabbed a portable room divider and yanked it between the girls. The classroom had come equipped with several, a fact for which she frequently thanked God and Mackie Sandoval. Mackie had scrounged them when a state office revamped its cubicle farm.

Dillon seemed amused. "Let 'em fight, for God's sake."

"Oh, hush up," Jeanie snapped.

Dillon's mouth shut and his eyes narrowed to slits. Snake eyes, just what she needed. Jeanie ignored him, zipping her own mouth closed before she said anything worse. Soon, rules or not, the girls would be rolling on the floor scratching out each other's eyes. She couldn't have that. One of them might break a fingernail.

Jeanie grabbed Sorrel's chair and pulled it and the screeching girl backwards. She kicked open the door to Mackie's office and towed Sorrel inside. Back out again, she grabbed two more partitions and boxed Brynna into a cubicle all her own.

The screams reached new crescendos. Jeanie marched to

At Risk of Being a Fool

Dillon's desk. "Excuse me," she said tartly, as she unplugged his earphones and grabbed his boom-box. She plugged it into the wall near the office door and turned it up as far as the knob went. Music blared, the raucous beat pounding its way through the screams. Jeanie blinked as the lyrics filtered into her brain, but shrugged. For drowning out screams, she couldn't beat it.

Jeanie stood by the boom-box and met four pairs of eyes. Rosalie and Quinto gave her the excited, joyful looks of small children at a slumber party; Dillon and Tonio were stony-faced. Two to two, then. They were tied.

Someone pounded on the classroom door. Jeanie opened the door and popped her head into the hallway.

An aggressively clean-cut young man stood there, his fist poised in mid-air. The inexpensive, immaculate suit, combined with the arrogance of frustrated superiority, marked him as a freshly graduated, professional something-or-other. She recalled the business listings in the lobby, and ran them through her mind. Not a dentist, social worker, or civil servant. They were all too accustomed to loud, angry people. Who did that leave? Ah yes, a lawyer, Mr. Oscar Kemmerich. It had struck her as an improbable name.

She couldn't hear his words. She raised a finger asking for his patience, and turned back to her room full of live wires. She pointed to the hallway and raised an eyebrow. Rosalie and Quinto took her invitation and bounded into the hallway. Dillon and Tonio glowered. Jeanie stepped out and closed the door. The shrieks dimmed.

"May I help you?" she asked.

"Would you *kindly* maintain some order in your insane asylum? This caterwauling is totally nonconductive to a professional environment."

Almost absently, Jeanie returned a soft answer as she

glanced to the end of the hallway. Rosalie tip-tapped back and forth, like Judy Garland on the Yellow Brick Road. Quinto wedged himself into the corner at the far end of the hall, next to the building's side exit. He wore his hunted look again. His eyes were riveted on Mr. Kemmerich.

"That's the boy who worked at the construction site." Mr. Kemmerich said, following her glance. He sounded darkly triumphant, as though vindicated in some private opinion.

Jeanie jerked to attention. "How would you know?"

Mr. Kemmerich stepped back half a pace and recovered himself. "It was in the newspaper."

"No, it wasn't," she stated. No newspaper would list Quinto's name. They couldn't publish Quinto's name or picture without Dandridge House's permission, and they would never give it. This man had special knowledge, either of the crime or of her students. "Excuse me, Mr. Kemmerich, but how did you know that?"

The classroom door bumped into her from behind. Prudently, she turned toward it and wedged the toe of her shoe into the crack under the door to jam it. The girls were still carrying on, and she didn't need Tonio or Dillon charging into the middle of this little confrontation. The door hit her again, and then shuddered with heavy blows. The door scraped over her toe. Ouch. It had to be Dillon, not Tonio.

The pounding stopped. After a moment, she relaxed her stance. She wriggled her toes, trying to get back some feeling.

Mr. Kemmerich leveled a finger at Quinto. "Keep away from my motorcycle, punk. If it goes missing, I'll sic the cops on you."

Oscar Kemmerich didn't have a brain in his head, she thought tiredly. Imagine saying such a thing to a kid with a

At Risk of Being a Fool

criminal record. "Quinto would *never* steal a motorcycle," she said. Spray-paint it, possibly, but not steal it. "Mr. Kemmerich—"

At the far end of the hall, Mackie's office door flew open and banged against the wall. Dillon erupted through it and checked his stride at the sight of Mr. Kemmerich. He straightened slowly, and stood there, immovable, stiff-legged, hackles raised, his fingers curved like claws at his sides.

Well, thought Jeanie, *it's about time to break this up.* She grabbed Mr. Kemmerich's right hand, which she pumped vigorously. "Thank you very much," she said, in the kindly but firm "teacher-voice" known throughout the world. He retreated without conscious volition. Mr. Kemmerich, newly out of law school, still had all the reflexes of youth. "I appreciate your concern for my young ladies," she said. "I'm sure they'll calm down shortly. Good day to you, Mr. Kemmerich. I'm sure we'll meet again sometime."

Mr. Kemmerich found himself on the stairs. "If they do not calm down shortly, the police will be here to investigate. I will see to it," he blustered. With a final scowl at Quinto, he left.

Jeanie walked down the hall. Dillon stared down at her with burning yellow eyes.

"Nobody touches my stuff," he said, voice grating.

Tonio appeared in the doorway behind Dillon. He rested his hand on the doorframe and settled there watchfully.

"Nobody touches my stuff, nobody. You took my box."

"I did, didn't I?" said Jeanie with an involuntary chuckle. "I apologize."

"You laughing at me?" There was a deep rumble through his voice.

The wolf is nothing to laugh at. The wolf is dangerous, and

23

attacks only when the moment is right. He's a wolf; I'm a rabbit.

"I'm not laughing at you. I'm laughing at myself, an old woman standing in a hallway, listening to a catfight. Maybe I should bring in a fire hose, and squirt them both. Or maybe we could sell tickets. What do you think?"

Dillon's eyes were unwavering. She tried again. "I'm sorry." Actually, she understood it. People confined him, leashed him up, and taught him tricks he had no desire to learn. Of course, he wanted her out of his stuff. "I'm sorry I took your box without asking. But things were a little," she waved her hand to the door, "hectic."

"Don't touch my stuff again."

"Okay."

He stalked past her and went through the classroom door. The volume decreased, held steady. Dillon had left his boom-box where she put it. Surprise.

"I think they're done fighting," Rosalie said. "You want I should go see?"

Tonio cocked his head to listen. "Can't hear 'em," he said. "Good music." Tonio glinted at her, with what might have been mischief.

"Never," Jeanie said, "in my life have I heard two girls carry on that way."

"Should have let 'em fight."

"I don't think their parole officers would be happy. Besides, I'm morally opposed," said Jeanie, "to getting blood all over my classroom. Did you see the length of those fingernails? I'm still not sure what started it. Sometimes I think I'm blind in one ear and can't see out of the other."

There was silence. Quinto said tentatively, "Uh, Jeanie? That don't make no sense at all."

"You're right, Quinto, it doesn't. My small attempt at

humor." It had been a hell of a day. She'd spent every second watching her back and her mouth. She was sick of it. "For heaven's sake, Tonio," she burst out, "work with me here. I joke with you, and you get it, I know you get it. And you give nothing back at all."

Unprofessional, she told herself angrily. She had no business seeking reassurance from a student. It was this rootless feeling she had, of walking in the sand and leaving no footprints. Everyone who loved her was so distant, one way or another. "Sorry, Tonio, forget it," she managed. Jeanie closed her eyes and dropped her head into her hands. Annalisa was dead; Shelley was far away, and so were the boys. And now there was this thing with Edward. *I am not alone,* she told herself. *I am not.*

"Me," Tonio said, "I think I'm deaf in one eye."

Jeanie's eyes flew open. "Must be the one I see the twinkle in, huh?"

"Must be."

Tonio turned to Quinto. "Hey, buddy, get back in, okay? Either of them does anything, we need to know. You're lookout, okay, homey?"

Quinto grinned. "Sure thing, man." He strutted into the classroom. Rosalie followed.

Tonio looked at her. "You got to watch it, Jeanie, with Dillon."

"And the others? And you?"

He seemed to make a decision. "It's just, shit happens, you know?" he said, jerking his head towards the room. "I know the guy Sorrel carved up. Maybe he had it coming, but still, Jesus Christ! You want to watch it. You could get hurt. These ain't your regular kids."

"But you're here, all of you," she said softly. "Studying."

"Court says we gotta be here."

"Maybe so, but Mackie says some kids fail their exams on purpose. She screens carefully before taking anyone in the work-study program. Why are you six here, while a dozen more aren't?" There was a pause. "That's it, then. That's where I come in. Isn't it?" She waggled an eyebrow at him. "Blind ears and all."

Rosalie bounced out of the room. "Phone's ringing."

Jeanie went to the office, skirted the stone-faced Sorrel, and picked up the phone. "GED School. Oh hi, Mackie. The testing schedule? We've only got one going in this week. Right, Thursday, Tonio's going in for Social Studies. Uh huh. Sure."

Jeanie gave Sorrel a lingering glance. The girl's leg swung spasmodically. Her chin jutted out and her cheeks were flushed. Her chest heaved with angry drags at the air. No doubt, Brynna was in a similar state. Rosalie was roaming; Quinto was ready to fly apart at any instant, and Dillon was in a royal snit. A man had been pipe bombed, and she was fairly certain three, if not four, of her students knew more than the newspapers, and so did a total stranger upstairs.

Habit held firm. These kids were hers. "Thanks, Mackie. Everything's just fine here. Not a problem in the world."

TWO

Maybe a midget could use this mirror, but Sorrel sure couldn't. Probably Torrez picked it out with the rest of this crap. Bright Futures Transition Home for Girls was stacked to the ceiling with crap. Sorrel snatched at the mascara and knocked it off the dresser. With a muttered curse, she grabbed it.

The clock sucked her eyes in for a moment and released her. It blinked its numbers, red and threatening. Like the rest of the furniture, it was institutional, barely sufficient and nothing more. The small bed sat in the corner, neatly made up. The dresser had two tiny drawers. A hook on the wall held her few clothes. The door stood open the regulation foot and a half, as it always did at six twenty-three in the morning.

The mascara fell onto the dresser. Sorrel inspected her face in the mirror, her fingers drumming the dresser top. She froze and inspected her hand. Good, she hadn't messed up the polish. It was decent stuff; it had a nice shine. It had better, at that price. Sorrel's eyes flicked to the clock, and back to the mirror. Pictures of her daughter Tiffany brightened the mirror. She was a pixie of a girl, with dark eyes and hair, and a gleeful grin, romping through an array of pictures: Tiffy at her second birthday party, ice cream plastering her mouth; Tiffy riding a trike; Tiffy jumping into a plastic wading pool. Sorrel's glance lingered painfully on shots of herself with Tiffany, her mother, and grandmother. At least *she* had family. Her little girl wasn't stuck in a cruddy foster home, like Rosalie's boy.

The door slammed back against the wall. Lisabet poked her head in the doorway. "Better get a move on girl, or you'll be in demerit city again. Hear me?"

Sorrel rounded on her. "Get the hell out of here." Her expression backed the girl out of the room. "Leave me alone, I've got five minutes left, and you know it." Lisabet acted like she was staff, the damned bitch. Sorrel adjusted the door to the correct angle.

None of the pictures were polluted with Carlos, Tiffany's father. Men were shits, and Carlos was a bigger shit than most. At least she'd gotten her baby away from him before he left. Left, huh. Two seconds before she'd kicked him out. It took a big man to hit a baby like Tiffany, a big man. Fuckin' asshole.

There were no pictures of the other one either, the "boyfriend." Damn Brynna and her big mouth. Boyfriend, like hell. He was gone, down Interstate 5 to L.A.—flying the Five. When they chased him out of Portland, he dropped by to see her in Salem before he split. Good riddance. He was trouble, big-time. Exciting, a good screw, but too risky. No way he was getting near Tiffany. He could take his guns and shove 'em right up his ass. Not that she'd dare say that, not to him. A girl watched her mouth around that one.

He didn't have nothing to do with that pipe bomb. Couldn't have, he'd been gone for months. And what would he care about some construction guy? Construction, staple guns, acetylene torches, pipe, nails, gasoline, maybe even welders . . . So what if he stole stuff, played with explosives, followed firemen to grin at blazing houses. That didn't mean he was still here in Salem, blasting some guy into bits.

If anybody knew about him, linked her up with him, she'd be in deep shit. Randy and Torrez between them—

she didn't want to think about it. She'd be lucky to see Tiffy at all, if that happened. She *had* to see Tiffy. She'd die without her.

Tiffy, Tiffy—Mustn't cry, can't cry, they'll all see it on my face. They'll laugh at me.

Nobody laughed at Sorrel. Nobody pushed Tiffy around either. The next man who tried it would be dead meat. She'd grab her a knife and carve him up good, like that one guy that grabbed her at the party. *Forget him, I heard enough about him and his medical problems in court. He had it coming.*

Damn Torrez and her rules. Seeing Tiffy twice a month was murder. Mama took good care of her, just like she had of Sorrel. *God, my heart's breaking. No demerits, can't get demerits—Two minutes left.*

She wiped away a tear and checked her mascara. She craned her head, trying to get a look at her body in the mirror. She threw her small store of makeup into her purse, and the purse in the top drawer of the dresser. She swung the door back into its daytime position and stepped into the hallway.

Locks and doors snapped shut behind her, cutting off the air, as she traveled from one prison to another. Why had Mackie put her in a courthouse, for God's sake?

A long countertop bisected the front office of the District Court Clerk. The public huddled on one side and the clerks on the other. Sorrel, her position ambiguous, spent her mornings balancing on a tight wire between them. She lifted the bar and crossed behind the counter, matching Hilda's baleful stare. Hilda, front counter clerk, spoke into the phone, and didn't have time for her customary digs.

Carol, office manager, and Dorrie, her assistant, had coated the desks with cutesy little decorations: beanie babies glued to computer monitors, and potted plants on the file cabinet. The attempts at a homelike atmosphere failed. It was all sugar coating on yet another prison. The falseness of it used to make her mad, but now it just tore at her stomach, along with the professional smiles and the security guards. Everything she ate, except chocolate and Coke, tasted like cardboard.

"Glad to see you, Sorrel," Carol said. "Your list is on the counter."

Working passed the time. If only it weren't so gut-wrenchingly boring. She couldn't answer the phone, or do filing, or sort mail, or handle paperwork. A criminal working with court papers? Oh God, no.

Sorrel crouched in front of the copy machine in the side room, loading up paper. Hilda brushed by her, bumping into her. Sorrel gritted her teeth on a sharp remark, and swallowed it unspoken. *Bitch, she does it on purpose.* Sorrel closed her eyes, shielding herself with a memory of Tiffany. Her anger leaked into the background, joining the deadly pool in the back of her mind. She picked up the copier paper, fanned it, and squared the edges.

A security guard entered and leaned on the counter, bypassing the three people waiting in line. He wore that casual look that meant something was up. Sorrel tensed in sudden calculation. Was he looking for her? Maybe Hilda got somebody's ear. What had she seen?

The guard tapped on the counter. "Carol?"

Dorrie looked at him inquiringly. He smiled and shook his head.

"Carol," he said again.

Sorrel closed the copier and slid behind the door, where she could still see him. Carol and the guard huddled together. A folded piece of paper, bright red, slipped from the

At Risk of Being a Fool

guard's hand to Carol's. The guard left.

Carol moved to Dorrie, nodding at the blond guy with the open briefcase. "I'm so sorry," Carol said, "but the 'powers that be' have decreed an evacuation drill. So annoying. I'm sorry to disrupt you, but we need to exit to the south lawn. If you'll all retain your number slips, we'll handle your matters as expeditiously as possible once we return."

The young man with the briefcase huffed loudly. "I must insist. The court hearing on this matter—"

"Yes indeed, annoying for you, but I'm sure the judge will understand. Dorrie, will you see our guests to the south exit?" Smiling, but as stubborn as Torrez, Carol got the small crowd moving. Hilda closed out a phone conversation.

"What's going on?" Hilda said the instant the door closed behind the public. She hunted for Sorrel, but didn't see her. "Did she do something?"

"Hilda." Carol shooed her to the door. "Out on the south lawn, you know the procedure. It's just a standard evacuation drill."

"It is not, we just had one three weeks ago. I saw that red slip Vic gave you. It's a bomb threat, isn't it?" Her voice rose. "Where is it, where did they say to look? It's these criminals, like her. In a normal office, we'd never worry about bomb threats."

"Hilda, outside, now. Sorrel? Oh, there you are. Go with— Never mind. Sorrel's with me. Move it, Hilda. Remember, they time us on these drills. The fire marshal's out there with his stop watch." Carol propelled Hilda out the door. "The south lawn."

The door closed behind Hilda's protesting figure. Carol muttered, "I can see why Judge Hodges got rid of her, but did he have to wish her on us?"

"I didn't do nothing," Sorrel said.

"Of course not," Carol said impatiently. "I should have sent you out, but I'm not putting you with Hilda without a referee." Carol whisked around the room, hitting hot keys on computers to throw them in emergency lock-down, snatching folders and a metal box with unerring accuracy. "Here, carry this." She handed the box to Sorrel and bent over an open desk drawer. "There, I've got it all. Out we go." Carol's entire safety protocol took twenty seconds.

Sorrel paced behind her, the heavy box dragging at her arms. Along the hallway, guards ducked into restrooms and storage closets, extracting stragglers. A prickling flush swept through Sorrel from her head to her toes.

"Carol? This isn't a drill, this is real."

"Keep it to yourself. I don't want Hilda to go ballistic."

Sorrel stopped. Carol tucked the folders under one arm and grabbed Sorrel's shoulder in a fierce grip. Sorrel jerked back, anger flaring, but Carol hung on and shook her hard.

"You listen to me, Sorrel. It's just a bomb threat. We get them all the time. They evacuate the building, check all the rooms and surrounding area, and that's it. We've never had a bomb explode. We've had the odd fire in the trashcan, yes, but no bombs. There are security cameras everywhere. They just have to check the tapes. If you know something, out with it, but don't, for God's sake, panic on me, because I've got enough to contend with out there on the lawn without you. Have you got that?"

"Yes," said Sorrel, gritting her teeth.

She followed Carol out the big double doors. Carol handed the guard the red slip of paper. The guard added it to his small stack, glanced past them to the lawn and back down the hallway. Sorrel rolled her shoulder, trying to erase the lingering pinch of Carol's grip. If the guard was looking for Sorrel, he was doing a lousy job. She drew a deep breath

At Risk of Being a Fool

and then another. The panicked flush subsided.

Clusters of people mingled on the lawn. A team of helmeted police with equipment bags trotted across the lawn, disappearing around the side of the building.

"That's a S.W.A.T. team," shrilled Hilda. "I told you it was a bomb!"

"Even it if it is," said Carol, "the building is evacuated."

"But all our records. And what is *she* doing with the key box? All our security is based on that key box, and you gave it to a criminal."

Damn that bitch, she was asking for it. Sorrel stuffed the metal box into Dorrie's arms. "You—"

Carol straight-armed her backwards. "Not a word out of you. Hilda, you'd try the patience of a saint. I asked Sorrel to carry the box for me. It's not strictly according to protocol, I'll admit, but you can't possibly think she's had a moment to make copies of them."

"You didn't give them to *me*, I notice."

"Hilda. Go to the Services building, borrow a phone, and arrange to shunt the calls from our office. Stay there and answer the phone."

Hilda stalked off, her head high, with a face like a prune.

"What about me?" Dorrie asked. She grinned, watching Hilda's rump twitch across the lawn.

"That depends. I have to say, this looks depressingly real." Two trucks and a sheriff's car pulled up simultaneously. Dozens of people swarmed around the side of the building. "We won't get back in there for hours. I guess we'd better set up shop over in Services."

"With Hilda? It's tight quarters over there."

"Hmm." Carol and Dorrie shared a rueful glance. "I'll go check."

Carol joined the other office managers converging on the

33

front door security guard. Sorrel looked for somewhere to sit down, but there was only grass. Grass left stains. She watched the action by the edge of the building.

"Want to take a look?" said Dorrie. "We'll just pretend we're supposed to meet over there. Come on."

Sorrel followed her, half unwilling. She searched for a familiar face, or a loose-jointed slouching walk. He wasn't here, thank God. Of course he wasn't. He was in L.A. like he said he'd be. The lying son-of-a-bitch.

She was being stupid. He hadn't set a pipe bomb at the construction site, and he sure wouldn't have set one here. He had no reason! Well, maybe he did. Her stomach lurched with dread. This wasn't supposed to happen. Look at all the attention Quinto got when a bomb went off at his work site. This would draw attention to her. She didn't need that: people staring at her, poring over her record one more time, looking to see who she knew, her "contacts." He'd know that, wouldn't he?

"Now, now, ladies, no rubber-necking. Back to the main staging area, please." Vic Dunlap scowled, the expression sitting awkwardly on his round, cheery face.

Dorrie laughed. "Come on, Vic, tell us. They found something under a courtroom window, didn't they? Must have been Hodges' or Matsuura's. I'd bet on Hodges. He's a mean old son-of-a-gun in a courtroom. What did they find?"

Vic raised his eyebrows. "What did *they* find, did you ask? Who says *they* found anything at all?"

Dorrie gasped, pleasurably horrified. "Come on, Vic, what's the story? Who found it? It wasn't you, was it? It was? Oh my word, what is it?"

"Probably nothing at all," said Vic, with self-deprecating humor. "I probably jumped the gun. If I'm wrong, they'll

At Risk of Being a Fool

never let me hear the end of it. Doesn't this place look like an anthill, though? Police jumping all over the place." He took on a melodramatic tone. "Who'd have thought I could release such forces!"

He seemed to be quoting from something. Sorrel didn't get it. She looked around the side of the building at the crowd of uniforms. Fear shot through her. *What the hell am I going to do?*

"Little lady?" Vic frowned at her. "Are you all right, miss? You look like you're going to faint. Don't you mind me, I'm just blathering on like always. I didn't mean to scare you. You need to sit down. There's a bus stop right over there, with a nice bench."

"I'm fine," she managed. Dorrie was looking at her funny.

"Well, my goodness, Sorrel, honey, I'd never have thought— But anyway, don't you fret, I'm sure it's no big deal. Look, Carol's coming back, she'll tell us what's happening. You going to be all right? Thanks, Vic."

"You just wait, it'll turn out I've been a fool," Vic called after them. "No big deal."

No big deal, Sorrel thought, just a pipe bomb, set at the courthouse where she worked, close to where the Bright Futures' van usually pulled up. Where the hell was a bathroom, when you really, really needed it?

Sorrel swung into the classroom, hips swaying. Tonio and Quinto watched her go by. Good. Guys were shits, but they had their uses. They never watched Brynna. Sorrel had it; Brynna didn't. *He* had thought so, too. Did he make bombs? Or just steal stuff, and drool over guns? She ran their brief conversations through her memory, but couldn't remember. They'd never done much talking.

35

She chose a desk two down from Brynna, and sat sideways to her. Jeanie brought an essay topic sheet, a notepad, and pencil. The essay questions were a lot of bull. She'd read the list often enough to know. "Should the age limit for purchasing alcohol be reduced to age 18? Discuss pros and cons." "Explain how education has affected your life." "Should violent television shows be restricted from daytime viewing hours? Explain your reasons."

Sorrel's fingernails rattled on the table. She caught herself and studied the fingernail polish minutely. She couldn't think, couldn't concentrate. Whenever she let her mind go, the courthouse bomb jumped right up and punched her in the face. She drew in a deep breath, and looked around. Brynna was staring at her, like usual. Let her look. Maybe she'd learn something.

Tonio, now, that was different. He picked up a helluva lot, almost read her mind sometimes. She kept her distance from him these days. And Quinto. God, that was a laugh. Jeanie had no clue about him, treated him like he was some sweet little kid. But then, Jeanie'd look at a cockroach the same way.

"Sorrel, time to get some work done. I marked an essay topic for you. Or would you rather choose a different one?"

Essay questions, for God's sake. She pulled the mirror from her purse and checked her eye shadow, peering at one eye and then the other. Her eye shadow exactly matched the purple nail polish. She shot a look towards Jeanie, who pretended to ignore her. Good, she'd gotten the point.

A circle marked one topic. Sorrel read it over, muttering under her breath. Her leg swung back and forth, faster, and faster. With a solid thwack, she slammed the paper against the table. "This really bites. Jeanie? This is a bunch of crap. You know it, don't you?"

At Risk of Being a Fool

"Afraid you're stuck with it. I don't make up the essay questions. It's just a practice one anyway."

"Yeah, well. But goddamnit—" Her voice shifted to a high-pitched singsong. "'Write an essay describing an important event in your life, and how it changed your outlook on society.' Huh. What the hell I'm gonna write about? Like how I got locked up? How's about that SOB jumping me? Bet they'd love that." Another incident came to mind, the one that might, just might, have resulted in a certain pipe bomb left at the courthouse. Panic surged, but she throttled it down.

Dillon walked in, sat at his desk, and opened a book. Sorrel found herself staring at him. They'd been tight, Dillon and the "boyfriend." She'd forgotten. Oh God, was that it? Was it him? She jumped involuntarily as Jeanie perched on the table next to her.

"Try a happy time, maybe," Jeanie said.

"Uh huh. Sure thing, like when I was a crackhead? I was real happy then."

"Right, Sorrel. Forget it. Just sit there. I'll go check on Rosalie."

"Okay, okay." She had to work. She didn't want Randy, her parole officer, on her case, too. "Just help me out here, okay?"

"Before you went inside, when you were back home—remember something fun. Parties, Christmas with your family? Taking Tiffany to the zoo?"

Sorrel leaned back in her chair, considering. It was kind of good, thinking about something else. "Well, there was this wedding we went to."

"Sounds good. Tell me first. Think it through."

"My cousin Angie, she married this flash guy, suit and collar kind of wuss, you know. This was before Tiffany,

37

three, four years back. Mama, and Grandma and me, we got all dressed up. Tia Lupe, she's all—" Her voice rose again, became fussy and affected. " 'Please, Sorrel, just for once, dump the makeup.' Only she don't say it that way, it's more 'unobtrusive coloring' or something wacko like that. She talks kind of like you, Jeanie.

"So we get all done up, fancy dresses. Man, we looked good, we really did. So, we got to the wedding, and that was okay, usual stuff. But the reception. What's-his-name's family, Angie's guy? They're all, noses in the air, looking down on us. This fuckin' bitch starts talkin' trash at us. Mama rolls right into her, nails, fists. You don't take shit from nobody, Mama taught me that. They got no respect, you got to teach 'em.

"We was rolling all over the floor, nails flying, kicking, tearing stuff apart, food all over everything. It was a *good* fight. We was really stoked. We won, too, 'cause Grandma got into it. Her and those high heels, bashing everybody who took a shot at Mama and me. It was a lot of fun, Jeanie. My grandma, she's a real scrapper."

Sorrel grinned at the look on Jeanie's face. Jeanie was such a baby. If she'd lived Sorrel's life, she'd have died. "What's the matter? It was nothing big. A few people needed stitches, but nothing big-time. No cops called in, nothing like that. Angie and her guy got out just fine, no trouble. You can bet, though, people showed some respect after that. They'd better. Grandma, she's something else."

"Actually, I don't think I've ever met your grandmother."

"No? I've got a picture, right here. Yeah. See? Me, Mama, Grandma, and Tiffany. That's Tiffy's party, when she was two, they let me out on furlough for it."

"How about Tiffany? You could write about her."

At Risk of Being a Fool

"Boy, yeah, Tiffany—" Sorrel's voice was low, gruff. "I remember, she was born, I was screaming, crying. I mean, I never hurt like that, not even when— Well. And then, they give her to me, all red and bawling, got this white stuff all over her head. God, she looked like shit. I touched her, and it was like, she quit crying, right then. Like she knew, somehow, it was me." Sorrel raised a hand and touched something invisible, shifted her arms and cradled it. "I was never so happy in my life, and there I was, just all bloody and hurting. 'Cause we was together. It's always been like that, her and me. Just like it was with Mama and me. Always."

"See, you could write about that. She touched your life."

"Yeah, I could. I could write about Tiffany." Sorrel picked up pencil and paper. "Tiffany." Fear and despair mingled. She couldn't run, not from the cops, and not from him either. If she ran, she'd never see Tiffany again. And if Dillon knew, she was in deep shit. What the hell was she going to do?

Time passed, and Jeanie was there again, crowding her.

"Sorrel? Sorrel, I'm sorry, I didn't realize—"

Her mascara must be running. The paper had blotches on it. God, she'd been crying again. She must look like shit. A room divider blocked Sorrel's view of the room. Brynna couldn't see her. Dimly, she felt this was a good thing.

"Sorrel, I really like that picture you showed me. Your grandma looks like a spunky lady. I'd like to meet her sometime. Sorrel? Sorrel, let me give you another piece of paper. Maybe you'd do better, writing about the wedding after all."

THREE

The house had the cluttered emptiness of a way station, of a temporary haven between catastrophes. It existed in a time warp, post-war tract housing for low-income families at a time when paint-splattered linoleum set the fashion. Jeanie's armchair, her sofa, and her table perched uncomfortably on the industrial carpeting.

She'd been lucky to find the two-bedroom house. The same property owner owned all the buildings down this side of the street, including three other houses and a few old apartment units. Given the contents of the back yards, it wasn't worthwhile to rip them down and replace them with higher density complexes. Train tracks weren't standard decorative items.

Geoff, her older son, had argued that she'd never sleep, with the trains coming through at night, blaring their horns through residential neighborhoods. She couldn't explain without upsetting him. Insomnia lurked in the darkness. She cherished the companionship of the twice-nightly trains. The steady clacking vibration shook the house and her twin bed. The sudden glare of the headlights through the window shifted sideways to leave patterns on her wall. Usually after loading her worries onto the train, she managed to collapse for a few hours' sleep.

Jeanie opened the freezer, groped for something of marginal nutrition, and threw it in the microwave. She got treats for the pets: a strip of rawhide for Corrigan, the longhaired dachshund, and a freeze-dried minnow for Rita,

At Risk of Being a Fool

snoozing on the bed. Jeanie rescued her pillow, making a mental note: Never feed fish to a cat on the bed.

A memory shot to the surface, of a cat bounced off the bed with an affronted yowl, as she and Edward tangled arms and legs in snuggling tenderness. The suddenness of it, and the cat's indignant commentary, reduced them both to helpless hysteria. They'd had the waterbed, and they'd had Tristan then. Eight years back?

The quicksand of despair sucked at her feet. Her life had diminished to treading water, and trying not to mire herself in memories. She taught for three hours a day, spent countless hours at Oriole's Nest trying to drag Edward from his mental pit, and yearned for the lifeblood of e-mails and phone calls from family. Then she woke the next day, facing it all again.

The microwave binged. The half-warmed manicotti filled a hole in her stomach. It was food, of sorts.

The computer barely fit into the corner of the smaller bedroom. Corrigan's ramp to the foot of the bed took up most of the remaining floor space. Geoff, her older son, a physicist with NASA, built the ramp so Corrigan could sleep on the bed. Dachshunds shouldn't jump.

She downloaded her e-mail and her heart lifted. She had notes from Geoff, Julianne, and Andy, all from their respective addresses: father, mother, and son. Geoff's daughter, Lillian, was only five, so her e-mails were hard-fought battles of love, with long silences between them. Keith hadn't written, as usual. Keith preferred to phone, tossing off his rapid-fire jokes while pacing around his apartment. She didn't have a note from Shelley, but time zones did screwy things to the transmissions between Germany and Oregon. Sometimes Jeanie heard nothing from her sister for three days, and then got several notes in a row, zip, zip, zip.

Her shoulders relaxed, and tension sloughed away as she wrote to her sister Shelley, in the habit of a lifetime. E-mail's fast, cheap transmissions were a blissful addiction. Everything either sister saw, heard, thought, or felt flowed through her fingers into a stream of detail. It was like journal writing, with a kindred soul inhaling the words on the other end.

> . . . *I've hired a nice boy, Cody, to help me chip away some of the rock in the front yard. I have to make room for Julianne's flowers. She sent another box, irises this time . . .*
>
> *Remember Sorrel, who works at the courthouse? Somebody set a pipe bomb against the outside wall under a judge's window. They found it while Sorrel was right there at work. They evacuated the entire building. Mackie told me all about it. She figures the police will pull Sorrel in for questioning. I said, that's nuts, she'd never plant a bomb while she's working there. And if she was after the judge, she'd never have put it under his window. Under his desk, maybe. Of course, she wouldn't have access to his desk, would she? But she could figure out where he parked his car, and in that underground parking structure with everyone coming and going, that'd be a safe place. Why would anyone put it under a window? It doesn't make sense.*
>
> *I asked Mackie about Dillon. She placed him at Delancey Brothers last May. He stuck it out for about three weeks, and then had a massive blowup with Bryce Wogan. Mr. Wogan insisted that hand tools were missing. One of those big drills for going through masonry and metal, a hundred-foot extension cord, and some other stuff. She pulled Dillon, had a lot of trouble placing him*

At Risk of Being a Fool

again (you can imagine!), and finally got him onto a loading dock for a frozen foods plant. Not a lot of temptation for theft there, I guess. They've got a lot of equipment, but most of it's not portable.

I said, what if Dillon didn't steal the stuff. If it was cut and dried, Delancey Brothers would have pressed charges, wouldn't they? And why would they be willing to take on Quinto? Mackie just gave me this look. If your Christmas tree fell over, she said, and ornaments were scattered through the house, wouldn't you suspect your cat? The company gives Bryce Wogan a free hand, because he's a great foreman but an ogre for everyone to work with—except for Danny Rivera. So if Danny said, Bryce, I'm taking another kid on, Bryce would roll his eyes, and let him do it. So, that's how she got Quinto into the program. Apparently, Danny knew Quinto's brother from years back, and he was happy to get Quinto.

Poor Quinto and poor Sorrel. I hate seeing them so stressed out. It's hard, not being able to just fix everyone's problems . . .

At last, the flood of words slowed to a trickle. She scanned the letter, and copied and pasted excerpts into a new message. A few whimsical comments and dozen more exclamation points wove the excerpts together into a lighthearted general newsletter. It was a third the length of the original, and certified "worry-free." She sent it to Julianne and Geoff's joint address. A similar concoction went to Keith.

She added a postscript to Shelley's letter.

Just wanted to tell you, I know you sicced Geoff and Keith on me last May. I'd probably have done the same to

you. So, quit pussyfooting around about it, sister mine.
                                            Love you, Jeanie

    She mouse-clicked the computer clock to check the time. Rita jumped in her lap. Rita was a ball of long fur wrapped around a sweet nature and a scatterbrained head. Rita could get lost in her own house. Corrigan plopped at her feet, hoping for a walk. The clock refused to change. She'd promised herself and Shelley that she'd take some personal time this morning. Well, she had, hadn't she? She picked up the phone.
    "Nadezda? Jeanie, here. Is he up yet? Oh, he is. Thank God, I'm going nuts here. I'll be there in ten minutes."

    "Lift your foot, Edward. Your foot, for the curb." Jeanie reached down and patted the back of his knee. "Lift your foot. That's it, great, here we go."
    Parkinson's was like that, as Michael J. Fox could attest. So could Billy Graham, Janet Reno, and countless people like Edward McCoy.
    "Here we are, Edward. Look, the ducks are waiting for you."
    "That they are," he said cheerfully. With the ease of long practice, Jeanie backed Edward to the bench. Edward half-sat and half-fell onto the bench, adjusting himself with a series of hitching moves. Five years before, Edward retired from Starfire Engineering. His joints stiffened, as though encased in layers of bubble wrap and packing tape. His world contracted. He couldn't drive, work in his shop, manage a keyboard or mouse. She had remained afloat on his courage. They found solutions together: the electric toothbrush, clothes that fastened with Velcro, and handrails in the bathroom. Fifteen months ago, her retirement had

At Risk of Being a Fool

come, to their unspoken relief.

The ducks clustered at the edge of the bridge, swimming in tight, eager circles. Edward fumbled a piece of the bread between his fingers. He drew back his arm in a series of jerks and threw the bread. It landed on the deck. Jeanie nudged it over the side with her foot. The ducks scrambled over each other.

"She's here again," said Edward, frowning.

A young woman with long unkempt brown hair herded two toddlers towards the slides and stood close by, her baby on her hip. Her eyes roamed the playground, catching every movement of squirrel, bike, or skateboard.

"It's nice to see the little ones play," Jeanie said.

"She's here *again*," he emphasized. "Notice how she watches everyone?"

"Now, Edward, she's just being careful." The young woman radiated fear. If they spoke to her, she scurried away with her children. Covertly, Jeanie had begun keeping watch for strangers on the young woman's behalf. "She belongs here. She's a neighbor."

"A neighbor? What's her name?"

Jeanie's paused, and recovered quickly. "Miranda."

Edward looked at her quizzically. He shook his finger at her, moving his whole hand with the effort. An engaging grin spread over his face. "You made that up."

"You got me," she confessed, laughing. She hugged his shoulders and helped him stand. With Parkinson's, the brain forgot which muscles were which. The brain said, *move the foot*. The foot said, *who, me?* After a moment's pause, Edward's foot remembered and moved forward.

"Ah well, I'll let it go, then. But you're far too trusting, my dear. Like my wife."

"I'm your wife, Edward. I'm Jeanie."

45

Edward frowned. "I'm afraid not. My wife's at work now. She's a teacher. I don't mean to hurt your feelings, but it's best to keep these things clear."

"But Edward—"

"McCoy," he said gently. "Mr. McCoy, that's best, isn't it? I remember your husband. I believe we once worked together, didn't we?"

"No, Edward."

"Yes, indeed. Years ago, when we were tracing chemical seepage in the water supply. Your husband was the state inspector, wasn't he? His name was Carl."

The dementia had defeated her. Senior moments finally mutated into another state. "Miranda" was a terrorist spy; Nate, the night security guard at Oriole's Nest, was trying to collect classified information on nuclear submarines. Edward's Navy days were long gone, but his mind clung tenaciously to the word "classified," and met the conversational gambits of nurses and doctors with polite suspicion.

"No," Jeanie's voice shook. "My husband's name is Edward."

"The same as mine? Oh no, it was Carl. Quite a man with a story, he was. Very fond of his wife." Edward patted her hand. "What was his last name?"

Jeanie felt sick at heart. "I don't know." A small but significant number of Parkinson's patients suffered from dementia. More suffered from depression. At least he'd escaped that.

Edward stopped and looked at her in surprise. "Your own husband, and you don't know his name?"

"Edward, you—" Forty years, but he didn't remember. In spite of herself, her eyes stung. So, she couldn't remember her spouse's name? She cleared her throat, and filed the bittersweet joke to tell Shelley. "Take a step, Edward. Let's keep walking, shall we? You wanted to walk to the oak trees, you said. Lift your foot."

The first step was always the hardest.

Edward studied a motorcycle crossing the street in front of them, turning his head to follow it to end of the street.

"I've seen that man before," he mused. "Several times."

"I'm amazed you can tell. To me, they all look alike in those helmets and billowing jackets." She helped him off the curb. "There's a young lawyer near my school who has a motorcycle a bit like that, but I can't tell them apart. Oscar Kemmerich. He worries me, Edward. He seems to know things he shouldn't know."

"Lawyers often do," said Edward dryly.

"But he knew where Quinto worked," she said. "I told you about Quinto, one of my students? He's doing construction. There was an accident at Quinto's job site, and his boss got hurt. We saw the lawyer at school yesterday, and he knew Quinto on sight."

"He knew the boy's name, or his face?"

Jeanie frowned. "His face, I think. I don't remember if he used Quinto's name. Quinto's never met him before." If Quinto hadn't lied.

"It's not really a mystery, is it? He probably saw the boy at the courthouse some time. If he's hungry for work, he probably gathers information by the ream. A young man?"

"Straight out of law school, I'd say. Frantically insecure."

Edward grinned. "I've heard my wife say that exact thing. You must be a teacher."

He seemed so rational, so easy to converse with; it was easy to forget his condition. "Yes, I am." The walkway to Oriole's Nest's front door curved before them.

"You're sure he wasn't the lawyer for your student?"

"I doubt it. Quinto says his lawyer was a woman. She

apparently spent Quinto's appointments with a cell phone pasted to one ear, arguing with her boyfriend. I suppose there are lots of people who knew about Quinto. The work crew, the company's administration, even the medical staff who took care of Mr. Wogan."

"Bryce Wogan? Construction chief? Dear Lord, what a small world."

Jeanie blinked. "You knew Bryce Wogan?"

"Well, hello," caroled Nadezda, holding open the door. "Long time no see."

"Right," said Jeanie, "It's been at least an hour."

"Will you be back this evening, or are you taking the night off?"

"I'll be back in a few minutes. I thought I'd bring Rita down."

"Great. So, Edward, how was your walk? Did you feed the ducks? They look forward to seeing you. Just like your lovely wife does, doesn't she?"

"I haven't seen my wife," said Edward.

Jeanie tensed, but Nadezda dove in first. "Of course you have, Edward. She's been walking with you. A nice long walk, just like when you first got married."

"No," said Edward. "This is the other one. Not my wife."

"Well," said Nadezda, putting an arm around his shoulder, "the other one will be back soon. The visiting nurse wants you all to herself for the moment."

Jeanie kissed him on the cheek. "Good-bye, Edward. I'll see you in a little bit." She turned quickly and started out the door.

Behind her, Edward said, "She shouldn't kiss strangers. My wife wouldn't care for that at all."

"Well, we just won't tell her then, will we?" said

At Risk of Being a Fool

Nadezda. "Hang on just a minute, would you, Jeanie?"

The door closed with a heavy click. Jeanie waited, sternly controlling the wobble in her chin. Edward's movements were a little looser with the new medication dosage. In a week or two, with his state more predictable, perhaps she could take him home for another overnight visit.

Nadezda stepped outside. "Thanks for waiting. Jeanie, your windows lock down, don't they? So people can't wedge them open?"

"What? Oh," said Jeanie, astonished, "yes, when the boys were here, they cut bars for them. They put about a thousand locks on each door. What's the matter?"

"Last night we had a prowler. Nate heard him and scared him off." Every night, Nate patrolled Oriole's Nest and the retirement complex next door. "The guy was in the back yard, looking in the windows. Fortunately, none of the residents saw him. He jumped right over the fence when he saw Nate, so hopefully he's scared off for good. We called the police, and there's no damage. But Kherra and me, we got a bit worried about you. Your place isn't even fenced. So you be careful, you hear me?"

"I'm always careful," Jeanie said, touched. "Probably somebody's after your drug cabinet. Maybe a burglar with high blood pressure? I'll check the windows when I get back, just to be sure. Don't worry about me."

Jeanie left, still mulling over Edward's recognition of Bryce Wogan. Perhaps he'd remember the name in an hour or so, but probably not. She dismissed Nadezda's warning. All her valuables were in storage. Who could possibly be interested in her?

He leaned against the building and gauged the shadows in the darkness. The security fence wobbled. His mouth

49

quirked as he vaulted over it. Maybe there were too many people climbing over it at night.

There wasn't much security on the construction site. Since Wogan's little accident, a couple of guys drove by at night. They got out of their cars and poked around with flashlights, but they weren't fast on their feet. Too many burgers and fries. They were no trouble. More to the point, Rivera was always the first on the site; poking things with long handles, wearing goggles and hardhat. That was Rivera, all right. He was so fuckin' conscientious. He was also predictable.

The question was, where *wouldn't* Rivera look. He gave the site a long look, watching for movement or red lights from security cameras. He prowled softly, keeping his hands in his pockets. Klutzes didn't make it for long.

The crew hadn't broken through into the building yet, to connect the new part with the old. It looked like a fort built with cinder block Legos. Framing two-by-fours filled the gaps with sharp lines, horizontal and vertical, like bars.

His stride broke for a moment, and recovered.

The scaffolding climbed around the construction, like a frame around a picture. Rivera left a neat site, especially lately. There was the trailer, of course, but it was too chancy. There was no telling who'd open it next. Supposedly, the new guy was foreman and Rivera worked under him, but you'd never know it from the way they acted. There was no rhythm, no method to their work, not like when Wogan was around.

He stepped into the open framework, checking out the crosspieces holding the window braces upright. His gaze traveled high into empty space. The trusses would go there. Trusses held a multitude of hiding places. That could work. He thought about the cinder blocks, with their neatly

At Risk of Being a Fool

molded holes, but gave them up. The blocks would mess up the explosion, rather than add missile force. The trusses were probably best, more effective.

It would take them another couple weeks to get that far. That was okay. He had lots of time. The important thing was to do it right, and get away clean. Not to get caught by the cops, and sure as hell not by Rivera. He had to keep his homeys out of it, too. It was safer, for them, and for him.

He tested the scaffolding ladder with one foot. It rocked some, but that didn't bother him. Noiselessly, he climbed to the top.

FOUR

Bright Futures Transition Facility for Girls squatted in the middle-class neighborhood like a sulking bulldog amidst poodles. An unnaturally clean bulldog. The pavement looked as if someone routinely scrubbed it with a toothbrush. It matched the landscaping, with every bush sculpted, not into beauty, but conformity. Clean, sterile, almost snobbish propriety was the order of the day.

Jeanie shifted to the other foot as she waited on the doorstep. Perhaps it was only Mackie's stories, Sorrel's sullen silence, and Brynna's paranoia that made her expect the worst at Bright Futures Transition Facility for Girls.

"Yes, ma'am, can I help you?" The girl bowed her head, presenting a view of perfectly clean hair and nothing much else. The blondish hair was dull and dry, separated into two exactly symmetrical portions, like a stick of butter sliced with a hot knife.

"I'm Jeanie McCoy. I teach at the GED school. I'm here for Sorrel Quintana. Mrs. Mahoney said she'd been delayed, and I offered to come get her." Last week Jeanie had offered to transport Rosalie from Esperanza. Esperanza's wide, bright halls and relaxed atmosphere had warmed her. Rosalie had responded to the sharp-eyed housemothers with mingled irritation and affection, just as Jeanie's sons had spoken to her in their youth.

The girl's fleeting glance lit on her face. "I'm afraid she's with Mrs. Torrez right now," she said, with the air of reciting a hard-learned lesson. "Would you care to wait in the rec room?"

At Risk of Being a Fool

"I haven't met Mrs. Torrez yet," Jeanie said cheerfully. "Why don't I join them?"

The girl's instant recoil took her two steps back into the hallway. Jeanie followed. This poor, nervous child was a juvenile offender? Still, perhaps Mrs. Torrez's extreme control was necessary, particularly if Brynna and Sorrel were a representative sample. The girls always took every inch offered and several miles that weren't.

The girl scuttled ahead of her, pausing at the end of a side hallway. "Mrs. Torrez's office is the last door on the right." She snatched up a basket of cleaning supplies and vanished, removing herself from any possible blame for Jeanie's actions.

The inexorable march of a single voice sounded from the office. Jeanie frowned after the girl and then at the closed door. With sudden decision, she knocked on the door and turned the handle without waiting for an answer.

Mrs. Torrez sat enthroned behind a massive desk of black metal. Her excruciatingly perfect black-and-white hair formed a helmet around the commanding face. Steel-gray eyes matched the metallic sheen of the tailored business suit. The curtains on the only window blocked outside light and roaming eyes. Sorrel sat across from her, peculiarly colorless under the fluorescent lights.

Jeanie might have been invisible, a speck on the floor to be mopped up later.

". . . Unfortunate behavior, Miss Quintana, especially following yesterday's expedition to the police station to make your statement regarding the courthouse incident. I hoped we had come to an end of this intolerable rebellion. But clearly not." The verbal dagger pricked with every word.

Sorrel looked fixedly at a knot in the floorboard between

her shoes. "I didn't do nothing." She clasped her hands in her lap, the knuckles white.

"Ah. And yet the girls were full of your little stories."

"We was just talking. It was rec time, we're supposed to talk."

"And I suppose," the soft voice went on, "you forgot our rule about war stories? About egging others on to acts of violence?"

"I didn't. It was just, you know, we was talking about our families, that's all."

The scene of debasement tore at Jeanie's gut. Without knowing the rights or wrongs of the matter, she ranged herself beside Sorrel. Mrs. Torrez's eyes never flickered in her direction.

"Your 'family'? Oh yes. Your disgusting story about a family riot. Perhaps you don't understand civilized behavior, Miss Quintana, but disrupting a wedding is hardly a usual topic in girls' recreation, at least at this facility, no matter what you may brag of at home. Of course, I suppose I can hardly expect true comprehension from one of your family background. Your grandmother, actually stomping—"

Sorrel boiled out of her seat. "You keep your fuckin' mouth off my grandmother."

Jeanie stepped in front of Sorrel with a warning look. Sorrel flinched, closed her eyes, and sank into the chair.

"I beg your pardon?" said the voice, detached, mocking. "Did you speak to me?"

Jeanie turned, her mouth agape. Mrs. Torrez reached towards a set of forms squared neatly on her desk.

"Because if you did—"

"No," said Sorrel. The words jerked out in spurts. "I mean, I'm sorry. I forgot, like, that we're not supposed to talk about before we . . . I mean, before."

At Risk of Being a Fool

"Estelle," said Jeanie, with determined good-humor. She'd be damned if she'd call her Mrs. Torrez. "I'm Jeanie McCoy. I'm Sorrel's teacher. I don't believe we've met."

"Ah yes," said Estelle Torrez. Her glance flicked the doorway and sliced across Jeanie's cheek. A slight rearrangement of her swivel chair brought Sorrel back into view.

"I'm afraid," Jeanie said firmly, "this misunderstanding is my fault. Sorrel and I were discussing essay topics, working on brainstorming techniques so she doesn't freeze come test time. The story of the prank at the wedding came up then."

"Prank."

"Yes, a prank. Some families pull pranks on each other at weddings. It's traditional. My own father carried a whip and shotgun to my wedding reception."

"Really. Well, Mrs. McCoy, I can't answer for what may be traditional in your family, but that's not overly important. You don't appear to be quite with the program, and that is important. By glorifying disorderly behavior, Miss Quintana is undermining the structure of this facility. She must adapt, because if this facility doesn't suit her, she will need to await placement elsewhere. Won't you, Miss Quintana? I believe you've been down this road once before?"

The naked pain in Sorrel's face shook Jeanie to the core.

"I'm sorry, Mrs. Torrez," Sorrel managed to say. "I didn't mean to undermine the facility. I . . ." Sorrel paused, peering at the desk as if hunting for an apology written there. "I think the things I'm learning here are important. I'm really sorry."

"Thank you. I appreciate your concern. This little matter will be noted in your file."

"Yeah." Sorrel said, almost inaudibly. "Can I go now?"

"Perhaps you—"

"Yes," said Jeanie shortly. "Here are the keys, Sorrel. Go get in the car."

"She will not—"

"Sorrel is late for class, which began ten minutes ago at a place several miles from here. Move it, Sorrel, the class is waiting on you." Sorrel escaped with the keys.

Estelle Torrez remarked, "She is to be supervised constantly. The police indicated as much yesterday, during that unsavory little ordeal. It quite threw our schedule to the winds. Letting her out with your keys is unwise."

"Sorrel was under my authority as of ten minutes ago. Humiliating young people is unproductive. Moreover," Jeanie added with malice aforethought and careful emphasis, "it's unprofessional." There! She'd thrown the gauntlet, with the ultimate insult of Jeanie's world. Brynna's pithy obscenities weren't even in the same league.

Estelle Torrez read the challenge instantly. "Mrs. McCoy, I don't require lectures on professionalism from a woman reduced to teaching juvenile offenders."

"Reduced? Oh Estelle, how utterly petty." Now that Sorrel had escaped the woman's clutches, Jeanie's anger drained away. "It's impossible to be 'reduced' to teaching." Prodded by an unnamable instinct, she added, "You must be a lonely woman. I'm sorry."

Estelle rose. "How dare you?"

Jeanie met her eyes with pity. "I'll be going now. If you ever need to talk, Estelle, just call me. Jeanie McCoy. I'm in the book."

She stood there for a moment. Estelle Torrez said nothing.

Jeanie left, closing the door gently.

Quinto drew a man's face, all angles and ill temper. Sorrel recovered her dignity with the help of a hand mirror.

At Risk of Being a Fool

Dillon listened to his headphones, his eyes at half-mast. Brynna studied a lipstick ad in a fashion magazine. Tonio wrestled with a math problem. Rosalie wandered around the room. Jeanie perched on a table, talking quietly with Mackie Sandoval.

They were waiting, all of them.

"I'm afraid there's not, Jeanie." Mackie looked at Sorrel, who examined her fingernails with complete absorption. "She had a different placement, the same place Rosalie's at now, Esperanza, wonderful people. But she loused it up good and bounced herself back to Corrections. Esperanza agreed to take her again after six months, if they had an opening, but they rarely do. The voluntaries all go there, like Rosalie, so there's not much room for the detainees. Torrez's place is rarely booked up, so she takes the overflow. I have to say she does stick to procedure mostly."

"She enjoys the power. Her little tantrum was sadistic."

Mackie nodded. "Yep, she's on a power trip. But it's rough finding people to do that kind of work. The supervisors have to live there, you know, at least part of the time. Randy told Sorrel to wait for Esperanza, but she couldn't stand it, never getting to see her kid. It's the last step, before parole. She said she'd tough it out with Torrez. She figures it's worth it."

Jeanie looked at Sorrel with new respect.

"There's a good side to all this, Jeanie. We do have successes, like Natalie and Maria. The girls respect survivors like that, who've been through the gutters and come out with a real life."

"Especially Rosalie."

"Yeah, that bit with the baby really got her. Did you know the foster Mom's trying to have Rosalie's rights suspended?"

"Can she do that?"

"Not easily. She's new at it, got all wound up about little Dominic. She's making a heck of a fuss. I guess Child Services will have to pull him out, place him in a different home, and that's a shame. It's hard on Rosalie. She's a lousy mother, but she adores Dominic."

"That's going to throw Rosalie right off the deep end." Not that Rosalie's needs outweighed Dominic's. But the decision reminded Jeanie too strongly of the old question posed to many heartbroken men. Which should we save, the mother or the child?

Mackie's mouth twisted, acknowledging the truth of the remark. "But we do have successes, Jeanie, that's the big thing. I'm so glad Ricardo Cervantes agreed to come. He used to be really big in the gang, high up in the pecking order. Same gang as Quinto and Tonio, up in Portland. He's Quinto's brother, you know. He got the rug pulled out from under him and turned himself around. He's at a big retail operation now, on the junior management track. They just love him to death. Works long hours, conscientious—all that and bilingual, it's hard to beat."

The door sprang open, and a young man strode in the room. *Han Solo,* thought Jeanie, *only Hispanic.* He wore that same engaging grin, the sense of adventure, as he coursed through life on his own cock-eyed mission.

Quinto and Tonio sprang up. "Hey man, good to see you, homeboy," Tonio said, his eyes shining.

"Right on, looking good. How about you, Flaco, hanging in there? You still fit your nickname! You're as skinny as ever. How's the artist? Whoa, is that your latest? Old Maldonado's face, right there on the paper. Want to hang it up? We can throw darts at it, huh, whatcha think?" Ricardo caught Quinto's head under his arm, and knuckled it. Quinto yelped in happy protest. Laughing, Ricardo shoved him away.

At Risk of Being a Fool

Brynna and Rosalie orbited the trio. Brynna actually looked attractive, as a brief animation lit her discontented face. Quinto and Tonio cleared tables out of the way. Dillon watched with detached interest, as though it were a television show. Sorrel's glance recorded the presence of each of the young men—Ricardo, Dillon, Tonio, and Quinto—and slid back to Ricardo. Her shoulders tensed. She seemed to be waiting for something.

Ricardo grinned at Mackie. "It's like coming home again," he said. Mackie threw a hand into the air. Ricardo grabbed it and swatted her on the shoulder. "Hey lady, you do good work."

"Did good work with you anyway. This is Jeanie. She replaced Sarah."

"Good to see you." Ricardo didn't offer to shake hands, but his open grin and sharp nod served the same purpose. "How's my bro doing?"

"Quinto's doing great," said Jeanie warmly. "It's a long way," she added, "through all five tests, but he's plugging away at it. One down, four to go."

"Cool." Ricardo raised an eyebrow at Quinto. "Which one?"

"Social Studies," said Quinto proudly. "Executive, Legislative, and Judicial."

"Right on, way to go. So Mackie, what's the drill? Haven't done none of these motivational speeches before. Listened to plenty of them though." Ricardo glanced around the room, spotted Dillon sitting in his corner, and ambled towards him. He turned a chair backwards and sat down, resting his elbows on the back. Ricardo noted the cell phone in Dillon's pocket. His gaze dropped to Dillon's ankle. "House arrest?"

"Nope. Off it, a month ago."

59

"Lost your jewelry, huh?" The wry comment referred to the locator bracelet, worn on the ankle, which pinpointed an offender's location on a twenty-four hour basis. "Congrats," he said. "Been there, done that. All of it."

The two regarded each other as the others dragged up chairs. Dillon dropped the headphones on the table, angled his chair towards Ricardo, and sat back, arms crossed over his chest.

Ricardo seemed to withdraw. "The gang was good to me," he said in a low voice. "Home wasn't so good. Quinto can tell you if he wants, I won't. You can guess, usual stuff: Mom on the stuff, no Dad that I could see. But the gang, that was good. I had a place to belong, people to back me up." His voice dropped further. "Guys I really cared about, you know." He glanced around, meeting one look after another. "Only, the gang, it's a dead end."

Ricardo slipped into a natural cadence, the swing in his speech like Tonio's, but with higher hills and lower valleys. "You got to get out of there, to have a good life. You don't got to leave your friends. What you gotta do, you gotta drag 'em along with you. That's what I'm trying to do here." He nodded at Tonio, and cuffed Quinto on the shoulder. "Detention facility is the pits. You know, you've been there, right? Prison's worse. The older you get, the more they shove you into the adult courts. And no matter how much I love my homeboys, I ain't going to spend the rest of my life in an eight-by-ten cell staring at 'em. 'Sides, they don't stick you with your homeboy, you know what I'm saying?"

Dillon snorted. "That's the fuckin' truth," he said. "Talk to my Dad, he'll tell you."

Ricardo nodded. "Once I was in the Dandridge craphouse, like my bro here, I got to thinking it through. I seen it, then. It's one side or the other. Me, I want a nice

At Risk of Being a Fool

car, a nice house, and money enough to go party when I feel like it. I don't want to be watching the door, keeping my head down, wondering who's coming through next. Get it? Maldonado, the son-of-a-bitch—"

Quinto let out a laugh and stifled it, with a guilty look at Mackie. Mackie flipped her hand, dismissing it. He relaxed.

"He done a good thing along with all the shit. He hooked me up with Mackie there. Mackie got me a couple jobs, and when I got my GED, she called a buddy or two in retail, and got me in with a national department store. I do promotional stuff, community relations, advertising layout, like that."

"They're real happy with him," Mackie confirmed. "Speaking Spanish, especially. Of course, he had to clean it up first, and drop the cuss words." Mackie and Ricardo grinned at each other, old friends.

The door swung open, and a burly man put his head through the doorway, wearing a hesitant smile. He was a homely-looking guy, his coarse black hair sticking out from under a baseball cap. His big, broad face wore the familiar crumple of the outdoorsman, with a sag around the eyes from squinting in sunlight.

Quinto jumped out of his seat, his face alight. "Mr. Rivera! You come to get me? Let me go back to work now! Huh?"

"Hi, Quinto." Laughter shot through the booming voice. "Hey, who's that I see?" At Mackie's welcoming wave, Danny strode into the room, exuding energy.

Ricardo grinned and held out his hand. "Danny Rivera, hey, like old times. Good to see you, bud. Quinto told me you got stuck with him. Still into the mentorship deal, huh?"

Danny Rivera pumped his hand. "I see Mackie pulled in our favorite success story. Quinto tells me you're hot stuff these days, Ricky." He glanced at the others, nodding to each. His smile faded a little. "Hey, Dillon, doing okay, are you?" Dillon examined him, cold-faced.

Quinto romped around them, an eager puppy with muddy paws. "So, am I back on the crew? Huh, huh? God, I'm sick of the House, let me come back, okay? I do good there, you know I do, I'm a good worker."

"You're a good worker, Quinto. Even Bryce said so." Danny's face sagged. "God, what a thing."

"Mr. Wogan?" said Quinto respectfully. "How's he doing, huh?"

"Yeah," said Mackie. "Sit down, Danny, tell us how Bryce is getting along. Ricardo, Bryce Wogan's the foreman at Danny's site. He got hurt, pipe bomb left at the site last Saturday. Touch and go, there, for a while, but last I heard, they thought he'd make a comeback."

"Well, he's a tough bugger," Danny said. "If anyone can, he will. It'll be tough, though. He lost three fingers on his right hand, and his right eye too. Gonna be a lot of scars, mess up his good looks. It could have been a hell of a lot worse. You know pipe bombs, the blast goes every which way. The worst of it went the other way, took a chunk out of the truck. Bryce was damned lucky. Old Bryce, I still can't believe it. He says he'll be back on the job, but I don't know." Danny looked bleak. Jeanie followed his thought without effort. Construction work with half a hand, and one eye. "He'll be in rehab for a long time."

"Rehab?" said Rosalie, frowning. "Like, for drugs?"

"Physical therapy, and like that. He's got to learn to do stuff all over again, because his hand won't work right."

"Oh," said Rosalie, uncomprehending.

"But you're still working, right?" said Quinto. "So I can come back!"

At Risk of Being a Fool

"Well, that's why I came. I'm having a little trouble, going to have to work on the new foreman a little. After the pipe bomb, he's a little nervous about mentorship."

"But I wouldn't. Hurt a guy? I never, you just ask anybody."

"I know, I know. I been telling him. What I figure is, give me the rest of the week, and then show up Monday, same job site. You stick close to me, buddy, you hear? Don't give him any grief."

Quinto nodded energetically. "Like always. He'll see. Mr. Wogan, he didn't like me much either, but he seen it, I'm a worker. When I get out, first thing I'm doing is get a job on construction with you."

"Lotsa jobs around, Quinto," said Ricardo. "Come up to Portland, back home, I'll get you in at the store. Better job." He looked at Danny apologetically. "Air conditioning, you know. Besides the kid's an artist. He could use it in advertising or something."

"Couldn't have said it better. There's lots of opportunities out there for a guy with Quinto's spunk," said Danny. He slapped his thighs. "Well, I'll be getting along now. Just thought I'd drop by. Glad to have caught you, Ricky. Bye Quinto, Dillon. Good-bye, Mackie." The door thumped closed behind him.

"Well," said Mackie. "That's good news, Quinto. Monday, it is! I'll let Mr. Maldonado know. How about Jeanie and I back off for a bit? We've got paperwork and phone calls to catch up on. That okay with you guys?"

Mackie retreated to the office, and Jeanie sat next to the office doorway, in visual range but out of earshot of quiet voices. Mackie dialed Maldonado's number from memory. Jeanie looked through student essays, keeping half an eye on Brynna and Sorrel. Estelle Torrez, reflected Jeanie, would have had a fit. Who knew what they were arranging between them? Something despicable, naturally.

Sorrel didn't have much to say, but she was listening. She'd been pale for several days, though it was hard to tell under all the makeup. Stress, probably. Quinto, though, was exuberant, barely able to confine himself to one section of the room.

You couldn't program emotional growth, just accelerate it a tad, here and there. So many rehabilitative efforts tried to make sows' ears into silk purses. And what happened, the moment the pressure let up? There'd be a bunch of pigs, running everywhere, tearing up the city, and everyone would be surprised. Jeanie grinned to herself at the foolish analogy.

"Excuse me, er . . . Jeanie?"

Jeanie looked up, startled. Ricardo Cervantes stood next to her, running his hand over his styled black hair.

"Hey, can I talk to you and Mackie for a bit?"

"Of course. Mackie?" She followed Ricardo to the office, and stood in the doorway.

"What's up, Ricky?" Mackie set down the phone.

Ricardo sat on the desk, one foot cocked up against the table leg. "Well, it's nothing, really. It's just, jeez." He sighed and shrugged. "Look, I wanted to tell you, one of the guys in our old gang, Matt Houston, he got sent up when I did. Only he got sent to the pen." He jerked his thumb to the east. "He was some older than me, got tried as an adult. He jumped the wall on a work release thing a few months back. Shit, you'd think they'd *know* he'd run. Work release," he snorted in disgust. "Anyway, cops called me, checking up on all his homeys, see if he called us. But I haven't heard from him since we got caught."

"Uh huh," said Mackie, a certain reservation in her voice.

At Risk of Being a Fool

Ricardo shot her a look. "Yeah, well, he sure don't fit into my life now, and that's a fact. I got no room for that kind of risk. Thing is, I figured he headed for Vegas, or L.A. or something, long gone, no problem. But with that bomb Saturday, I got to thinking. He wasn't just the easiest guy to get along with." His eyes flicked around the room, settled on Mackie, jerked away. "Look, Mackie, just keep an eye on Quinto for me. And you, too, Jeanie? My bro, he's not, he's—" He stood up, and hooked his thumbs into his belt. "He's an artist, he's got no . . ." He loosed his hand, and swung it up into the air helplessly.

"No survival skills," Mackie said.

He exhaled. "That's it. That's it, right on. I keep wondering, what if Matt grabs Quinto, gives him some shit story. Matt'd sucker him right in." He shook his head. "This is nuts, he's gone, he's off in Mexico for all I know. It's just, I got to thinking. That's why I called you a few days ago, figured I'd ask. Then I couldn't say it, and you asked me down, and I figured, what the hell. Made more sense to talk to you face to face. So just, kind of, watch out for my bro, will you? He don't always got good sense."

"No problem," said Mackie.

Ricardo looked at Jeanie, questioningly.

"Absolutely," said Jeanie.

Ricardo sighed. "Great, that's good. You call me if he gets into something, I'll come down and shake him up. It bugs me, him being so far away. I get down to see him a good bit, but what's an hour or two a week? You got a better chance than I do, keeping tabs on him."

"Jeanie does. I don't, not so much."

"Right, I figured. And Mackie, maybe you'd talk to Danny for me? Ask him the same? I couldn't catch him right now, the kid would've seen it."

"Sure thing," said Mackie, warmly reassuring.

Ricardo clapped a hand on Jeanie's shoulder, and the other on Mackie's, grinning his relief at them. Jeanie hid her surprise. He'd even overcome the "never touch" rule. Perhaps Quinto would too, in time.

"We'll watch out for Quinto," she vowed. "Never you fear."

FIVE

Sorrel's fingers shook as she wrote on the tablet in sprawling letters. One box of file folders, almost full; one and a half boxes of pencils; a bunch of printer cartridges. Mechanically, she looked at Carol's list of printers, hunting for spare cartridges for each one. It was stupid, all those different kinds of printers. Why couldn't they use the same kind? Or use that big laser printer down the hall? But no, Carol had a printer. Hilda had a printer, hauled down from the judge's office. Most of those anal-retentive types down the hall had printers, and they were all different.

God, she couldn't think. What the hell was she going to do?

She lined up the cartridges on the counter, sorted them, and started again.

"Are you all right, Sorrel?" asked Dorrie, resting a hand on her shoulder.

Sorrel slid out from under it. She closed her eyes and throttled down the anger. Dorrie didn't mean anything. She was trying to be nice. "I'm fine. Thanks." Sorrel had to force out the words.

"Boy, doesn't the security get to you? Seems like every time I head to the restroom, they're running that metal detector over me." Dorrie's laugh floated over her shoulder as she ran her fingers over the shelves of file books. "I told that one cop, John, his name is. I said look, if I wanted to kill Hodges, I wouldn't use a pipe bomb. I'd use rat poison in the coffee like in that old movie, who was it? Lily

Tomlin, I think. He didn't think it was funny. Security guards have no sense of humor."

That's for damned sure. "It's pretty bad," Sorrel said, making an effort. "But I'm okay with it." The cops thought Judge Hodges was the bomb's target. It was only a coincidence that it was so close to the van's drop-off point. She hoped they were right. She really, really hoped so.

"Well, don't fret about it. Even the judges have to go through the metal detector. Funny, huh?"

"Yeah." The security guys bugged her, always staring, as if their eyes had rubber bands on them, hooked to her ass. They counted her sneezes, her trips to the crapper, noticed every place her hand touched a countertop. If she snatched ten minutes to use the phone, somebody scribbled it down in a little book. Twenty fuckin' months in Correctional, a month at Esperanza, one month back in Correctional, now almost six weeks at Torrez's house of horrors. No wonder she was schizoid.

Sorrel gave up on the cartridges and filled out the order sheet by guess. If she had to count them again, she'd scream. She rubbed her sweaty hands on her jeans and inspected her nail polish. Dust drizzled everywhere, floating through the windows from the courtyard where they yanked out all the bushes. That way, Carol said, there'd be fewer hiding places for bombs.

A guy at the counter waved a paper in Dorrie's face. Dorrie patted the air in front of him. Sorrel would have hauled off and slugged him, if he treated her like that. Maybe that's why they didn't let her work counters. A moment's humor flared and extinguished itself. Sorrel moved into Dorrie's line of sight, pointed to her watch, and held up five fingers. Dorrie nodded, her stream of talk uninterrupted.

At Risk of Being a Fool

Sorrel slid out the door and down the hallway past the security guard. Habit took over as Sorrel gave him the eye, and a swing of the hip. She might as well make his day for him. Once in the bathroom, she took care of a few things and repaired her face. The panic in the mirrored face shoved her back, suddenly breathless.

It wasn't the security guards making her crazy. It was the fear, the fear that he was looking for her. She didn't used to be afraid of him. But when they'd evacuated the building, the fear had zoomed out of nowhere, that he was out to get her. She couldn't shake loose of it. She wouldn't nark on him. He had to know that, didn't he?

Worse, yet, the other fear had sprung up, full-blown. She hadn't even thought of it until yesterday, listening to the guys shooting the bull. All of a sudden, it hit her, and she'd had a hell of time hiding her thoughts. She'd kept to herself, being inconspicuous. Damn, that was Torrez's word, inconspicuous, and here she was using it.

Had the others caught on yet? Jeanie didn't have a clue, but like Quinto said, what else was new? Mackie was smarter. What if they knew, and were hiding it? They'd tell Randy, and Torrez. Her breathing came in short, hard pants. If Torrez found out, she'd be in deep shit. Torrez had had a cow, just with the story about the wedding.

The door opened and a woman walked in. Sorrel Quintana smoothed her face into emptiness and retouched her eye shadow with meticulous attention.

Tonio stopped short in the classroom doorway.

"That dog," he said.

"Looks funny," agreed Jeanie. "So I've been told, several times this afternoon. He's a nice dog, nonetheless. He can't help his looks. His name is Corrigan."

Tonio flashed her a look she couldn't interpret. Corrigan took a sniff or two and bumped his head under Tonio's fingers. Tonio rubbed his ears. "Friendly," he remarked.

"Oh yes. He's a longhaired dachshund, about twelve years old. He's my sister Shelley's dog, but she's in Germany right now, so I've had him for about a year. He gets lonely by himself at home, but if you guys don't like him, I won't do it again."

"No, bring him, bring him," said Quinto. "I never had no dog."

"Germany?" said Rosalie, as if she'd heard the word on a game show, and couldn't quite remember what it meant.

"He looks deformed," said Sorrel. "Like he got caught in a door and stretched out."

Jeanie nodded. "My sister took him through a revolving door once. His front end wound up in one section, and his tail two sections back. It took forever to get him out of the works."

Five faces showed identical looks of shock and even Dillon gave her a measuring look. Rosalie frowned. "Boy, that must have hurt him, poor baby."

"Actually," Jeanie said, "my sister is known to exaggerate, on occasion."

Over the next hour, Corrigan trotted from one student to the other. Jeanie made her own rounds, soothed by the counterpoint of the dog's travels. Rosalie, regrettably, was delighted to have yet another legitimate distraction.

"Come on, Rosalie," Jeanie said, removing Corrigan from the girl's encircling arms. "Essay time. Pick a topic. Close your eyes and point."

With a rippling laugh, Rosalie stabbed her finger onto the sheet and read the words under her finger. " 'Should laws be enacted to prevent the sale of handguns in the

At Risk of Being a Fool

United States? Explain your reasoning.' " Rosalie blinked. "Gee, I don't know. Who cares? Everybody's got guns. My Dad, he's got guns. He goes hunting every year, gets deer mostly. He got an elk one time. They got big horns."

Guns were not Jeanie's favorite topic. "So your Dad has rifles, right? The long ones," she added, seeing Rosalie's bewilderment. "Handguns are the little ones, like you see on TV."

"For holding up liquor stores," said Dillon unexpectedly.

Jeanie forced herself to relax and shifted her chair to include Dillon in the conversation. He'd have to take the same test. All of them would, and the Lord only knew what topics they'd have. "Among other things," she agreed. "Though homeowners buy them, to protect themselves. What do you think, Rosalie? Is it a good thing for people to buy handguns, if they want them?" Rosalie looked wary, perhaps from too many talks with police and parole officers. "The test graders don't care what your opinion is. They just want you to explain your opinion."

Jeanie cast a glance at Corrigan, presently engaged in sniffing Dillon's boots. As she watched, Corrigan leaned against Dillon's leg briefly, and wandered off again. Dillon, he'd concluded, was not a wolf, regardless of Jeanie's opinion.

"What do you think, Dillon? Should ordinary citizens be able to buy handguns, as they do now?" At his sardonic look, she replayed the sentence from his viewpoint, and answered it. *Should a regular guy be able to steal a gun if he wanted one? Damned straight.*

"Who needs guns?" he said. His fists clenched a time or two, pocked scars standing out livid white against the dark tan.

Corrigan stretched across Brynna's feet, and yawned.

Perhaps he knew Dillon was no threat, but perhaps he was being as perverse as Shelley contended when she'd named him for the rebellious pilot, Wrong-Way Corrigan.

"You're doing that on purpose, to scare me," she accused, pointing to Dillon's flexing biceps.

He grinned at her, white teeth flashing like summer lightning, and as quickly gone. For one instant, he looked like a normal kid, the kid he might have been, raised in different circumstances. Brynna moistened her lips. Sorrel angled herself a bit, displaying her ripe figure.

Jeanie cleared her throat. "So, what do the rest of you think? It's a topic you may well see when you take the Writing test. On handguns, Brynna."

After a moment, Brynna dragged her eyes from Dillon. "I don't see what all the fuss is about. I know a guy, he's got all kinds of guns. I don't think he ever uses them, he just collects them." She snorted. "Once I seen him holding one with a long barrel, rubbing his hand over it, like it was—" She checked herself, glancing at Jeanie. "—a dog or something."

"All a gun's gotta do, is work," said Dillon. "It's a backup plan, that's all."

"I don't trust no one behind me with a gun," said Tonio, joining the conversation. "If a homey shoots some sucker, that's all of us in prison for life."

"Accidental firing is a great danger," said Jeanie, striving to move back to safe ground. "If it's a tool, then it should be used safely, not left around loose. Is that right?"

"Any moron can shoot a gun," Tonio said. "If I'm gonna do a job, I'll do it myself. Like on my motorbike, when the sprocket broke, I didn't take it to no dude in a shop somewhere. I took it to work with me, and welded it back together. It's my life on that bike, you know. Same reason I

At Risk of Being a Fool

don't trust no fucker with a gun, either."

"They let you use the welder at the Yard?" Dillon said, interested.

"Yeah, on my own time. The guy there, he's okay. I done some stuff for him, too."

"My Mama's got a gun," said Sorrel. "She keeps it at the apartment in case some dipshit breaks in, thinks a bunch of women's an easy target. It's handy getting rid of the shits too, like Carlos, damn him."

"You waved a gun at him?" asked Quinto, wide-eyed.

"Grandma did. She let off a couple shots over his head, right into the wall. Said she'd go for his balls next. God, it was funny. He ran like hell, forgot his stereo, too. Of course, we had to move after that. Landlady got shitty about the holes. But screw her. A woman's gotta take care of herself, don't she?"

"Don't you worry Tiffy'll get hold of the gun?" asked Rosalie. "My Daddy, he always took the rifle apart and locked it up when he came home. He hid the black powder and bullets, too. We never found 'em when we looked that time." Her eyes shifted.

"We hide it from Tiffy, top shelf of the back closet. When she gets bigger, we'll teach her to use it right, let her blow the hell out of some pop cans. That's what Mama did with me."

"Quinto, what do you think about handgun control?" Jeanie asked.

"I don't like guns," Quinto said. As he spoke, his hand drew faces along the edges of his paper. Jeanie recognized a few of them. Danny Rivera, Tonio, Ricardo, two of the men at Dandridge House. "The only thing a gun's for is killing people. So I don't like them," he said unequivocally. "Not ever. Some guys I know." His glance flicked up, hit Brynna,

Tonio, and Dillon, and skittered away. "They robbed one of them QuickStop places. They wanted me to go too, be lookout. But I didn't, 'cause one of 'em had a gun." He shot a look at Dillon, dropped his gaze to his drawings. "I wouldn't nark, though. I wouldn't do that. No names, no nothing."

Sorrel leaned forward and slapped the table. "My Mama works in a convenience store, dipshit. Anybody turns a gun on her, I'll kill him."

"I didn't go, I said so. They said I was just scared," he muttered. "They was right, too."

"So," said Jeanie bracingly, "Sorrel's brought up a fine point. If a handgun can be turned to violence, that's one thing, but when it's your own family, it matters a lot more."

Brynna, whose family was her own worst enemy, rolled her eyes. Quinto's hand jerked, marring a sketch. She recognized Bryce Wogan from the newspaper write-up on his therapy.

"What I mean, Rosalie, is that guns don't seem like a big deal until your own family is threatened. Right, Dillon? I mean, hearing about a shooting on the news isn't nearly as important to you as if some guy threatens your grandmother with a gun. Or your mother, right, Rosalie?"

A stillness smothered the room. Rosalie flinched as Dillon boiled out of his seat.

"Any fucking son of a bitch touches my grandma, I'm gonna kill him," he bellowed. "I'll waste his whole family, you hear me? Don't matter if they got dogs, tear gas— Fucking hogs'll need assault rifles to take me out—"

"Dillon, I didn't mean—"

A hard hand grabbed her arm and dragged her away from Dillon. Tonio shoved her out the door and yanked Brynna through after her. Quinto and Rosalie skidded

At Risk of Being a Fool

through the doorway as a loud crash sounded behind them. Sorrel emerged with more dignity, snatching her arm away from Tonio with an offended look.

"The dog," said Jeanie, starting forward.

Tonio yanked the door shut. "He ain't gonna hurt a dog. His grandma'd get mad."

"His grandmother. Ah," said Jeanie, as realization swept over her.

"He lives with her. Most everybody else in his family's in prison or dead." Another crash sounded over the growl of Dillon's curses. "Just a chair," Tonio remarked. "I figured he'd go for the windows."

True. Dillon hadn't come through the door after them, either. In fact, in Dillon's own distorted way, he was striving for a modicum of self-control. "I'm afraid that was not one of my more inspired analogies."

Tonio's eyes twinkled at her. "Afraid not."

They heard a polite scratching sound at the door. Tonio opened the door a crack and Corrigan emerged, ruffled by the noise. Rosalie snatched him up, careful of his weak back. Corrigan licked her chin. She buried her flushed face in his fur, his long fur clinging to her damp cheeks. Rosalie's arms were as thin as celery sticks. She might be off the drugs now, as Esperanza hoped, but her appetite had yet to return.

"He's so nice. Wish he was mine. But I'd be lousy at taking care of him. Like Dominic."

"That's your son."

"Yeah. Nine months old." Tears rolled steadily. "He was a drug baby."

Brynna and Sorrel disappeared into the women's bathroom. They'd probably be there for half an hour, but that was okay. Jeanie doubted the classroom would be useable

75

for a while. Quinto collapsed in the corner again, wrapping his arms around his knees. Tonio strolled down the hallway and crouched beside him.

"I didn't mean for him to get hurt," Rosalie mumbled. "I cleaned up when I saw him hurting after he was born. I couldn't stand it, that I hurt my own baby. And I *wanted* to take care of him, be a good mother. I did, Jeanie, I really did."

The imploring look tore Jeanie's heart. "I know that."

"Only, my Dad and Mom, they wouldn't even see us. Well, Mom, she did, when I saw her in grocery stores, but Dad, he said I was," the words sank into a singsong chant, "a disgrace, a whore, dishonor to the family. Before the baby, my Dad caught me with Dominic's Daddy once, and chased him off with his gun.

"All my life, I was Daddy's girl, and now he won't say nothing to me, nothing at all. Hangs up if I call, yells at my Mom if she says my name. I thought I could do it, be a mommy, but that money come in, for the welfare, and I spent it all on meth. There's my baby, crying, needing stuff, and I spent it all. Every dime."

Corrigan squirmed closer and rubbed his nose against the girl's face.

"Dominic's safe now, and so are you. You're doing well at Esperanza."

"I guess. But the judge, he took my baby away, gave him to foster care. The lady there, she wants to adopt him. Maybe I should let her, my baby don't need no fucked-up druggie. His Daddy sure don't want him. You should've heard him cuss out the judge about child support. Judge Hodges threw him in jail for thirty days. Jeanie, I love my baby. I do love him."

"Sometimes," Jeanie said, "the best love there is, is to let someone go to a safer place." Her throat closed, as the parallel overwhelmed her. Edward lived in a safer place. *But I need him so much. No one else knows me.*

"Hey, don't you cry, too. You're twisting your ring, like you do when you're worried. It's no good crying, Jeanie, it don't change nothing." Rosalie shook Jeanie's wrist.

The touch, from one of her "untouchables," made her dizzy. Jeanie drew a shaky breath, and wiped the tears from her cheeks. "Hey, we're twins, with our blotchy faces. Don't we look awful?"

Rosalie managed a chuckle. "Maybe you should wear makeup, Jeanie. Want to borrow mine?"

"No thanks. By the time it covers all the freckles, it looks like a mud pie on a snowman. Hang on a minute." Jeanie went to the bathroom and retrieved several twists of toilet paper. Sorrel and Brynna were completely engrossed at opposite ends of the mirror. She blew her nose and took the rest of the tissue out to Rosalie.

Rosalie unslung her purse from her shoulder and rummaged through it. "Hey, Jeanie, how about a tattoo? One of the girls, she got a bunch of tattoos at those little machine-things? She gave me one."

A business card fell onto the floor. Oscar Kemmerich, Attorney at Law. A scribble in Rosalie's unformed handwriting read *Silvio*, followed by a phone number. Dominic's father, perhaps?

Rosalie snatched it up, stuffed it into the bottom of her purse, and extracted the stickers. "Here it is, see? You stick it on, and press hard, and the paper comes off. It's a butterfly."

You are a butterfly, thought Jeanie.

Rosalie smiled. "Here, let me, please? I want to." Her sadness had vanished.

"Well," said Jeanie, "all right." She held out her arm.

"No," said Rosalie, with a teasing note. "There, right there."

Jeanie found a paper pressed to her cheek. Fingers rubbed and pried carefully.

"There, it looks great. Hey, Quinto, Tonio, look at this. Don't she look great?"

Chuckles spread through the hallway, in melodic counterpoint to the fist pounding the walls of the classroom.

"Only a few more steps, Edward, we're almost there. Now a step up. Foot up, up, up; there you go."

"I do believe we've made it," said Edward in surprise.

Jeanie beamed at him. Kherra was right; he was having a good day. She'd said other things too, less palatable. "Don't you go foolin' yourself, Jeanie girl," Kherra warned. "It's not an improvement. It's an oasis in the desert." Kherra, of milk-chocolate skin and many-braided hair, was a lady of infinite heart. Emergencies flooded into her hands on a daily basis and emerged as gentle streams sliding through her capable fingers.

"Yes, of course," Jeanie said. But Kherra looked troubled as they left.

An apple-blueberry crisp was baking in the oven, as was Edward's favorite hot chili casserole. He loved strong flavors, to do battle with his fading taste buds. Jeanie had cranked up the spice on her chili until she feared a visit from the fire marshal. Edward looked around the small living room. He'd been there many times, and even stayed overnight in the hospital bed that took up so much room in the larger bedroom. The unfamiliarity still threw him.

"The house looks smaller than it used to," he said.

"After the boys grew up, we didn't need such a big

At Risk of Being a Fool

house. And now you stay at your club so much, it seemed better to get a smaller house."

"Ah. I see. I believe I have a new investor, did I tell you? A young man came by late last night. I saw him through the window, admiring the club's garden. I rapped on the window and invited him in, but he left suddenly. No doubt he'll return during regular business hours." Edward was always in "business" of some sort. Lately, it was an environmentally conscious energy producer.

"A new investor? How encouraging." Now he was seeing phantoms in the garden at night. The floor seemed to tilt, as it did when she faced his delusions. It was like living in a house of mirrors, where everything was askew by a few vital degrees.

"Yes," mused Edward. A vague frown furrowed his forehead. "I'm not quite sure how he left. I didn't think there was a door just there, in the garden. A gate, I mean. Is there?"

"I'm sure there must be, if he didn't come inside," she said with false cheer.

"Tell me about your day. You seem a little stressed," he said.

She sat on the floor and pulled off his shoes. His feet were like blocks of wood. She rubbed his feet, trying to loosen the stiffness in his ankles, as she rambled on about her day. The flow of words seemed to relax him.

". . . So, I took Rosalie home. After all that uproar, I didn't want her to get sidetracked on the way to the bus. Mackie says there's at least one drug house about a block away, and Rosalie could sniff it out in a flash. Corrigan calmed her down a great deal."

Rita jumped onto the sofa, and settled into Edward's lap, purring loudly. Jeanie found herself watching his wrists, assessing his joint movement as he stroked her. "Yesterday, I found Rosalie down the hall talking to that lawyer,

Kemmerich. I called her back to the classroom, and she bounced right in, the way she does . . . you know, like a little girl skipping rope. I asked if he was bothering her. I thought maybe he was hitting on her, but she said no, he was just asking about the bus schedule." She sighed. "It might even be true, but you can never tell, with Rosalie. I just hate it, the way he hovers, as if he's waiting for us to do something illegal. Lawyers!"

"Some of my best friends . . ." Edward said, letting the sentence die suggestively. *Some of my best friends are lawyers, but I wouldn't want my son to marry one.*

They both laughed. Edward sobered, staring at her intently. Jeanie met his eyes. *Please love me, Edward,* she thought. *Please show me that you remember me.*

Slowly a smile engulfed his face. "Why Jeanie, my love, it appears that a butterfly has landed on your cheek." He touched the ink tattoo with a gentle finger.

Jeanie clutched his hand. She lowered his feet to the floor, and snuggled next to him on the sofa, her arms around him. "Edward, my darling, I do love you so."

She was home again, for the moment. Thank God.

It was fun, being invisible. He hid his grin. Some of the guys bragged about how good they were, how they could mooch around looking like regular kids. He didn't say nothing, just listened to 'em talk. Because they were wrong. You didn't want to look like everyone else, be part of a crowd. People noticed crowds of young guys. But no one noticed him.

He lay on the grass on his stomach, waving his feet in the air. With a pen wedged between his teeth, he studied a magazine open on the ground, where anyone could see it. He wasn't looking at guns, like a hood, no way. No, he was just dreaming about the cars he wanted, circling engine features,

At Risk of Being a Fool

and making little notes inside the back of the magazine, of prices and car parts. He'd seen the feet pause near him, the looks landing on the open magazine, the casual dismissal of a thing noted and promptly forgotten. Besides, he liked cars.

He liked a few other things, too. That was what it was all about, wasn't it? Improving your life, getting what you wanted? A high school teacher had told him that, like she never realized what a guy like him might want. She was thinking about her safe little house, her two-point-five kids, her guy in the armchair, pretty painted pictures on the wall, and a nice ocean cruise. God, what an idiot.

He looked down the hill and watched this one, the new teacher, hanging onto the old guy at the bridge over the lake. He'd asked around, broke into the classroom one night, and poked around in the office. He'd asked the others, to see if he'd missed something, but they agreed. She never talked about her family, or stuck pictures on her desk. He'd found some names and phone numbers, but not many. Kherra, Keith, Geoff, and Shelley. Shelley's didn't look like any phone number he'd ever seen, had periods in it instead of dashes. Maybe it was a web site. He'd written it down, so he could check it out. Mackie's Rolodex had the teacher's address and a phone number for Oriole's Nest. That turned out to be an old folks' home.

The wiener dog walked stiffly beside her. He'd checked for the leash, right away. If the dog nosed him out, from the smell in the classroom, it would be big trouble. It was twelve years old, he'd heard. He had an idea that was kind of old for a dog, so maybe it couldn't smell people as good as it used to. The dog couldn't run too good, either, so if he kept his distance, he'd be fine.

A couple of times, he'd parked down the street, and done a little following. Both times, she'd gone to the old folks' home at dinnertime, so today, he'd figured to poke through her house, while she was gone. But she was at home, after all. It was a helluva shock to see her come out of her house with the old guy.

It was the same old guy, too, the one who saw him last night. That was a bit of a coincidence, but maybe not. There weren't many men at the place. It worried him some, that the guy might remember him. He'd doubled back later, but the guy just stood there, staring out the window like his brain got flushed down the toilet. So, he'd quit worrying. Mostly. Anyway, he'd solved the little mystery of why she kept quiet about family. And, along the way, he'd found out a thing or two. It was handy, knowing where to hide things, what places no one would suspect. She wasn't a danger to him, not now anyway. But things changed when you didn't expect it, and you had to be ready.

A guy jogged his way. He pulled the pen out of his mouth, circled the price on an intake, and dog-eared the page. The guy threw him a glance, registering the non-threat, and passed by.

No threat, that was the idea. Never look like a threat. The stupid sucker.

He liked to plan. His probation officer called it being proactive. Proactive, he liked the word. There were a lot of problems you could prevent, by watching people. It made him smile a little, the things his P.O. didn't know.

The bomb went fine. Well, there had been two bombs, but one hadn't gone according to plan. If he'd done more preparation, if he'd been more "proactive," he'd have caught the problem before it happened.

He'd learned, though.

His probation officer said it more than once, admiring. He learned from experience.

SIX

"Boy's over there," Mr. Walker said, jabbing his finger.

"Over there" hulked a vast mechanized rig. Under it, reaching into the belly, stretched two forearms. Tonio, it appeared, was in the pit.

"Ah," said Jeanie. "Working on a—what is it?"

"Road grader. Scheduled maintenance." Mr. Walker adjusted the toothpick in the side of his mouth with a thoughtful air.

Silly me, of course it's a road grader. Tonio didn't work on cars and trucks, but road graders, cement mixers, flatbed trucks, street sweepers, and . . . er, things. Mackie said he worked in the County Yard doing maintenance on motorized equipment, but the County owned a good deal more than she'd thought.

"We get a few of these kids in every year. They put in these charity cases, knowing we don't got nothing better to do than baby-sit them." She looked at him quizzically, and his derisive sniff turned apologetic. "Well, not him, but some of them can't work worth beans. Always on a coffee break, or gabbing away. This one, this Tonio of yours, he's pretty quiet, stays busy. Stays late sometimes, off the clock. If he don't know what he's doing, he asks, and more than that, I don't expect at this stage." The methodical crunching of his jaws reduced the toothpick to mangled splinters. "We're good, I'd say. Who knows?" He spat the remains of the toothpick onto the gravel and gave her a wintry smile. "We may try to keep him on later. Handy with tools, more than I'd expected, considering. Like he's had a lot of practice, you know."

Good news, overall, Jeanie concluded, as she trundled her car along to the cannery. Local businesses blurred past her as she composed her mental notes. This wasn't her bailiwick, visiting employers and filling out interview forms. Mackie had planned to do it today, but an emergency at Hills of Glory cropped up and Mackie was off to settle it. Hills of Glory was a religious nursing home for low-income families. Precisely why this affected Mackie escaped her. Still, if it related to poverty or crime, Mackie had her hand in it somewhere.

Jeanie leaped at the chance to meet the employers. She was suffering a bad case of maternal overload. Grudgingly, the police had conceded that Quinto was an unlikely suspect, and apparently they'd never seriously suspected Sorrel of engineering the bomb scare. Still, shivers went down Jeanie's spine. If one more incident occurred, one more bit of violence connected with her program, official eyes would zero in on her kids and never look away.

Hence the employers. She didn't know why she sensed this urgency to see her kids in other settings. She felt like a helpful beaver, gathering thousands of small sticks in hopes of building an unbreakable dam. A beaver didn't wait until after the flood. Perhaps some bit of knowledge could prove innocence, if another crime occurred. Perhaps she could prevent violence, pour oil on troubled waters, cap the volcano before it erupted. Her efforts might be fruitless, but she couldn't sit back and do nothing. She couldn't help meddling. It was what teachers did.

The cannery's loading docks were a sight to behold, with bay after bay of open doors and ramps. Huge trucks backed up to the docks, gaping open like vast baby birds awaiting

At Risk of Being a Fool

Mama or Papa's offering. Workers mobbed the trucks, the ramps, and the open bays, operating dollies and forklifts. In each bay stood a sharp-eyed clerk, checking items on hand-held computers.

Dillon manned a small forklift, virtually invisible beyond the stack of crates he hoisted onto a truck's liftgate.

"He's a touchy bastard," said Millie Flores, warehouse supervisor, "but he's settled into Manuel's crew. We did have a little fuss about a crate or two that went missing, but Manuel says your guy's clean." Millie started to say something else, and caught it back. Jeanie smiled encouragement. "Manuel would know," said Millie, but her voice was doubtful.

"Manuel's been with you a long time."

"Ye-es." Millie looked over Jeanie's shoulder and drew back. "Well," she added, her voice raised. "Doing fine, he's just fine. Did you need me to sign something?"

"Yes, if you'd initial here?"

Jeanie stole a look over her shoulder as Millie scrawled her initials. Dillon glowered at her from his forklift.

"I, uh, I've got to check something." Millie beat a retreat to the third truck in her row.

"Hi, Dillon," Jeanie said, waving her hand. He flipped a lever and rolled to the next stack of crates. His total involvement in his work denied her presence. She waved anyway, and headed for Rosalie's workplace.

Rosalie worked at an experimental childcare run by the State. Or was it nonprofit, with government funding? At any rate, it served children from foster homes, or neglectful homes. Parents attended as well, to learn how to play with their children. The concept startled Jeanie. Didn't everyone know how to play with children? You made silly faces, rolled on the floor, tossed them in the air, and made darned sure you caught them as they fell. Apparently, not everyone knew the basics. Mackie hoped that Rosalie's fractured maternal skills could get a boost by working here.

Rosalie stood by the window, picking dead leaves from a large potted plant.

"You see what I mean," said Elizabeth to Jeanie. Elizabeth moved rapidly, cutting paper jack-o-lanterns out of construction paper. "Rosalie. The children are waiting for you. The paints, remember? And the plastic coveralls?"

"Oh, that's right," said Rosalie, the sunshine breaking out in her face. "Come on, kids, around the table." She thumped two tubs of finger paints on the table and turned to get more from the cabinet, oblivious to the small hands reaching for disaster.

Elizabeth slapped the jack-o-lantern on a stack of black cats with unnecessary force. "Candy, help Rosalie out, would you?"

Candy lifted the paint tubs out of reach. She poured yellow paint into a small bowl, capped the tub, and reached for the green. Over her shoulder, she spoke to Rosalie. "Plastic tablecloth first. Now the coveralls."

Rosalie enveloped the children with affection. The coveralls did not, in fact, "cover all," especially when Rosalie arranged them.

"She's gentle," offered Elizabeth. "And kind. But she can't concentrate."

"She seems to like children," Jeanie said.

"Oh yes, that's the distressing part. I really had hopes—However, last week I left her with them while I took a phone call, and when I got back half of them were outside, and she hadn't the least idea of it. She had a man in here, and was off giggling with him in a corner."

"Do you know who he was?" Jeanie asked, aware of a

sinking feeling. Dominic's father? The one Daddy had chased off with a rifle? Or perhaps he was the mysterious Silvio.

"I didn't even ask, I was so mad. I've never seen him before. She's bright enough; she understands things when you tell her. But it never occurs to her, the things that can happen."

Butterflies aren't maternally inclined. "You don't think, with a little more practice?"

Elizabeth began tracing witches. "It's not going to work. Tell Mackie to find her another placement. She can finish out the week here, but that's the end."

Jeanie tried to think of a job somewhere, anywhere, which didn't demand an attention span of more than five minutes. Nothing came to mind.

Brynna had been the devil to place. Retail establishments, service organizations, and government offices were prejudiced against abrasive people with sticky fingers. Mackie had pumped her fist in the air triumphantly when she nagged the nurseryman into accepting her. Work skills first, people skills later, said Mackie, and greenhouses held precious little temptation to a city girl, as long as she didn't lay hands on marijuana seeds.

Brynna grumbled. She hated scrabbling in the dirt. Still, it got her out of Estelle Torrez's clutches every morning. Brynna lived at Bright Futures, like Sorrel, and her expressed opinion of Estelle Torrez provided Jeanie with a unique education in current cuss-words.

Jeanie passed the first rank of greenhouses, looking for the geranium sign. Geraniums, said Mr. Harris, the owner, were less touchy than most other plants. Possibly, he had said with the weighty air of a man considering an expensive gift, Brynna might advance as far as begonias in time, although she wasn't to depend upon this. Jeanie understood things like tulips and daffodils. Begonias were just the fuzzy things with reddish leaves. Nonetheless, Jeanie gave this pronouncement the hushed reverence it deserved. Mr. Harris had nodded, a benevolent Buddha bobbing over his round stomach.

A voice pitched well above soprano screeched from a building down in the row. This solved the question of Brynna's location. Jeanie made a beeline for the shuddering greenhouse and opened the door. At the far end of the aisle stood a woman, quivering with outrage from the toes of her sensible shoes to the top of her dandelion fluff hair. Her plump cheeks flushed an unbecoming purple.

". . . Flinging yourself at him, corrupting him! He's far too good for the likes of you! Dragging yourself out of the gutter, and mucking—"

Long trays of plants ran down each side of the building, and again down the middle, leaving two aisles. At the opposite end, the shelves stopped short behind the combatants, leaving an alcove with workbenches, bags of potting soil, and high stacks of pots. Brynna stood with her back to the bench. The older woman barred her way, shaking a finger at her. She was either brave or exceedingly stupid.

"Jason's a jerk," growled Brynna. "That fuckin' son of yours grabbed my ass. Lucky for him I didn't kick him in the balls."

The woman gasped. "My Jason would never demean himself by touching such a—such a—"

"Like hell. Get real, you bitch. He grabs everything with boobs."

"My Jason has been raised on the strictest principles—"

"Hello-o-o," sang Jeanie with apparent delight, as she

At Risk of Being a Fool

trotted to the rescue. Although, come to think of it, which one of them actually needed rescuing? "You must be Laramie Cooper. So nice to meet you in person."

The other woman favored her with a cold look. "My name is Mrs. Cooper. I have no idea who—"

"Mrs. Cooper, my name is Jeanie McCoy." She seized Mrs. Cooper's limp hand and pumped it up and down. "I'm Brynna's, er, program leader for the day. I've come to see how she's doing. Repotting geraniums, I believe, is that right, Brynna?"

"Yeah," said Brynna. She plunged her hands into a huge bin of soil. Her intent, Jeanie decided, was not to plant geraniums.

One thing about Brynna, she certainly added liveliness to each and every day. Jeanie swung into place between them by the simple expedient of hanging onto Mrs. Cooper's hand and pivoting her out of Brynna's reach. Regrettably, this put Brynna back in Mrs. Cooper's line of sight.

"You're supposed to use gloves," snapped Mrs. Cooper. "Not that you should be potting geraniums. Only the good Lord knows what you'd plant! I saw you with that bag this morning, girl, don't you think I didn't. When I—"

"I gather Brynna hasn't worked with you before," Jeanie broke in.

Mrs. Cooper swelled like a balloon. "I am not accustomed to being interrupted."

"I can see that," Jeanie said. "Don't worry, it gets easier with practice. I've taught for thirty years." Brynna snickered. She scooped dirt into a pot with unconvincing innocence, her battle plan suspended. "So, this is your first day with Brynna?"

"Yes, I was out for a week, and that ham-handed Alyssa—however, that's neither here nor there. This, this girl has been supposedly working with my son, Jason, mixing fertilizers." Her nostrils flared. "Until this morning. I went to get her, and discovered her plastered on my—"

"Jason's a slime ball," said Brynna. "Get your fuckin' story right. He did the grabbing, not me. Think I'm going to mess with a geek with bad breath and a sloppy mouth? Keep him, for God's sake, I don't want him." She closed her hands over a large ceramic pot.

"That will be enough out of you, young woman," shrieked Mrs. Cooper. "Decent conduct is a closed book to you, but let me tell you—"

"You're not actually the greenhouse supervisor, though, are you?" asked Jeanie. A note in her voice pulled up Mrs. Cooper in the midst of her rampage. "You'd be Brynna's co-worker."

"I hold a position of considerable responsibility."

"In geraniums." said Jeanie. She edged Mrs. Cooper away from Brynna's large ceramic pot.

"And just what do you mean by that? Martha Washingtons are among this nation's most treasured horticultural—"

"Exactly. Brynna? Why don't you come with me? It appears that Mrs. Cooper doesn't need your help with the Martha Washingtons. Let's go talk to Mr. Harris."

Brynna released the pot and stripped off her gardening apron. She headed down the other aisle. "Yeah." She threw a final jab over her shoulder. "Maybe he can find me work in begonias." The door shut smartly after her.

"Begonias?" said Mrs. Cooper, outraged. "That little snippet could never, not even possibly, why even I rarely—"

"I'm sure you're right, Mrs. Cooper. The most important thing to do is separate her from your son. I'm sure you agree. And since he's mixing fertilizers in geraniums, she's

At Risk of Being a Fool

better off elsewhere. I'm sure Mr. Harris won't put her in begonias. A nice hosta greenhouse, maybe."

"Well, then," said Mrs. Cooper, mollified. "Hostas, perhaps."

"I gather you don't work with hostas."

"No, of course not."

"Naturally not." Jeanie retreated slowly, giving Brynna time to evacuate.

Mrs. Cooper followed her, brandishing a finger. "You don't seem to realize the affront of that young woman's presence, let alone the temptation to the morals of every man on the premises. Not all men are as gentlemanly as my son, when faced with a prostitute."

"What makes you think she's a prostitute?"

"Well, I, um . . ." Mrs. Cooper averted her gaze. "I happened to be in the office one day, when that girl was talking to Mr. Harris. Quite blunt she was, totally unashamed. Well, of course, when I finally had the opportunity, I decided to advise her, give her a helping hand, you know."

"Ah," said Jeanie, enlightened. "So your son, really—"

"Humph." Mrs. Cooper straightened her shoulders in offense. "I was discreet, of course—"

"I beg your pardon?" said Jeanie, anger bubbling up from deep inside her. "That was discreet? Did you ask Jason what happened?"

"I didn't need to ask him, it was obvious that hussy—" Mrs. Cooper stretched a shaking finger in the direction of the shut door.

"I'm afraid the term 'hussy' is outdated." Jeanie paused as she opened the door. "Some messages work better than others. You can coat them in honey and chocolate, and ease the bitter taste with laughter. Or you can coat them in shards of glass, and force them down with a fire hose. Which message, do you suppose, will digest better? Good day to you. I'm sure you do wonderful work with plants." Jeanie snapped her mouth shut before anything else escaped. She closed the door on Mrs. Cooper and bumped into Brynna. "Sorry, Brynna. Let's go see Mr. Harris about a different placement." Preferably several acres away from any man under sixty.

Brynna folded her arms across her chest, and marched alongside her. "Go ahead, say it!" Her voice shook with rage. "How I should be grateful for this job, and for that jackass back there pawing me. Check the greenhouses, damn it, like Harris does, looking for marijuana and mushrooms."

Jeanie said nothing. Brynna jumped ahead a couple paces and whirled in front of her, throwing her fists down to her sides. "Go ahead, yell at me," she screamed, "like everybody else. Do this, don't do that, mind your tongue, and for God's sake SMILE at the SOBs. Go on. Ask me what was in the fuckin' bag I brought to work. You're thinking it, aren't you? Go ahead and say it."

Jeanie looked at the convulsed face. If she really wanted to know what was in the bag, the last thing she'd do was ask Brynna. Tenderness swept over her, as it so often did at inconvenient moments. The silly girl. "Brynna, I wouldn't know a hallucinogenic mushroom if it bit me on the nose. You have survived in a world that would have flattened me. I respect you, I even like you, and I wish to heaven you'd quit trying to pick fights with me."

"Heaven? Heaven? What is it with you, Jeanie? Can't you even cuss? Are you afraid of me?"

"Afraid of you?" Jeanie gave a short laugh. "You think I'm an idiot? Of course, I'm afraid of you. Of you, Sorrel, Tonio, Dillon, and all the people in your lives I'd shiver to meet. Look at this arm of mine. These muscles are made out of Play-Doh. Think I'm going fight? No way, girl. Is that what you're after? Go ahead, Brynna, hit me. Pull out those claws of yours, and scratch."

"Hit you?"

"Hit me, Brynna, or give it up, and decide you're not going to."

Brynna narrowed her eyes. "If I did, you'd report me to Torrez."

"Give me a break, Brynna." Jeanie couldn't help laughing. "What do you expect out of me?"

Brynna grimaced and fell back to her side. Silently, they walked towards the main office. After a long moment, Brynna's fists unclenched.

"It was makeup," she said. "In the bag. Jeanie, you're crazy."

"Boy, tell me about it. Seems to me I've heard that about a thousand times in the last month." Of course, it could have been makeup. But it probably wasn't.

"Yeah." Brynna gave her a sidelong glance. "Maybe you're not a wimp after all."

"Ha. Look at my hands shake!"

SEVEN

Jeanie shaded her eyes and applied Mackie's rule of thumb to the construction site. Look for the large, muscled figure of Danny Rivera, and there would be Quinto jogging behind, with his hardhat, shining eyes, and endless stream of questions.

Danny waved. His grin made the world seem like a better place. "Hey, good to see you, Jeanie. Come to check out my guy, here?" Danny hauled a heavy cardboard box under one arm. "He's a great young man, one of the best I've had. Never wears out on me halfway through the morning."

"Soon's I get my GED, I'm gonna come on full-time, ain't I, Mr. Rivera?" The great brown eyes looked like Corrigan's when he was hoping for a walk.

"We'll see about that," said Danny heartily. His eyes, meeting Jeanie's, expressed some doubt. A subtle tilt of his head indicated a tall gray-haired man with a sheaf of papers. "We'll have to see what Mr. Browning has to say, but I'd sure recommend him in a flash."

"Quinto, don't you already work full-time on Saturdays?"

"No, just a couple times, when they was behind, like they was last week," said Quinto. He tensed and studied the ground between his feet.

That, she realized suddenly, was the day Bryce Wogan had been hurt. She hurried on, trying to ease his embarrassment. "So, what are you doing today, Quinto?"

"We been checking out the supplies of rebar. We got lots

At Risk of Being a Fool

a them cinder blocks to go afore we get to the rafters. I been framing out windows, cross bracing, you know. Hey, let me show you something sharp. I just learned me this, just this morning, been working on it real good." Quinto ran off to the trailer.

"So, what do you really think?" Jeanie asked Danny.

"Gotta love that enthusiasm. He's got some good stuff in him, Quinto does. Not the brightest, but sometimes he surprises me." Danny indicated Quinto jogging back, a loosely rolled sheet of paper tucked under an arm.

"See? Look, Jeanie. Them's blueprints, see? They tells all there is to know about this building. There's a cut-away, shows what it's gonna look like, kind of three-D, you know." Quinto threw his hand in front of his face, and framed the building between thumb and forefinger. "See? Just like that, ain't it great? Then these marks here, they tell about stuff like the plumbing, and the inside walls. Look here, see? That there's a support wall." Quinto pointed to the drawing, and then to an empty space in the middle of the floor. Danny nodded approvingly as he scrawled his initials on Jeanie's paper.

"It ain't there yet, but it's gotta go in before they get much higher. Real important, Jeanie, 'cause if it ain't there? The whole second floor will come crashing down, soon's they get the furniture on it. This stuff, this blueprint, it's important. It's like people live, or die, depending on if these guys done their pictures right. Ain't that something?" Quinto shook his head. "And it's all math, Jeanie. How come none of them teachers ever told me that? Math ain't just counting apples and money. It's people living or dying, and I never knowed it before, 'til Mr. Rivera showed me this morning."

Behind him, Danny said, "You stay here for a bit,

Quinto, talk to your teacher. I'll be up on the scaffold."

Quinto turned instantly. "Hey, I'll go with you, Jeanie don't care."

"No, no, in a minute or two, okay? She's probably got questions to ask you, about me, how mean I am, stuff like that." He gave Quinto a wink, and strode away.

"Damn, Jeanie, I hope I get to stay on, after the program." His eyes tracked Danny. "You think I could?"

"I guess it depends on how well you do while you're here."

"Yeah, only that Mr. Browning, he don't like me."

"You said Mr. Wogan didn't like you either, but Mr. Rivera said otherwise."

Quinto turned the blueprints in his hands. "Well, yeah, but that was different. Mr. Wogan, guys like him, you got to prove yourself. Mr. Wogan, he kind of waits, watches you, and if you do good, he's okay with you. This guy, though, this Mr. Browning, he watches me too, but it's like he thinks I'm gonna do something. He probably thinks I did that pipe bomb, but that's crazy. Wouldn't catch me near no pipe bombs, I ain't stupid. Guys get their hands blown off making them, just like Mr. Wogan got." His face clouded. "Mr. Wogan, he liked the picture I drew him, of his truck. Mr. Rivera took it to him. It was hard, 'cause they don't let me near none of them trucks, and that one, it's in for repairs, and besides, I couldn't come to the site last week. But Mr. Rivera, he said I got it down good, dents and all. Mr. Wogan, he stuck it up on his hospital wall, so he must have liked it."

"You're quite an artist, Quinto."

"Yeah." His voice slowed. "Jeanie, I'm all messed up. I don't know what to do. Ricky, my bro? He's always telling me, you gotta use that talent, come to the store, work in

At Risk of Being a Fool

advertising, soon's you finish the program. There's this art school, Ricky knows some guys there."

"That could be a great opportunity."

"Mr. Rivera, he said that too. Ricardo, he's really going up, he's gonna make the big bucks afore he's done. And Mama, you know, she's up there in Portland." Quinto scuffed the ground, his gaze straying after Danny. "Advertising, you gotta sit around all day. This stuff, here, it's real, you know. I'm really doing something, not drawing pictures."

"Isn't it great that you have a choice?"

The thin face turned to her with a big grin. "Ain't it? I got *way* more choices than I did a year ago. Don't you worry about me, Jeanie. I'm gonna make it, one way or another. I gotta go, okay?"

"Sure thing."

Quinto darted back to the construction trailer with the blueprints. As Jeanie left, he was swarming up the scaffold calling, "Mr. Rivera, anything you need?"

Jeanie sat in the big front office of the courthouse, waiting for Carol. Unfortunately, Carol was stuck with a weepy, middle-aged woman half-lying on the counter, sobbing out her life story.

"I can't believe he'd do a thing like that to me. I want a divorce, I told him, and he said, why baby, I love you, I love you, I'll never leave you, and fool that I was, I took it for true. Come to find out, he was seeing her on Tuesdays, not going to the gym. Little tramp like that—"

"Really, a lawyer is your best option," Carol said, "If you want a divorce. Yes, dear, I know, I know—"

Sorrel walked through the back of the room, and paused in mid-step. Jeanie waved. Hesitantly, Sorrel stepped forward. "Hi, Jeanie. I can't talk, I got so much to do right now. Really backed up, all right?" She slipped into the copying room.

Jeanie's anxiety hiked up a notch. Sorrel's family came down on Sunday afternoons every other week, and yesterday had been their day. Ordinarily, Jeanie could trace the visitation schedule by Sorrel's attitude. She was calmer on the Mondays after a visit, and Jeanie had sincerely hoped that would be the case today. Instead, she seemed more wound up than ever.

". . . had our ups and downs, but when he threw the pickle jar at my windshield, I realized. Not that he's violent, he's so sweet, you know, it was just . . ."

Carol patted her hand. "I have the phone numbers for marriage counselors. What do you think?" She didn't look hopeful.

Jeanie checked her watch. Five visits down, only this one to go. Jeanie caught Carol's eye, pointed to her watch, and held up ten fingers.

Carol nodded. "Maybe anger therapy," she was saying, as Jeanie closed the door.

Vic Dunlap, Mackie Sandoval's favorite security guard, sat near a desk at the main door. Vic knew all the gossip about everyone in the building. Vic was nearing retirement age, and had thankfully quit fretting about his waistline. Mackie said that his wife called him the Pillsbury Doughboy. The legendary ticklish side of the Doughboy was part of the joke.

Jeanie joined him and leaned against his desk. "Hello again, Vic," she said.

"Hi, need my report, ma'am?" Vic said, with mock solemnity. "Nothing new since ten minutes ago."

Jeanie laughed. "Good."

At Risk of Being a Fool

"Couldn't get through to the clerk?"

"No, unfortunately. I need to talk to her about one of her employees. One of my students works here."

"Student? Oh, the girl with the black hair, and the, uh . . ." he cleared his throat, "the purple eye shadow?"

Jeanie raised a tolerant eyebrow. "The one with the figure, you mean. Yes, that's her. Sorrel Quintana."

He poked his tongue into his cheek, considering. "Dorrie likes her. Mind you, it was touch and go there for a while, but she's doing okay, I'd say. Of course, Hilda doesn't like her, but Hilda doesn't like me either, so what does that tell you?"

"A lot about Hilda."

"Damned right. Hilda was pretty jumpy after our little scare last week. Can't blame her, really. That little present in the bushes wasn't the most calming thing."

"How did you guys find it? Or can't you tell me?"

"No secret. Somebody called in a warning. Then during the evacuation, we each took our regular assigned rounds, and I found that sucker myself. A suspicious briefcase, right there outside the judge's office."

"My goodness. It's a good thing you didn't try to pick it up."

Vic looked embarrassed. "Well, yeah. Glad we got the phone call. Briefcases aren't that uncommon around a courthouse, you know. That thing was hell warmed over, just waiting to take our heads off. You should've seen the bomb squad. They brought in this robot gadget to get the bugger, little remote control thing. Absolutely amazing. I've read about 'em, but never seen one before. They blocked us all off, though, couldn't see what they were doing. No biggie," he said, with a wave of the hand. "Glad someone wants those S.W.A.T. jobs."

"Why would someone set a bomb, and call in a warning? It doesn't make sense."

"Probably a threat, I figure. Like he's saying, 'See what I can do, watch yourselves, because next time's for real.' Or, could be, one person set it, and another person tipped us off."

They looked at each other. "I'd like to think so," said Jeanie.

"Me, too."

Jeanie checked her watch. "I was afraid, from what Sorrel said, that all the landscaping was gone."

"Oh, no, just bushes next to windows, and the window boxes. Janna, Judge Hodges' new clerk, she was fit to be tied when they pulled out her window box. But that's where it was, you know, under the judge's window."

"Any fingerprints? Other evidence?"

"Not that I know of. Not likely to find it, either, in my opinion. Don't usually get stuff like that here in Salem. More a Portland kind of thing, big cities." Vic's face sagged. "Pitiful, what our world's coming to. You elect a judge, let him see all the vicious stuff in the world, let him try to protect us, and then you throw a bomb at him. It's not right."

"He handled violent crime, huh?"

"They all do. He does juvenile crime, some domestic relations. You'd think juvenile wouldn't be so bad, but I've heard stories. Like I say, it's pitiful."

"Some of them come from hard lives," said Jeanie.

"Yeah, that's what my wife says. What goes around, comes around."

"I'll go try to catch Carol again. If she's still busy, I may come back and bug you some more."

"No trouble, no trouble at all."

At Risk of Being a Fool

★ ★ ★ ★ ★

Sorrel watched Jeanie and Carol. They were in close, serious conversation. She opened the front of the copy machine, and crumpled a sheet of paper. If someone came in, she'd just be clearing a paper jam.

Jeanie *never* came to work sites. Mackie must have sent her in, to see if she could spot something.

I must be crazy, Sorrel thought. *I couldn't even play with Tiffy yesterday, I'm wound up so tight. Mustn't cry, mustn't cry. They'll know, they're watching me. They're always watching me. Especially now.*

Could they tell? Just by looking at her? If Torrez found out, she'd be back in Corrections in the blink of an eye. If she only knew for sure about that bomb. If it was him, she'd have to run. She'd be dead meat, if he was after her. She'd have to leave Tiffy behind. She couldn't lead him to Tiffy . . .

Sorrel pulled the mirror out of her purse. The bags under her bloodshot eyes were worse than Jeanie's. With trembling hands, Sorrel repaired her makeup and botched the eyeliner. She swore and dropped her hands. She had to ease up some, or she'd go off the deep end for sure. Carefully, she corrected her makeup. She still looked like hell. Fear did that to you.

Guys were shits, no two ways about it. Some were worse than others; some were worse, some were worse . . . Oh God. Jeanie was still out there. What could they find to talk about? They had to be talking about her. They knew something.

Sorrel sidled through the back door and into an unused office. She punched a number on the phone, waited for it to pick up, waited for the recorded message, and the beep of the voice mail.

"You were right," she said. Desperation drove her voice up, made it shrill. "I can't take this any more. Help me, would you? I need help, real bad."

She hung up, wrapped her arms around herself, and rocked back and forth.

Tiffany. Oh God, Tiffany.

"Hey, Jeanie, you got any books on them blueprints?"

"Well, no, I don't think so," Jeanie said, stymied. "I'll call Mr. Rivera, and see if he can loan us some books. Maybe he's got some software. I wonder if our machines would run AutoCAD." The two computers sat at the back of the room, under dust covers. Jeanie's efforts to incorporate computers into the study programs had all failed. They didn't talk, chat, surf, or play games. It would be nice to have a valid use for them. "I do have some books on areas, and some problem sets on computing amounts of wallpaper, paint, and boards. How about those for now?"

Quinto flipped through the books. "Hey, here's some stuff on triangles. Mr. Rivera, he says the triangle is strong. They use 'em all the time in buildings."

"Good idea. Go ahead and start with that." Quinto set to work with a will.

Jeanie caught Tonio staring at her, a frown on his face. Dillon slammed down his book and thrust out his jaw. "Jeanie. How come you were checking up on me?"

"I was at everyone's workplace today," Jeanie said. "Mackie couldn't make it this time, and she asked me."

"Yeah, sure."

"Dillon, I don't know what you think I was doing, but I went to every student's workplace this morning. Ask them."

"Yeah," offered Quinto. "She saw the stuff I was doing. I showed her all about them blueprints, that tells about buildings. It was cool."

"She came to the child care too," said Rosalie. She bounced on her toes behind Jeanie.

At Risk of Being a Fool

I need shackles for that girl, thought Jeanie. She made small herding motions, and Rosalie went back to her seat. "See? Ask the others. Tonio? Brynna, Sorrel?"

Brynna and Tonio nodded. Sorrel looked from Jeanie to Dillon. "Yeah," she said finally. "She was at the courthouse too."

"Are you feeling all right, Sorrel? You look ill," Jeanie said.

"I'm fine." Sorrel ducked her head towards her book. "Didn't sleep well last night, that's all."

Dillon gave Jeanie an unreadable look. "Huh," he said. Corrigan ambled up to Dillon and nosed his hand. Dillon pulled back as though his hand burned.

"It's okay," said Jeanie, smiling, "if you touch my stuff. Even my dog."

"I don't like dogs." Despite that, he was careful when he shifted his chair, avoiding Corrigan's paw. He seemed to have finished talking.

"Rosalie, essay time. Come on, girl, let's get going. Which one did you choose?"

"This one here."

Well, wonder of wonders, Rosalie had actually read the essay topic list. "Discuss a happy childhood memory, and how it relates to your life today," read Jeanie. "Have you decided what memory to write about?" Jeanie rather hoped it wasn't about breaking up a wedding reception.

"My Dad used to take me to the park, and push me on the swing."

"Oh, that's nice. I always liked swings. I felt like I was flying."

"Yeah, that's it, Jeanie. Like I was flying. It was exciting, but I was safe, you know? Because my Daddy, he was always there to catch me."

Rosalie's lip quivered. Oh no, not again. "That's a wonderful memory, Rosalie. So, now, if you start out talking about the park, and your feelings—"

"He's not there to catch me, now, Jeanie."

If she only had a dollar for every time she and Rosalie had gone around this mountain. "What other memories do you have, Rosalie? Playing with your sisters? Did you take any trips?"

"Jeanie, I miss my Daddy something awful. Why won't he talk to me no more?"

"For God's sake, drop it, Rosalie," Brynna said. "I'm sick of it. You whine all the time about your shitty father."

"Don't you say that about my father," Rosalie said, her voice shaking.

"I'll say what I want, girl."

"Brynna," said Jeanie. "Hush."

"But she's always going on, like he's some kind of angel or something. It makes me want to puke. Daddy, Daddy, Daddy," she mocked. "Grow up, will you? Catch me, crying about my father, don't even know who the fucker was. Don't need him, not with uncles like I got." Her face went red, then white.

"Brynna, stop, honey." Automatically, Jeanie reached for the nearest room divider, dragging it between the two girls. "Rosalie, sit down now, and write your essay. Your subject is just fine. Don't get off track, hear me? Now stay put." Jeanie pulled an extra chair next to Brynna's desk. "Sit down, Brynna. Here." She grabbed a Kleenex box, and dropped into the chair. The barest outline of Brynna's history was in the files, and a ghastly reading it made. "It's okay, Bryn, you're not living there any more. You're safe."

Brynna grabbed a wad of Kleenex. "Safe. Like hell. The whole world's like that. Draggin' kids into the back room—"

At Risk of Being a Fool

"It's not, Brynna. The world isn't like that. I've taught kids for years and years, and raised boys of my own. There's a huge world out there, and in most of it, none of those dreadful things ever happen."

"I want to hurt 'em, Jeanie." The vicious, yearning note seemed to echo through the room. "If I had my way, they'd be hamburger, just like that construction guy. All of 'em, any man'd do that kind of thing! Rip 'em to shreds, plastered on the walls, all of 'em. I want to hurt 'em so bad. Minute I get back to Portland, I—"

"So, stay here in Salem, no problem. Keep away from them."

"Happens here, too! This girl at Futures, too, her daddy was always doing it. Her mother didn't give a damn, any more than mine, the bitch."

"Brynna, you never have to see any of them again." Jeanie fought the urge to pat Brynna's hand. Brynna had had too many people touching her, too many ways.

"Them and their damned parties. Dishing out all their good stuff, drugs, booze, and me. Maybe I'll get me a pipe bomb, God, I know just who to call—"

"Brynna, it was their fault, not yours. You're a survivor, Brynna. Don't let them control your future." It was all words, just words. Brynna had heard all of it before, many times. How could words fight the destruction her family had inflicted? "Brynna, I admire your strength. You haven't let them crush you."

Brynna shot her a sarcastic glance. Her eyes wavered and dropped. "Huh."

"Just keep plugging away, Brynna. And don't go back to Portland until you can put the memories behind you."

Corrigan, with his nose for difficult situations, appeared by her feet. Jeanie picked him up and offered him to

Brynna. After a moment's hesitation, Brynna held him. Corrigan nestled close, licking the salty tears from her face.

After a time, Jeanie retreated, leaving Corrigan to continue the counseling session, while she moved on the familiar rounds of helping Tonio with grammar, Dillon with graphing, Sorrel with spelling, Quinto with triangles, and Rosalie with the ever-present problem of staying in her seat. After a time, she saw Brynna back at work, with Corrigan asleep on her feet. Jeanie tucked the room divider back against the wall.

Dillon's phone beeped. He flicked it open. "Yeah." He held it out to Jeanie, eyes still on his book.

"Hi, Randy. Yes, he's here. That was good news, wasn't it? Three tests down, two to go. Sure thing. Bye." She placed the phone on his desk.

Dillon picked up the phone. With a twist of his mouth, he punched an autodial number. "Hey, Gram. Yeah. She's here. Right."

Dillon stood up and held out the phone to Jeanie. "My grandma, she wanted to talk to you." His look challenged her.

"Sure, I'd be glad to speak to your grandmother."

Jeanie reached out a hand. Dillon pulled the phone back, and advanced it again slowly. Tug-of-war? Jeanie closed her fingers around the phone. After a long moment, Dillon released it.

"Mrs. Otero? Jeanie McCoy here. I'm delighted to speak to you."

"Thank you. I am so pleased."

Dillon stepped closer, his face threatening.

"Hold on just a minute, Mrs. Otero. Excuse me, Dillon." Jeanie walked to Mackie's office, and turned in the doorway. Dillon was right behind her. He hulked over her, fists clenched at his sides.

At Risk of Being a Fool

"Dillon, I can't talk to your grandmother with you hanging over me. Trust me." It was a stupid thing to say, she realized instantly. Dillon didn't trust anyone.

Dillon spoke, in a low, rumbling voice "You don't upset my grandma."

There was a sudden growl. Jeanie jumped. At her feet stood Corrigan, fifteen pounds of aged protection. Jeanie stooped to pick him up, cradling Corrigan in her arms, a living shield against violence. Mutely, she held out the phone to Dillon.

He didn't take it. "She wants to talk to you."

"Then you'll have to let me talk, won't you? I'm not going to do it without privacy." She knew she was pushing him, but there were times when a teacher didn't dare back up.

"Anybody upsets my grandma," said Dillon distinctly, "is gonna be real sorry."

"Mrs. McCoy?" The distant voice from the receiver insisted. "Are you there?"

Corrigan whined. He poked his nose at Dillon. Dillon stepped back. Corrigan thrust his head forward, his tail wagging furiously. Dillon looked at him for a moment. He turned on his heel, and said over his shoulder. "You remember what I said."

Jeanie pulled a chair into the doorway and sank into it. She set Corrigan on the ground. "You, Corrigan, are an utter fool," she muttered. "Your instincts are totally screwed up." Corrigan yipped, and sat between her feet, defending her from predators. Five pairs of eyes looked from her to Dillon and back again. Dillon put on his headphones, turned up his music, and bent to his book. One by one, the heads bent to their books as well.

"I'm sorry, Mrs. Otero," Jeanie managed. "One of the

students had an important question. I'm sorry to keep you waiting."

"Oh, it is no problem." Mrs. Otero's speech was slow but precise, and sang with the unconscious melody of the native Spanish speaker. "I like to talk to teachers of my Dillon. When he was in school in Portland, I could not. But now, he lives with me, so I say to him, Dillon, I talk to your teacher."

"That's a good idea." Jeanie was baffled. Why had Dillon thought it necessary to threaten her? Her fright passed, and she threw him a puzzled look. "Dillon is doing fine here. His progress is quite steady. He's passed three of his tests. He's told you, hasn't he?"

"Oh yes, but," a small chuckle floated from the other end, "I think, best to call, to be sure, yes? My grandson, he is sweet to his old grandmother, but sometimes, he does not tell me all the truth. Boys are like that. They hide away, and keep their little secrets."

Jeanie felt disoriented. Were she and Mrs. Otero talking about the same young man? "Well, he's telling the truth about this. And I went to the cannery today, and his supervisor says he's a good worker."

"Ah. It is good to know." She sounded exhausted and old. "It is good that my Dillon tries hard. This time. My little one."

Jeanie watched the "little one," hunched in his heavy jacket, the thug's face capped with headphones. His alien yellow-brown eyes turned on her. "He's an excellent worker, when he puts his mind to it. He seems to have changed a great deal, from what Randy tells me." At least, his behavior had changed. His internal change was open to question.

"Yes, I would say so. They agreed, the officers, that he

At Risk of Being a Fool

could stay with me at home instead of at the res-i-den-tial fac-i-li-ty. He went there last time. Did not work," she said. "But with me, maybe. Just an old Mexican lady," she said, laughter weaving through her words, "but he is my boy. He likes my pancakes, do you know?"

"I'm sure he does."

Across the room, Dillon watched her. For a moment, she almost read the expression on his face, but the shutters fell and there was no one home. "Your grandson loves you. He loves you so much."

"Yes," said Mrs. Otero softly. "*Es mi hijo,* my little one. He will do good this time." Her gallant words couldn't hide the undercurrent of doubt.

"Yes, he will."

"Thank you, Mrs. McCoy. I talk to you again, later, yes?"

"Yes. Call any time at all."

With a toe, Jeanie shifted the dog on his way. Corrigan ambled off to see what Quinto was doing. Jeanie put the phone on Dillon's desk. "Why don't you go out in the hallway, Dillon? Call her back."

Dillon snatched the phone and left the room in great strides.

Indignantly, Brynna burst out, "Hey, he's not allowed to leave for private phone calls."

"Brynna. Hush."

The darkness wrapped him like a blanket, warm and secure. He'd always preferred darkness to the light. In the light, people demanded, insisted, begged, and cried. They wanted actions, words, emotions, or loyalty. He resisted them all in small, hidden ways. In the nighttime, he was himself, alone and free. In the daytime, he worked, learned the book stuff, and went through the motions. Every move seemed to carve away a little of himself, to make him less of what he could be.

Once, his grandma told him a story, about a statue in a church. She'd gone there with her women's group, gone for a week or two, he didn't know where. There was a huge statue of some saint, all in granite or marble. St. Peter, maybe, or Paul. He could never keep them straight. The front foot of the saint was worn down, lots thinner than the other one. Grandma said it was worn down from kisses, just hundreds of years' worth of kisses. He hadn't believed it, but she'd showed him a picture.

He thought about it sometimes, about rock wearing thin, just from people getting too close. That's what he'd felt like, backed into a corner by the judge, his boss at work, the teacher, the parole officer, and even the gang when it flocked around him. That was crazy, thinking his homeboys were like the judge, but they didn't understand, any of them. They'd wear him down, all of them, until the day came when he crumbled into dust.

He got through the days somehow, and survived all the people pulling at him. But he watched the windows, waiting for the nighttime, his old friend. It was the worst thing about being locked up, never being outdoors at night. He'd missed the glow of the streetlights, the sharply-cut shadows of the apartment buildings, the screech of brakes, the smell of sweet-and-sour from the dumpsters behind the Chinese place, the leftover heat from the asphalt on the soles of his feet, and the breeze whiffing around his ears, humming to him.

He could scarcely breathe sometimes, until night fell.

He strolled around the car, his shoulders back, looking casual for any who might see him. It wasn't likely, not

At Risk of Being a Fool

there, not at this time of night. Like chickens, they all roosted at night, until the fox came by. He snorted and shook his head. All this education messed him up. He'd never seen a fox, except on TV.

He shoved his hands in his pockets. She'd locked the car. Without using his hands, it was a bit harder seeing how the hood opened, and the trunk latched, but they were standard for these little cars.

The question was, where the thing should go. It was a nice little scientific experiment, like Jeanie would say. There was this much metal in a car, and that many angles to affect the blast. If you wanted to hit your target, you had to think it all through. You had to be proactive.

Why did she have to stick her nose in things?

Why did they always do it? Push and prod, until a guy couldn't breathe.

It was like that natural selection thing he'd read about in the textbooks. There was the predator and the prey. The predator, he'd lose his place to live because of all the people crowding around, filling up his space, scaring off his natural prey. If the rabbits were all gone, what was the fox supposed to eat?

That was easy. Where the people were crowded together, there were chickens.

And any fox knew what chickens were for.

Eating. Preferably fried.

EIGHT

Shelley's e-mail was true to form. Jeanie chuckled her way to the end. Shelley had such courage, taking a hut-to-hut hike across the Alps at the age of sixty-one. The account could so easily have been a litany of complaints against aging, but not for Shelley. Why live in Europe for two years, she said, if one couldn't be a fool and try new things. If her explorations entailed imaginative uses of Ace bandages, and small children who propped her up against large boulders, so be it.

> . . . *So glad to hear you sounding like your old self. I've spent so many years reading your teaching stories, I'm addicted. Edward is a dear, sweet man. He loves you for who you are, even if he doesn't remember your name. And who you are, dear sis, is a teacher, retired or not. I'm happy you found that job.*
>
> *Love, Shell*

So was Jeanie. Teaching was a good half of her soul. She'd almost lost touch with the other half. In the last decade, only three people had known Jeanie through and through. One of them was dead, one was in Germany, and the third and most dear couldn't remember her name.

Except for Annalisa, her friendships with other teachers remained at work. Annalisa, with her great gales of laughter, taught biology down the hall from Jeanie's math room. When Annalisa died of throat cancer four years ago,

At Risk of Being a Fool

school life lost much of its zest. Then Michelle, her dear Shelley, faced her own marriage crisis, and moved to Germany for her self-discovery adventure. Letters and e-mail bound them together, then and now. The ocean, though, was wide. She dreamed of it often enough. She stood on one shore. Edward, Shelley, Annalisa, and her sons stood on the other. She screamed her throat raw, but they couldn't hear her. The waves thundered, roared, and surrounded her until she stood on the remains of a tiny sand castle, alone forever, cold salt water dragging her feet from under her.

But at least she could teach. Her drive to love total strangers had rushed back full force, staving off the loneliness. Now at one in the morning, along with the familiar worries about Edward, she faced the nightly parade of faces of her students. Her sons wouldn't consider it an improvement, probably, but she did. Shelley understood. She typed her response, running through her students in her mind, showing Shelley what she could see, and what she couldn't.

Quinto's thin, mobile face was always the first in the nightly parade. Appearances were deceiving. People heard the naïveté spouting from his every sentence, and shook their heads with a half-smile. Nice kid, just totally brain-dead, they figured. Jeanie knew better. His mind might skip a few gears now and then, but his hands had brains of their own. Once he sensed a connection between knowledge and the skill in his hands, the information soared into his brain like an electric shock to the heart. Quinto and blueprints went together like cocoa and marshmallows. Ravenously, Quinto had begun swallowing the practical world of spatial geometry with great, satisfied gulps.

Sorrel, on the other hand, was in dreadful shape. She rattled her fingers on the tabletop, swung her leg incessantly, and combed her hair until little shreds of it blanketed the floor around her desk. After her breakdown over the essay on Tiffany's birth, Sorrel raised her barriers, and peered over them suspiciously. Sorrel had a hell of a life in front of her: pain and agony everywhere, it was easy to see. But soft places filled her heart, evidenced by the semi-circle of her daughter's pictures around her workspace.

Jeanie hoped to God she never met Brynna's mother. The uncles were the mother's drug pipelines. The woman ignored their abuse of her daughter, and threw Brynna out when she dared to fight back. Brynna lived on the street, and found her safety in a girl gang. Jeanie had thought that girl gang members were girls who slept with guy gang members, but it wasn't so. Many girl gangs relished their family atmosphere, with their own "family" businesses in drugs or larceny. Despite Brynna's snarls to the contrary, she'd generally steered clear of prostitution. After numerous arrests for larceny, burglary, and possession, she plea-bargained her way into Bright Futures. With her gang connections stripped away, she had no identity left except as a sniping backstabber. Brynna's unhappy future seemed foreordained.

Rosalie's emotions were real, but transitory. She was fond of her mother, and fond of the baby she'd barely seen, but her father's rejection tore at her soul. Jeanie couldn't blame Mr. Perea. Rosalie's drug-scarred brain was a permanent liability. It didn't take a rocket scientist to know that reconciliation would bring him a lifetime of pain. Who was the man at the day care, for whom Rosalie had ignored every child on the premises? Who was Silvio? Was he Dominic's father, who swore at Judge Hodges? Had he set the bomb, and she, perhaps, called in the warning?

Tonio was the mystery. He was on probation of the

At Risk of Being a Fool

loosest sort, living with his uncle. He smiled and joked sometimes, and gave Jeanie bits of advice, but she never understood him. He reminded her of the ornaments her boys made for their Christmas tree. Styrofoam balls with glitter and paste and colored ribbons made engaging decorations, but underneath there was only a Styrofoam shell. What hid inside Tonio's core was beyond knowing. Jeanie joked with him, taught him what she could, and let him keep his privacy. Still waters ran deep.

Then there was Dillon. Hook a wolf onto a five-foot chain, anchor him to a stone wall, and hit him with a club a few times, and you had Dillon. Rage, suspicion, danger, and madness had to be expected. Still, once she'd glimpsed his deep love for his grandmother, Jeanie's defenses against him withered. Of course, Ted Bundy, the serial killer, seemed to love his mother, too. Dillon's love for his grandmother didn't guarantee his morality. Jeanie prayed that Mrs. Otero would live a good, long time, and die an easy, natural death several decades in the future. She typed another line.

Shelley, tell me truly, am I a bleeding heart? Am I blinded by what I want to see?

Love, Jeanie

She reread the words and hit Send. The e-mail soared into cyberspace, and began its dizzying trek across the world to Shelley.

The familiar rumble of the train shook the house. Rita was fast asleep in the middle of the pillow. She always shoved the cat over when she went to sleep, but often as not, Rita got it back again, drowsily purring her contentment. Corrigan slept neatly at the foot, having climbed up the ramp a couple of hours ago. The train didn't bother them.

She leaned against the windowsill, and watched the engine approach, the huge moving cars shadowed against the trees. Sometimes, if she thought to block the headlights with her hands, she could just make out the engineer in his lighted cab. Most of the time, he was a dim figure guiding the train, carrying who knew what kind of produce and hardware as it connected a line of dots on a map.

It was calming, counting the cars as they passed. Twenty-five, twenty-six. Tankers, boxcars, and plastic-wrapped plywood strapped into flatbeds. Thirty-one, thirty-two. The train slowed, and her thoughts slowed with it. Thirty-nine, forty, forty-one. Forty-one cars, exactly.

The train rumbled down the track and rounded the curve. After a time, the vibrations ceased. With a sigh, she shut down the computer and got into bed.

"Move over, little one." She tugged Rita down, tucking the warm ball against her stomach. Rita's purr rattled the bed, a miniature locomotive covered with long gray fur. Amidst the comforting vibrations, Jeanie slept.

Estelle Torrez turned on her dishwasher. A faint smell of bleach rose from the kitchen counters. She glanced through the window of her downstairs apartment into the tiny fenced yard behind it. Closely packed arbor vitae backed with chain link fence rimmed it on two sides. A six-foot chain link fence separated it from the left-hand neighboring yard. She'd insisted on the chain link when she bought the condo, had bulled her way through the building managers, and they'd yielded. It went against the grain to provide the managers with a key to the single gate between the two yards, but she'd done so. They'd never

At Risk of Being a Fool

used it. They had better not.

She checked the window lock, closed the blinds, and moved through the rest of the two-bedroom apartment, securing it for the week. The bedroom, with its twin bed, leather armchair, and reading light; the office, with its shelves of reference works, the solid mahogany desk, and state-of-the-art computer; the bathroom, polished and shining; the living room, with the second leather armchair, small television, magazine rack, and the stereo.

Estelle removed a CD from the stereo and put it in its case, slotting it into the rack with the others. She approved of Bach: calm, orderly, and rarely sentimental. Schubert's marches, and a few of Tchaikovsky's dramatics filled out her official music library. A few other CDs, confiscated over the years, lay tucked into a drawer where she didn't have to look at them. An illicit vice, but at times their savagery appealed to her, demanded that she listen.

The apartment secure for another four days, she set the burglar alarm, left a message on building security's voice mail, and walked to her car. Her mind shifted gladly from the simmering state of three days' relaxation to the full boil of complete engagement. Three days with Dolores Cuthbert would have softened the girls, though Estelle's frequent visits inspired at least a minimal efficiency. Dolores lacked energy and discipline. No adult should require more than six hours' sleep, and certainly not all in one stretch. A correction supervisor owed her charges full vigilance.

A supervisor must instill good habits and excise bad ones. The word "reform" meant just that: taking a formless soul and shaping it into one compatible with society. Those girls beyond Estelle's capacity to repair returned to Corrections. No doubt, they served their full terms and formed the criminal core of the next generation. So be it. Bright Futures was just that, a venue for girls with futures in society.

Last night, Estelle had spent two hours in her car down the street from Bright Futures. She'd recorded vehicle descriptions and license numbers of three cars and one motorcycle, though doing so entailed leaving her car to scrape the mud off two of the licenses. She'd compared them to notes in her journal, marking the dates against the arrivals of her twenty-three current charges. Double-checking her files was a mere formality. She held every detail of every girl's record in her mind.

She placed her suitcase in the trunk, mulling over the girls whose adaptability was in question. Lisabet Peters, Francia Millinger, Brynna Gallagher, Tatiana Romero. Tentatively, she'd pulled Sorrel Quintana and Kylie McMurray off the transfer list. She'd seen an encouraging sign or two. But it was time to step up the pressure, to see which of the six would survive firing in the correctional kiln, and which would shatter in the heat.

Estelle turned the key in the ignition, threw the car into reverse, and hit the accelerator.

And her world exploded in shrieks of metal, splintering glass, and pain.

"The important thing is not to decrease the profit margin so much that we suffer an overall loss. Contain the costs, put out a quality product, and the public will come, even with submarine plumbing fixtures."

Around the breakfast table, three elderly women agreed. It was nice for them, having a man around. There were only two male residents in the facility. Edward had a lovely speaking voice, kind and compelling.

Jeanie cut his sausages into small pieces, and stirred the Citrucel into his orange juice. "I'm sure you're right, Edward."

At Risk of Being a Fool

Kherra, popping by with a plate of toast, joined in effortlessly. "Defense spending is way up these days, good time for sellin' parts to the Navy. Gotta to keep our soldiers safe and healthy." Kherra's slight Southern drawl gave a cinnamon-nutmeg comfort to her most simple remarks. She moved on, joining in the next table's fantasy with equal ease.

"You raise an excellent point," said Edward, unaware that his "guest speaker" had departed with the toast. "Perhaps we should consider expanding into ship redesign. I'm sure the plumbing in aircraft carriers could use our attention as well. What do you ladies think?"

By the time breakfast was over, Jeanie's nerves were frayed. Edward found his bedroom, and shooed her away with a disapproving air. The over-familiarity of the nurses, and even his wife, often troubled his dignity. Jeanie sat in the foyer next to Kherra, who was matching socks from a basket of laundry.

"So tell me something," Kherra said. Conversations in Oriole's Nest rarely had a beginning or an end. They were a long-run affair, interrupted constantly. "How long you two been married?"

"Forty years last August." Jeanie turned a sock over in her hands.

Kherra's eyes flew wide. "You tell the *truth*, girl. Were you lyin' to me? Or did you really get married at eighteen?"

"The day after my birthday."

"Humph. No sense at all, just a baby when you got married." Kherra wrinkled her nose ruefully. "Welcome to the club. I was seventeen myself. Didn't last, though." She matched another pair of socks. "You know, it's a problem, workin' a place like this. A lot of people never visit their loved ones, 'cause it hurts too bad. Others keep expectin' their folks to get better. Like you. The thing is, honey, that puts a stress not only on you, but on Edward too. He keeps tryin' not to disappoint you. He's going to get worse, Jeanie." Kherra's voice was soft. "He may know he loves you, but he won't know why."

Jeanie sat rigid, restlessly twisting her wedding ring around on her finger. "I know that."

"I'm not tryin' to rub it in. What I'm tryin' to do is show you, you got to build other resources. You need other friends in your life."

Jeanie stood up abruptly. "Kherra, I—"

"Jeanie?" Nadezda called. "Telephone. It's Mackie Sandoval."

Jeanie escaped Kherra and dashed to the phone. "Hi, Mackie."

"Jeanie." Mackie's voice was distorted by a sharp exhale. "Good, I caught you. Look, I've cancelled class today. We've had a disaster. Estelle Torrez is in the hospital. She was leaving her condo about an hour ago, and her car exploded when she started it."

Jeanie gasped. "Another pipe bomb?"

"Hey, you're a lot faster on the uptake than you were a couple of months ago. Yeah, that's it, another pipe bomb. The blast knocked her out, but neighbors heard the explosion, and called the police."

Jeanie sank into a chair. "Will she be okay?"

"Probably. Her feet took the worst of the blast. I think the bomb was under the seat, but I'm guessing. The police won't say."

"First Bryce Wogan, and now Estelle," said Jeanie.

"You've got it. And there's the judge too, don't forget, I know my security buddy told you about him. Somebody called in a warning, but it would have done a lot of damage."

At Risk of Being a Fool

"Nobody's been killed though." Jeanie knew what Mackie had called to say. Maybe if she kept talking, she could avoid it. "Is that on purpose, do you think?"

"I wondered about that too, but the police say pipe bombs aren't predictable. Though I guess the amount of stuff in it would at least affect the degree of damage. Our problem, Jeanie, is the connections. There haven't been pipe bombs in Salem in years. Now there've been three in less than a month. Bryce and Estelle were both connected to kids in our program. So was the courthouse."

Jeanie stifled the instinctive teacher's retort. *Not my kids. My kids wouldn't do that.* "What about the judge?"

"I don't know. Except for Rosalie, they all came from Portland, and the only judges they faced were there, I think. Jeanie, we're canceling school for today."

"Just today," said Jeanie, half-questioning, half-stating.

"For now. Besides, you'd have a small class. Bright Futures is in lock-down, and Randy's pulled Dillon in to see the police—pre-emptive strike. Dillon didn't want the cops to come bug his grandmother."

A small smile forced its way up, and disappeared again. "Quinto? Rosalie? Tonio?"

"I'm going to call Tonio, and suggest he get his butt over to the station, check in with them before they come find him. I called Esperanza, asked them to keep Rosalie today. They're going to stick her in group therapy or something. I've got to find her another job anyway. Quinto could come, but he's the only one."

"Maybe Danny would let him work the whole day. He started there again yesterday, and it seemed to work out all right with the new boss."

"Good thought. I'll give him a call. Can you solve my Rosalie problem, too?"

"Actually, I did have an idea. Maybe a dog kennel? She'd still need supervision, but she does love animals. She could clean pens, walk dogs, things like that?"

"Well, well," said Mackie. "That's an idea."

"She likes Corrigan a lot."

"Everybody likes Corrigan. He's so—"

"Funny-looking, I know, I know. So, tomorrow, then, for class?"

"I'll give you a call, but I think either tomorrow or Thursday. God, it's only Tuesday. I don't know if I can survive this week."

"You always do, Mackie."

"Yeah, but I'm getting older by the minute. Enough of these emergencies, and my brain is going to retire permanently."

"Join the club. I've got just the place for you to move into." Mackie chuckled, as Jeanie hung up.

A third bomb, definitely connected to her classroom. Brynna and Sorrel hated Estelle, but neither had transportation or any interest in Bryce Wogan. Buses didn't go near the construction site. Dillon and Tonio lived with family. Tonio had a working car, and a motorbike upside down in the County Yard with its wheels off. Dillon had a bicycle, but his grandmother had a car. Both of them had time to make pipe bombs, and a means of transportation. Any idiot could get the ingredients for a pipe bomb. She'd looked it up on the Internet one night when she couldn't sleep. It was horrifying, what one could find on the Internet. As soon as authorities closed one site, another popped up.

She went back to Kherra. "I've got to leave the Nest early. I'm sorry."

"Hey, it's okay. Bad news?"

"Mackie called to say class was cancelled today."

At Risk of Being a Fool

Kherra studied her face. "I bet she said more than that. You're not lookin' too good."

"You're right. A woman I know was hurt by a pipe bomb."

"My word. She going to be all right, poor thing?"

"They think she'll be all right. Anyway, some of my kids—" She ran her hands through her hair, disordering the neatness of the last hour. "I've got to hit the phones, find out some things. I don't want them railroaded into anything."

"Good idea. They could use a good advocate. Hey, Jeanie? You be damned sure you keep your windows locked, hear me?"

"Sure," Jeanie said, not hearing. "I've got to go." She paused mid-step, glancing at Edward's closed door.

"Move it, girl," Kherra said, smiling. "Your kids need you, even if they don't think so."

"Right." Jeanie was trotting by the time she got to the door.

NINE

Sorrel sat upright in the cracked, hard plastic chair. Her pounding headache fought the Excedrin and won. Even the pills were out to get her. She was out of coffee, too. She held the empty Styrofoam cup in one hand, and set a perfectly arched fingernail close to the rim. Painstakingly, she rolled it against the cup, leaving an arch in its wake, and then another. Double arches, like McDonald's.

Randy's office was small, hot, and stuffy. Where the hell was he? Mrs. Mahoney had walked her right to the damned door, and called him on her cell phone. Five minutes, he'd said, so she'd left. Cuthbert, Mahoney, and the two temps were all twitchy over Torrez, and the fuckin' cop interviews. So far, Tuesday'd been crappy.

She turned the cup, adding overlapping arches. Pain stabbed through her temples, as the familiar pattern struck home. Concertina wire looked just like that, when you looked through the barred windows of the pen's so-called rec room. She punched a curve into the side of the cup, a second, and a third, in time with the throbbing in her skull. Three curves formed a perfect circle. She extracted the bit and placed it on the desk. She returned to her cup, punch, punch, punch, keeping time, marking time. Killing time.

The narrow window beyond the desk was stuck. She'd nearly broken a fingernail trying to get the damned thing open. What the hell, she didn't work here. Besides the institutional plastic chair, swiped from the County cafeteria downstairs, the office held a desk and a rickety swivel chair.

At Risk of Being a Fool

The desk, if you could call it that, barely managed to support the ancient computer. A limping fan stirred the loose papers on the desk. The air lay heavily, beyond the fan's muscle power.

Huh. You wouldn't catch *her* working in a dump like this, if she had Randy's chances. He'd been to college, and done all that geek stuff. Going to college was stupid, a waste of time. Still, if she'd done that, she'd want a helluva lot better office than a dump. Randy said his office had a locking door and a closet with a refrigerator, and beyond that, it didn't matter. Probation officers were screwy.

Randy crossed behind her, opened the closet, and disappeared inside. "Hot enough for you, Sorrel? I'm getting a Coke. Want one?"

"No." She looked up for a moment. A bird swooped past the window. Her eyes caught on it, sailed with it for a split second, and stuck on the window frame. The bird was gone. She swallowed past the lump in her throat, and turned back to her cup. Punch, punch, punch. Nice neat circles, lined up on the edge of Randy's desk.

"I thought I was going to die out there. Ninety degrees at the end of September, in Oregon, with this humidity. I can't believe people pay good money to go to saunas." Randy stood behind the desk. He popped his Coke open, letting a tiny puff of cold air into the room. He threw back his head and drank in long gurgles. He rolled the cold can across his forehead, the moisture melting indistinguishably into his sweat. He reached across the desk, and plopped a second can in front of her. "Have one anyway. How can you drink coffee on a day like this?"

Sorrel kept her eyes on the cratered coffee cup.

Randy sat down, effortlessly countering the chair's attempt to throw him onto the floor. "So," he said, "what's up?"

The cup developed another pit. *Potholes,* she thought.

"Sorrel, you called me, remember? I didn't call you. Surprised the heck out of me, too. First time you've ever called me, and asked for help."

She broke the silence with a jagged voice, bumping over the words. "I gotta get out of there, Randy." She had to get away from Bright Futures, away from Salem, away from that fucker who turned her dreams into nightmares.

"Yeah, well, you know how to do that. We've been all through it, Sorrel. It's up to you."

Sorrel glanced at him, calculating her odds. Randy was in his thirties, but he looked way older with all those lines in his face, the sagging on his neck. She'd asked him once, pretend-innocent, why he was a probation officer. He'd joked, said he was out to save the world one criminal at a time. She'd screamed at him, and he'd laughed, but he hadn't reached for a form to record it, as Torrez would have.

She'd given up trying sexy stuff on him. He must be gay, or else his wife had him by the balls. Randy never even gave her a look. She could say a lot to Randy, she'd learned, but she had damned well better do what he said, or the shit hit the fan at high speed. Grudging respect tempered her resentment. A sense of safety grew within her, hidden where she didn't have to see it.

"Come on, Sorrel, talk to me. Is this something to do with Torrez's car bomb?"

"No." Their eyes locked. "That bitch, I never touched her. I got more brains than that."

"I'd like to think so."

"The cops were all over us, every girl at the house. Do you think they'd have let me come see you, if they thought I done it? Yeah, like I just said, sorry officers, can't talk now,

At Risk of Being a Fool

gotta go see my P.O. like a good little girl." Her tone dripped with disdain.

"Ease up, Sorrel. It's too hot for this. If they'd found a single minute of your time unaccounted for, they'd have you locked up. You know it, and I know it." He took another drink. "Of course," he said, lazy-eyed, "there's always the phone. Probably, somebody got it done that way. Word has it, Torrez came to, gave the cops a list of license plates a yard long."

Her heart skipped a beat, then thumped hard and fast. "I want," she said, with biting emphasis, "to get out of there. Not to kill Torrez, not to get slammed back into the court for murder as an adult. Give me credit for brains, you bastard."

Randy's face twisted into a grin. "Well, you got Jeanie's vote of confidence. She's rattling a lot of cages. I've heard from Dolores Cuthbert, and Dorrie at the courthouse so far. Also a policeman who wanted to know who the hell she was."

"She's a fool," Sorrel snapped.

"How's that?"

She dragged her eyes away from him. "No reason. Forget it, will you? I didn't come here to solve the damn case for you."

"No, you came to hear the same thing I've told you before," he said. "Apparently."

Sorrel looked back at her cup. Punch, punch, punch. Another little circle, extracted, placed in the line. Randy reached unerringly for a fat folder midway down a stack. He shoved the others back into a rough pile and flipped the folder open. He tapped the paper stapled into the left-hand side.

"Three parts. First, satisfactory work experience, good

reports from an employer. Fine, you're doing that. I talked to Carol this morning, she says you're fine, a good, willing worker. She did ask that you modify your attire—her words. Seems those tight blouses of yours attract a little too much attention from some of the lawyers."

"Bummer." The word was flat, off-key.

"Cool it, Sorrel, it's a valid request. So, assume you do that. There's one down. Second, good effort at your place of residence to assume responsibilities related to . . ." Randy slid a glance at her, and half a grin, "let's call it civilized behavior, shall we?" His grin faded at the lack of response. "Basically, that means Bright Futures has to sign you off as a reformed character. I talked to Estelle Torrez a week ago, before her fiasco." He grimaced. "God, that's a hell of a thing. Looks like she'll be gone quite a while."

"Good." Another white foam circle joined the others on the edge of the desk.

"Sorrel."

"You want me to lie? Sure, no problem. Gee," she said, in a little girl's singsong, "it's really too bad she got hurt like that, and I really miss her, and hope she'll come back soon. Like shit."

"You don't sound much like a reformed character."

"I didn't do it, Randy. I didn't get it done, and I didn't know nothing about it. Am I supposed to get all upset about it, if she's gone for a while? No way."

"Hmm. Well, as it happens, I talked to Mrs. Torrez, and she had a few things to say."

"I'll bet."

"Yeah, well, for Mrs. Torrez it wasn't too bad. Pretty good, actually, in spite of your wedding story. I'd say you're on the road there, too. So that's two down, or at least it will be in a couple of months, I'd say."

At Risk of Being a Fool

Sorrel's head jerked upwards. "Couple of months."

"Maybe. Of course, there's also the third one."

"Education. Progress to the GED. I'm doing it." Sorrel gripped the edge of the desk. Her knuckles turned white. "A couple of months, you said."

"No, Sorrel. Complete the GED. All five tests. Jeanie says you're three down, two to go, and almost ready for number four. One more after that, and you're home free."

"Randy." Sorrel's makeup stood out in mismatched blotches. "I'm making progress. That's what you wanted, right?"

"It's not me, girl, it's the judge." Randy tapped the paper.

"I'm never," her voice scaled up an octave. "I'm never going to pass that fuckin' math test, not in a million years. Randy, you gotta hear me, I gotta get back to Mama, and Tiffy." Her voice was ragged with panic. "I'll run, I'm telling you, I'll run the hell away from here. You've got to get me out!" She heard her words echo off the walls, heard rejection before he said a word. Her face twisted in despair. The cup crumpled into a tiny ball, strangled by fingers with blood-red nails.

"Sorrel. It doesn't work that way. And I can't see you hauling Tiffany with you, while you're on the run. She'd hate it, all that driving, and hiding. You'd always wonder who'd seen you. You'd never see your mom or grandma again. Think it through, girl."

She dropped the cup and covered her face with her hands. A dry, racking sob shook her shoulders. Randy shoved the box of Kleenex in front of her, and developed a sudden interest in the many pages of her folder. A sullen gratitude surfaced in the girl. Tears were not her weapons; she scorned them. Sorrel blew her nose and wiped her face. She wadded up her tears, snot, makeup, and hopes into a ball of paper. She picked up the crumpled cup and each mangled bit of Styrofoam, and dropped them in the trashcan by the door. She sat down, reaching for the Coke can. The sharp icy feel against her cheek cooled the fever. She popped the lid. The sweet acid taste brought her back, reminded her of many things, like childbirth, like men. Sweetness and acid.

"Sorry," she muttered. She brushed at her cheeks. "I must look like hell."

"It's not your lovely face that brings me back to you. It's your charming personality."

"Shut up."

Randy leaned back. "It's going to be okay, Sorrel. You're doing all right. It just takes time."

"I'm going to be there, in residence, until I'm twenty-one and the sentence ends. I'm not going to make it through that math test. I can't even multiply, for God's sake. Twenty-two more months, Randy."

"Looks like you can add and subtract all right." There was a pause. "Sorry. Bad joke. You're wrong, Sorrel. You'll study and you'll make it. In a couple months, maybe Esperanza will have an opening. You could go back there, if they're sure you won't louse it up again. Linda said they'd take you, if Estelle passed you."

Sorrel's eyes shot to his face. Two months. She shook her head, and her shoulders slumped. "Even then, I'd be stuck for the rest of the sentence. Two more years. You think I'm trying to con you," she said intensely. "Okay, I tried before, but that was before I knew you. This is not a fake. You've got to believe me."

"It doesn't matter if it's a fake or not. How hard do you want to study? Because the whole thing is in your hands. And I'm not kidding."

At Risk of Being a Fool

★ ★ ★ ★ ★

She got through the rest of Tuesday, in spite of cops, suspicious eyes, and a dozen girls ready to nark on her for being in the bathroom for an extra minute, or not separating the silverware.

Wednesdays were a bitch. She'd have thought, with Torrez gone, Cuthbert would ease up, take a break for once. But no, Cuthbert was afraid to step out of Torrez's little hopscotch squares. Wednesday morning came, and rain or sun, she was out policing the grounds before breakfast. Weeds, cigarette butts—where the hell did they all come from? Nobody around here got to smoke—papers blown in from the street. The regulation three girls swarmed the kitchen. Three more vacuumed the life out of anything that didn't move. Two polished all the Venetian blinds in the building, except in Torrez's office. Four of them manicured the grounds.

God, it was endless, the crap they dreamed up for the girls to do. Whether a girl worked and went to school, or whether she just went to therapy and cried all day, she still plowed through the morning chores. Why did it have to be on Wednesdays? Why not clean everything on the weekends, like regular people?

Becca looked out of the kitchen door. "Breakfast," she said. The door shut.

Sorrel tied the top of her trash bag in a knot, and slung it over her shoulder. Lisabet was already at the trashcan. *Cut out early, didn't you, whore?* Sorrel thought. Lisabet flinched away. Sorrel lifted the lid on the trashcan and threw in her bag. She went inside and washed her hands at the bathroom sink. She pulled a nail file from the small box of toiletries sitting on a shelf. *Sorrel Quintana*, it blared in black print. That was another of Torrez's nitpicky rules. She couldn't leave her stuff in the bedroom, oh no. She had to leave it in the bathroom, where anybody could use her comb on their greasy hair, and get lice all over everything. Well, they weren't getting their hands on her makeup. That stayed in her purse, and the purse stayed in the bedroom. There was one good thing about Torrez's rules. No one dared go in her bedroom except Torrez, Cuthbert, and the aides. If a girl set foot in another's room, it was five demerits. The trouble was, she couldn't get her purse until it was time for the van to leave, and so she never got her face done before she left.

Breakfast was nauseating. They'd rushed cleanup because Cuthbert detailed the wrong girls, and these couldn't do sausages without grease blanketing the kitchen. Cuthbert was a nervous wreck, with Torrez gone. Cuthbert didn't do Wednesdays; Torrez did. Cuthbert was a flurry of waving arms, like the routine actually mattered. How was Torrez going to know if they'd picked up cigarette butts before breakfast or after dinner, or even on a Wednesday?

Just a few days ago, Sorrel had seen Torrez staring at her, those gray eyes of hers like stones from a slingshot. She'd wanted to vomit; she was so sure Torrez knew. But the car bomb took care of it. It didn't matter what Torrez knew anymore; she couldn't do anything about it. And Cuthbert was as good as blind.

The van dropped her at the courthouse. As she got out, Mrs. Mahoney held out a hand, stopping her. "Now, Sorrel," Mrs. Mahoney said, "we're short-handed today, so here's a bus token. Since Mrs. Cuthbert's covering for Mrs. Torrez, I have to cover for Mrs. Cuthbert. Things are really messed up right now."

"Yeah," said Sorrel. She strove to sound sympathetic. "I'm sure it's hard on you guys."

At Risk of Being a Fool

"Uh huh," said Mrs. Mahoney, undeceived. "Anyway, we're asking our working girls to take the bus home, until the State loans us a driver. I'm sure you won't mind."

"No, that's fine." She tried to keep her voice even. "Thanks."

Mrs. Mahoney raised an eyebrow. "Just remember, we know the bus schedules, and when you get off work. Check in when you get back. Don't blow it, Sorrel."

"I won't." Sorrel stood frozen, staring after the van as it swung away. She closed her hand tightly over the bus token. God, if only Mahoney knew. What a piece of luck. Maybe she could sound things out, or make some plans. If she could get to Carol, and the woman let her off a few minutes early, she might actually live through this.

Sorrel paced up and down the sidewalk. Again, she checked her watch, and the distance to the bus stop. She had half an hour. It was only down two blocks, and across the street. How hard could it be? She eyed the door. All she had to do was step inside, go up the stairs, and knock. No one would know.

It took all the guts she had to open the door. Her feet were blocks of concrete, dragging up the stairs with clanks that shook the building. At the top of the stairs, a plain wooden door barred her way, with its discreet, unrevealing sign.

She looked over her shoulder at the light filtering in through the entry door's window. She could leave. It would be so easy. There was Torrez, though. Cuthbert was clueless, but that wouldn't last. She thought of Tiffany, growing up without her, for two more goddamned years. The inner door seemed to open by itself.

"Hello," said a cheery voice. The woman had fluffy gray

hair and a perpetually surprised look, like a cat under a blow dryer. Sylvia Palenski, her desk sign read. "I'm Mrs. Palenski, so pleased to meet you. We've had such a dull day, just manning the telephones."

Sorrel found herself seated in front of the woman's desk. She wasn't sure how she'd gotten there.

"What can we help you with?" The delighted look on Sylvia Palenski's face left no doubt that she would be of the greatest help to anyone who walked through the door. Sorrel had met a social worker with the same expression. She'd nearly swept Tiffany out the door into foster care.

"Um. I thought maybe, like, you could tell me some stuff?"

"Of course," said Mrs. Palenski warmly. "We'd be happy to, that's why we're here. Tina? Bring the intake forms with you, dear."

Intake forms. Sorrel edged sideways, ready to flee.

Mrs. Palenski smiled at her. "I have a young volunteer with me today. She's in training. She's a little nervous still. Would it be all right if she helped us out?"

"Um."

"Tina!"

Tina bustled in from an adjoining office, intently scanning the paperwork in her hands. She looked up, saw Sorrel, and grinned at her, a perky expression, a duplicate of Mrs. Palenski's. Oh God, they were twins.

Tina pulled up a chair next to Mrs. Palenski, across the desk from Sorrel. She fanned the papers out. "Are these the right ones?"

"Perfect, Tina. Excellent. Why don't you begin the interview?"

Tina squared the papers together self-importantly. She picked up a pen, and turned to Sorrel with eager eyes. "Hi.

At Risk of Being a Fool

I'm so glad you came in. I was afraid I wasn't going to get any practice today at all. We've got just a few questions first, if that's okay. It's for our funding, you know." She shot a glance at Mrs. Palenski, and became suitably grave. "Of course, everything's confidential. I've just been through the training on it. Confidentiality is a really big deal. So you can trust us."

Yeah, sure. Sorrel edged back further. She closed her eyes for a moment. She had to get home. It was killing her, not seeing Tiffany, or Mama. Grandma was getting so old. What if she died while Sorrel was inside? How would Mama cope?

"So, if you don't mind, could you give me your name?"

Sorrel's eyes flew open. "Brynna," she said. Not fair to use Gallagher. She hated Brynna, but not that much. "McCoy. Brynna McCoy."

Mrs. Palenski looked hard at Sorrel. "McCoy?"

"Yeah. My Dad was a McCoy," she said stiffly.

"Thanks," said Tina, oblivious to the significance of a Scottish name for a Hispanic girl. She stuck out her tongue, frowned at the paper, and wrote "Brenda McCoy." With similar care, she obtained a false address and phone number. "Now, Brenda, we've got lots of information we can give you—"

Mrs. Palenski cleared her throat. "Excuse me, Tina? Did you forget something?"

Tina looked at her blankly.

"The warning? About classes of information? Their availability?"

"Oh." Comprehension lit Tina's face. "Right. I've got to ask you, how old are you? Because if you're under eighteen, we have to get parental permission for some stuff."

"I'm nineteen."

"Could I see your ID? You know, just for the forms."

Sorrel's ID lay in her purse. Sorrel Quintana, it read, aged nineteen, in care of the Oregon Youth Authority. "Didn't bring it today. Taking the bus, you know, not driving."

"Oh," Tina said, stymied.

Mrs. Palenski recovered for her. "Well, we don't really need the ID right now. It's possible it will be required if we meet again. Now Brynna, what information can we offer you today?"

Dust motes danced in the air. Sorrel's head began its daily throb. She lifted a trembling hand to her temple. She hid her hand in her lap. Tina looked puzzled, vaguely concerned. She began to speak, but Mrs. Palenski rested a hand on her arm.

"The door is right there, Miss McCoy," Mrs. Palenski said. "You can leave at any time."

Just for a minute, Mrs. Palenski looked approachable, like Mackie, like Randy, like Jeanie. Torn between fear and hopelessness, Sorrel opened her mouth, unsure what would come out.

"I wondered if you could tell me, like, about abortions."

TEN

"Hi, Mike. So how's everything at Starfire these days? Hmm, well for goodness sakes. I never thought she'd do it. That must be tough, training a replacement mid-job like that. Oh, really? That's a bit of luck." Jeanie leaned back in her armchair, doodling on a notepad on her lap. "I wanted to thank you for coming down last week. I know Edward appreciates it, even if he's a little confused these days."

Mike's deep voice boomed across the phone wires. "My pleasure. He's still a great conversationalist. We got to talking about the Navy, and the time just flew."

"I'm really glad you came, Mike. Women surround him, and there's not an engineer among us. Look, after you left, he brought up a story, and I never heard the ending. I thought I'd heard all his stories! I even pumped him yesterday, and got a bit more, but then it was time for his meds, and that derailed us. It's been bugging me ever since."

Mike chuckled. "You always were a nosy parker. A work story, was it?"

"Yes, about a construction job. You guys were overseeing removal of one of those old underground gas tanks down on the south side. Delancey Brothers bought the site at a distressed property auction."

"Yeah, it happened a lot then. The expense of pulling a tank sometimes wiped out the property value. Owners just walked away, and let the banks foreclose. They figured that was the end of it, poor fellows. Delancey bought a few that way, rebuilt them."

"Right. And Edward was talking about a construction chief he met just a few years ago, Bryce Wogan."

"Wogan . . . I don't quite—"

"Something about a gang, Edward said, and Bryce Wogan's daughter? A teenager."

"Oh, that one." A long exhale. "Poor guy. Yeah, Wogan came by one day, to see when the site would be ready for building. He was grumpy as all hell, picking fights, got everybody's back up. The backhoe operator was all set to walk off the job. Then this guy, a friend of his, big Hispanic guy, what's his name? Romero? Maybe it was Padilla. Shoot, why can't I remember . . ."

"Danny Rivera." Jeanie scribbled on her notepad.

"Yeah, that's it! By God, Edward's memory's better than mine is! Rivera, he kind of lassoed Wogan, rounded him up, shoved him in the truck, sent him off to bug somebody else. Then he apologized to everybody. I got the impression he'd been doing that a lot lately. Seems Wogan's daughter tangled herself up with some gang kid. He had her selling drugs at the high school. I don't know if she was hooked, or just selling it. Cops got her, but the guy split to the winds. She's in the reform system somewhere."

"Do you know her name?"

"Oh geez, Jeanie, this was a couple of years ago. How am I going to remember that?"

"I just thought you might. You've got a couple of daughters yourself, Mike. Carly's about that age, isn't she?"

"Not quite, couple years older. I remember the girl went by her mother's last name, not Wogan's. Divorced right after he married, I bet! Shoot, what was the name? Liz? Elizabeth? Something like that. Wasn't in the newspapers."

At Risk of Being a Fool

"No, it wouldn't be, if she was a minor."

"Oh God yes, sixteen, I remember that! Kind of struck home hard, you know?"

Jeanie wrote a few more notes, thanked him, and hung up. She flipped back to the front page on the notepad, and checked off Starfire Engineering. She added a page number, so she could find her notes on Mike's conversation later on. She scanned her list, covering some thirty lines. She'd marked off about half of them. Most showed cross-references to other pages. Nancy Zernel, at the top of the list, had put her on to half of them, while Ann and Janine filled in the blanks. God bless the teacher network. Their inquisitive fingers dug deeply into the guts of any community, and Salem was no exception.

The head counselor at Jeanie's old school had a network of her own. If anyone could zero in on a nameless girl two years back, somewhere in the Salem/Keizer School District, it was Susan McLain. She added a star to Susan's name. But before that, Jeanie needed a broader understanding of gang activity in the area. Ah, there it was. The Marion Area Gang and Narcotics Enforcement Team. MAG-NET.

Jeanie turned to a fresh page, and dialed another phone number.

"The wheel's turning, but the hamster's gone," Jeanie remarked.

Tonio turned his eyes on her. They seemed blind, out of focus.

She cleared her throat. "How about this. The phone's ringing, but nobody's home."

"What?"

His toneless response worried her. "Tonio, Tonio, Tonio, wake up and smell the coffee. Usually you get my dumb little jokes. What I'm saying is, you seem lost in thought. Having a problem with the essay?"

"Essay? Uh, no." Tonio shook himself, reminding her of Corrigan after he'd walked under a sprinkler. "I was just, uh, thinking real hard."

"Yeah, I figured that out about ten minutes after the pencil quit moving."

"Pencil?"

"This thing here," Jeanie said, tapping his pencil. "Masquerading as a miniature yellow flashlight? Yeah, that thing. That's a pencil."

Tonio gave a short laugh. "Jeanie, you're a nut."

"So you keep telling me."

"What was that about a hamster?"

"The wheel's turning, but the hamster's gone. Means, like, the exercise wheel is going around by itself."

"Huh."

Jeanie rolled her eyes. "A hamster is a little animal—"

"I know what a hamster is."

"Good. So, what's up? You don't seem to be getting far with the essay. Want a different topic?"

"No, I'm fine."

He didn't look fine. He looked like a rug that had been beaten, hung out to air, and then run over by a lawn mower two or three times. Naïve she might be, but she'd seen a thing or two in her day.

"Look, Tonio, if I saw a high school kid looking the way you do now, I'd haul him to the counselor." Jeanie felt his stare burning into the top of her head. She had dirt under one nail. She occupied herself in prying it out with another nail. "I'd like to help."

If it had anything to do with Estelle or Bryce, he wouldn't tell her. If it were any of a dozen things, he

At Risk of Being a Fool

wouldn't tell her. She looked at her nails ruefully. "I wish they looked as good as Sorrel's. I just never seem to pay attention to things like that."

Yesterday had been a frustration, start to finish. Jeanie had made dozens of phone calls, and dropped in on several people unannounced. Mystery books notwithstanding, police had no interest in sharing information with civilians. She'd had a trifle more success with parole officers and substance abuse counselors. There was a limit to what she could ask employers. If she drew their attention to possible risk, her students' jobs were at stake. On the other hand, some were already at stake, and a friendly voice did no harm. She'd made those contacts in her cheery, chirpy persona, the sort of persistent lovey-dovey maternal type that people found it hard to reject. Annalisa claimed it made people feel as if they were stomping on a bunny rabbit.

In terms of facts, the day had netted little. In terms of her students, she'd saved a job or two. Possibly, she'd convinced a few people not to let her students fall into a bureaucratic abyss. If they came after one of her kids, they'd better have clear, compelling reasons, or surrogate mama would be all over the radio stations and the newspapers. Of course, she hadn't said that. But they weren't stupid. They'd been that route, seen her like before.

Sorrel and Brynna would be late today, but they'd be here. Some sort of plumbing disaster at Bright Futures. Dillon was gone, too. Another official was grilling him. Jeanie didn't know why. Teachers never knew the whole story. Perhaps it was fair. She never reported all she knew, either.

"Never mind. I just got to fretting about you, that's all. Just promise me one thing?" She looked up at him. "If a student of mine committed suicide, I'd never forgive myself. So don't, okay? Deal?"

Tonio frowned. "Why?"

"I beg your pardon?"

"I'm not saying I would. I'm just asking, why does it matter?"

"I'm a teacher. I care. That's why I teach."

"No." His head turned slowly from side to side. "All my life, my teachers were scared of me. I never did nothing to 'em, not ever, but they were scared." The flat monotone added an odd emphasis to the words. "I could never figure it out."

A lump in Jeanie's throat shifted and settled into her stomach. It lay there like a snake, writhing and turning. This memory mattered deeply to Tonio. He'd wadded up his observation, sour and spiked, and handed it to her, a double-edged gift. Now he waited to see what she'd do with it. Protect her colleagues, or care about him?

"I'm sorry, Tonio. If they'd known you better, they wouldn't have been frightened." Teachers cared, but they had choices to make, between ten easy students or one difficult student. If you worked with the one, you were cheating the ten. If you worked with the ten, you cheated the one. She shouldered the vague guilt. "You matter to me. What happens to my kids, matters to me." She didn't know what else to say.

His eyelids dropped to half-mast. "I'm kind of tired, that's all. Been camping out in my car. Don't sleep good."

She blinked back the moisture in her eyes. She'd failed his test. "Your car? I thought you lived with your uncle."

"Yeah, well, usually. Only we got into this thing a few days ago. I lit out. Give it a few days, I'll go back. It happens, no big deal."

Tonio was only nineteen. "Have you been able to get to

At Risk of Being a Fool

work all right? Got enough to eat?" Silence. "Let me rephrase that. When did you eat last?"

"Yesterday," he muttered. "Morning."

"Idiot," she said, without heat. "Blast you, you're the one who told me not to carry money in this neighborhood. Stay put, will you?"

Tonio's head jerked up. "Hey, I'm not—"

"Oh, hush up." Jeanie rifled her purse, Mackie's desk, and the closet. With a bang of the door, she disappeared. Shortly, she reappeared at his desk with a can of pop, a bag of pretzels, a candy bar from the vending machine, a dollar and seven cents in change, and a plastic bag under one arm. She looked at him doubtfully. "Look, all I've got is this stuff. I'll go upstairs and borrow a ten from—"

"No," he barked.

She let loose a sharp sigh. "Okay, be a martyr. What about these things?" She dangled a bag of corn cakes, caramel-flavored.

Tonio laughed, and snatched it. "Listen, lady, I'm hungry enough to eat the plastic bag."

"And tomorrow?"

"Tomorrow," he said, his eyes glinting, "I'll ask my boss for a loan. He'll do it, I done him some favors on his truck. I just, you know, I didn't want to ask."

"Thanks." She smiled. To an outsider, it would seem odd, thanking him for letting her feed him. But Tonio had trusted her, briefly. For someone of his background, that was a great gift to give.

"Hey," he said, as she walked away.

"Hmmm?"

"Suicide, it ain't my way."

"Deal, then?"

"Deal. The hamster thing, I get it now. Pretty good."

"For a teacher?"

"For a teacher."

Jeanie turned to lighter problems. She'd had a few misgivings about bringing the cat. Rita was more of a distraction than Corrigan was. Currently, Rita was having a wonderful time chasing paper balls that Quinto thoughtfully threw to her. How educational. Quinto's "essay" held few words, and many sketches of Ricardo Cervantes and Danny Rivera.

"Quinto," she prodded.

"Hmm? Oh, yeah." He flipped the page and wrote laboriously.

Dillon stalked in, handed her a note from Randy, and sat down. Jeanie ushered Rosalie back to her seat for the third time, and tried to extract an essay from her. Regrettably, the topic she chose had led, once again, to memories of her father, and the loss she now felt without his love. This was a poignant story, and had affected Jeanie greatly the first half-dozen times she'd heard it.

"Rosalie, Rosalie," she said bracingly. "Come on, girl, quit the tears. You'll get salt in the potatoes."

"Potatoes?" said Rosalie, startled. The tears stopped.

"Life is like a potato, Rosalie, didn't you know?" Jeanie felt like a fool, pulling out the old family joke. It never made sense to outsiders. "Potatoes have a rough life. They're mashed, baked, fried, or scalloped in a cheese sauce."

"Huh?" said Quinto, interrupting from his table. "How's that? Life's a potato?"

"Back to work, guys. Come on." Jeanie cast a glance around for the cat. Rita had discovered Dillon, and crawled into one of his large coat pockets. Jeanie savored Dillon's unnerved expression.

At Risk of Being a Fool

Brynna shoved her way through the door, looking over her shoulder. Jeanie stood involuntarily. Brynna was her own personal weathervane. Whatever was going on, Brynna always knew it. Was the girl sadistic? Or calculating, always looking for an angle? Or was it just the suspicion of a trapped animal, watching for hunters? Jeanie's hand settled on a room divider. Without conscious thought, she pulled it behind her, closing Brynna off from Tonio.

"Hi, Brynna," Jeanie said.

"Hey," said Brynna. She settled at a table, and sat watching the door with the alert look of a vulture waiting for something to die.

There was a shuffling step in the hallway. Sorrel walked in stiffly, jerking from side to side, like a wind-up doll whose interior mechanism had fragmented. Brynna's alert look sharpened.

"Hi, Sorrel," Jeanie said.

Sorrel gave no sign of hearing. She passed all of them and fumbled her way into a chair in the furthest corner of the room. The students generally avoided the corner desk. It was too isolated, and had no nearby windows. It accumulated the usual clutter of homeless debris: empty Coke cans, crumpled assignments, even a wrench and a spray can of paint.

Brynna swiveled to watch, her face bright with malicious curiosity. Jeanie closed the door, grabbed two more room dividers, and boxed off Sorrel from the others. Brynna gave a wordless protest, and subsided into a sullen lump.

"Here, Brynna," said Jeanie, plopping books on her desk. "Science today, I thought. A little change of pace."

Her wandering eye settled on Tonio. Tonio glanced from Sorrel's divider to his radio. He edged it towards Jeanie with a questioning look. It was a trade for the food, thought Jeanie, and nodded gratefully. Tonio turned on the radio. The beat of gangsta rap drowned out the background paper rustles. Rita squawked at the noise, and dove into Dillon's jacket. Dillon flinched, but his hand, pursuing the cat, was unexpectedly gentle.

Jeanie slipped between the dividers. Sorrel hung in the chair, her hands lying loose on the table. She might have been dead or comatose, and tied into her chair for some barbaric ritual. Jeanie lifted the clutter from the desk, dumping it on the floor.

The roar of Oscar Kemmerich's motorcycle cut through the music. Jeanie noticed it with vague irritation. Since she'd broken up a cozy conversation between Mr. Kemmerich and Rosalie, he'd gone to some trouble to disrupt the class. In one of his more inspired antics, he'd brought a friend of his, a police officer, on a tour through the building, and introduced him to her class. The officer was polite, if baffled, but her students' varied reactions had taken her most of an hour to overcome.

"Sorrel, I talked to your boss," Jeanie said, trying to break into her self-absorption. There was no flicker of understanding. "Carol's really happy with the way you're working out." Where were the girl's restless movements? The tapping of the fingers, the impatient slap of books onto the tables? There was something obscene about the dreadful stillness. "Sorrel? Sorrel, are you feeling all right?"

"Sure." The voice was distant, vague.

Was she in shock? Sugar was good for shock. "Sorrel, can I get you a pop? Some coffee, maybe?"

"No." With a visible effort, Sorrel looked up. "I'm fine. I got work to do."

"Yeah, sure." Jeanie's glance slipped over Sorrel's eyes, the color of the skin around the vivid splotches of makeup.

At Risk of Being a Fool

She ticked off the warning signs she'd read a hundred times in the last months. Nothing matched. "You look sick. Do you need to lie down? Should I call the clinic?"

"No." Sorrel's voice was still, lifeless.

Jeanie waited for the automatic reach for purse and hand mirror, but the purse lay disregarded. Rumpled clothes, uncombed hair, uneven makeup, applied with an absent mind and careless hand. There were scuffs on her fingernails. There were actually *scuffs* on her fingernails.

"Sorrel? Honey?" Jeanie's hand edged out over the desk and hesitated. Her instincts fought with her hard-won knowledge.

Never touch, Mackie said. Never.

Very lightly, Jeanie rested two fingers on the back of Sorrel's hand. Sorrel's hand was still. It quivered, turned, and closed tightly on hers, fingernails digging into the back of Jeanie's hand. Sorrel's face convulsed, and a tremor wracked her body. She dropped her head onto the joined hands. Her forehead was hot and damp.

"What is it? Whatever it is, just tell me."

"I'm pregnant." The words were scarcely audible.

Words leaped to Jeanie's mind. Who, when, how? She bit back the words. All it took was ten minutes and a broom closet.

She brushed a tendril of hair from Sorrel's hot face. "You're sure."

"Yeah." The tortured voice was nearly inaudible. "Shit, what am I going to do? They find out, they'll kick me out of Futures, back to the Tank. 'Til I'm twenty-one. Two more fucking years. I can't do it. I'll kill myself."

Jeanie strove to keep her voice calm, detached. "Maybe an abortion, Sorrel? I'll help you sort it out. No need to tell anyone." Jeanie was putting herself out on a limb, but it seemed like a natural place to be. A student needed her.

"No." The word wrenched loose. "I thought of that, I thought maybe— I snuck out of work at lunch today. I went to this place and asked. They had these pictures, you know. Babies, all cut up."

"You can't be far along, just a few weeks—"

"I've been thinking." Sorrel's tone was dreary, exhausted. "But I can't do it. It's like, if it were Tiffany."

Or Geoff, or Keith. A wave of kinship washed over her. She stretched out an arm across Sorrel's back, and leaned her cheek against Sorrel's fevered one. "We'll work it out. There's always ways."

Sorrel's keening sobs rocked Jeanie back and forth to the beat of the crashing music from Tonio's radio. After a time, the tremors eased. Jeanie sat up, letting her free. "God, I must look like crap," Sorrel muttered.

Jeanie smiled involuntarily. "Just about," she said. "How about you go clean up some, and we'll figure things out. Go out through the office," she added, remembering Brynna's eager look. "Sorrel?"

Sorrel's eyes looked like Tonio's: deep, mesmerizing, a dark cave with a bottomless pit. Jeanie kept her footing. "We'll figure something out," Jeanie said. "We will. Believe it, Sorrel." The cave wavered and disappeared, leaving behind a girl, stunned and bereft. Sorrel nodded and fled.

Jeanie watched her go. A month ago, she'd gotten this job, walked through the door, and started going through the motions. A student acted this way, and the professional teacher reacted that way. It was a complex dance, the moves choreographed through years of practice. When had that changed? When had these six students wormed their way into her heart so completely? Randy Firman and Dolores Cuthbert weren't going to hear about this, not from

At Risk of Being a Fool

Jeanie. They were colleagues, but on opposite sides of the same fence.

How could she help Sorrel hide her pregnancy? The girl's clothes emphasized every curve. That had to change. Then there was the Writing test. She was nearly ready. If she could recover her balance, she could take it Friday. It was best to get that over with as soon as possible, since it took so long to get the scores back. She could study for the math test while waiting.

How far along was she? It was a second pregnancy, and she wasn't showing yet. She might have another month of grace. Of course, if she failed either test, they were up a creek. The problem would be obvious before she had time for another try. Meantime, the main problem was keeping her out of the sight of suspicious people. At least Estelle, with her sharp eyes, wouldn't see her.

Jeanie's mind stilled. Her fingers rattled on the desktop, the sound indistinguishable from the crashing music. Oh dear Lord, she couldn't have. She half-rose, eyes frozen on the door through which Sorrel had escaped. Surely not. Sorrel couldn't bear the thought of an abortion without getting sick. She couldn't order a pipe bomb set for Estelle, just to get her out of the way. Could she?

But there was that man she'd attacked at the party. She severed an artery, nearly castrated him, and left him in the bedroom. If no one had found him, he'd have died. He hadn't recovered the use of two of his fingers, and walking remained uncomfortable a year later. Sorrel said she'd defended herself. The guy said that she'd answered a joke with a knife.

That was different, wasn't it, from a pipe bomb? A knife attack was an instant's fury, slashes with the knife close at hand, and the instinct to flee. Arranging a bomb took plan-

149

ning and intent. Or perhaps it didn't, if all it took was a phone call. Had she called someone because she was scared Estelle was onto her, would kick her out, and toss her back into Corrections?

No. She couldn't have.

Sorrel came in and sat down, drawing the shreds of her dignity around her. Her freshly scrubbed face looked naked without its customary armor of makeup. She looked at Jeanie, with hope and fear mingled.

"All right, here's what I'm thinking," said Jeanie. "Stop me if you disagree. I know you have to pass the tests to get out of Bright Futures, right? I'm assuming you can handle living there, and working for a while? You're going to take the Writing test on Friday, so you're going to have to live and breathe writing for the next two days. We'll have to wait from one to three weeks for those results, and I figure that's all the time we've got. Now for the math test, that's bad news. To get to that level, in a month, means a lot of work, lots of concentration on your part." Doubts rose. Sorrel had the basic skills and the intelligence, but not the patience to apply them. "More than you've shown me in the past."

"I will, I will. I can do it. If I don't, God, I'm back in Corrections and the baby's in foster care. I want my baby." She clutched her abdomen protectively. "It's ours. Tiffy's and mine."

"And the father?"

Sorrel sealed her lips and shook her head. "He's got nothing to do with this. The baby's mine."

"But Sorrel—" Sorrel half-rose, looking ready to bolt. Why was the father such a touchy issue? "All right then. That's your business, not mine. Sorrel, you'll need to fill me in on a few things, especially on how your sentence reads.

At Risk of Being a Fool

Then I'll hit the phones while you hit the books. I'm going to line you up enough homework to keep you out of trouble."

Sorrel gave a watery chuckle. "A little late."

Randy replayed his voice mail. He shifted his shoulders against the car seat, propped the bag of fries on the dashboard, and took another bite from his hamburger. Fast food parking lots were his second office. He gathered the burger into one hand and thumbed his cell phone with the other.

"GED School." Jeanie sounded a little strained.

"It's okay," Randy said, through a mouthful of burger. "Sorry." He swallowed. "They've cleared him, at least for now. He'll be there soon."

"Dillon?" She sounded startled. "Oh, right, he got back a while ago."

"They got a search warrant for his house."

"His house? Dillon would never build pipe bombs in his grandmother's house."

Randy grinned at the acerbic tone. "Yeah, well, they don't understand about Mrs. Otero."

"If they think he did it, they should be checking his friends' houses."

"They'll get there."

"Yeah," she said, depressed. "Actually, I called about Sorrel."

"Sorrel? I saw her yesterday. What's she pulling now?"

There was a momentary silence. "She's working really hard. She'll be taking the Writing test this Friday."

"Wow, she's really putting the pressure on. Can she pass it?"

"I hope so. Probably."

Possibly, Randy corrected her mentally. Sorrel must be pushing Jeanie, too.

"She's really eager to get out. We were talking about ways she could increase her chances. There's work, school, and a positive report from Bright Futures, right?"

"That's the basics, yes."

"What about community service?"

Randy paused, a load of fries halfway to his mouth. Ketchup dripped onto his shirt. "Say what?"

"If she were to put some hours in, on community service, wouldn't that help her chances? Show she's a reformed character?" The chuckle was subtly reassuring.

Randy munched, brain spinning in a new direction. "Maybe. But I haven't got time to arrange stuff like that. And transportation's impossible from Bright Futures, with Torrez out of commission. They're short-handed. Mary Mahoney's about out of her mind."

"How's Estelle doing?"

"She's off critical, out in the wards. She'll be off work for a while. Six weeks, minimum."

"Oh dear. Poor thing. Sorrel said something about license plate numbers. Have the police had any luck?"

"If they had Mrs. Otero's, I'd have heard about it. Otherwise not. Jeanie, I don't think community service is workable. She has to be under constant supervision. Once she meets the criteria, she'll be better off. Down to supervised probation, like Dillon, but in her case, that'll be up in Portland where her family is."

"Ah. Well, about community service, I had a sudden notion. There's this memory loss facility near my home. I do a lot of volunteer work there." The strain was back in her voice.

"They'll let a felon work in a nursing home?"

"If I bring her, they will. Talk about short-handed! Retirement homes are so depressing, a lot of people won't

At Risk of Being a Fool

work there, and the ones who do are collapsing under the load. So I thought, why not kill two birds with one stone? I'll take Sorrel with me sometimes in the evenings, to help with dinner and activities. Maybe a Saturday or two? If that's all right?"

"She's okay with this?" He heard the suspicion in his voice, and tried to downplay it. "She *wants* to volunteer?"

"She seems to. I suppose it's mostly the idea of getting out of Bright Futures. It's not the most congenial environment, especially now. Besides, I can make her study more if she's under my thumb."

"Ah, so you'd be there all the time. You'd have to sign papers and stuff, acknowledging supervisory responsibility. Are you sure you want to bother?"

"Yes, I do. Most definitely."

"Listen, it sounds to me like she's trying something. She was pushing me a day or two ago, but I didn't give her any happy answers. If she is pulling something, she's going to get bounced right back to Corrections. She'll be worse off than she is right now."

"Randy, I know what you're saying. But this is important."

Randy reran the conversation in his mind. "Do you know something I don't know?"

"Possibly."

"Do you know what this is about? For real, for sure?"

"I think so." More strongly, "Yes, I know for sure."

"So tell me."

"You don't want to know."

"I have to ask."

"You have to ask, but you don't want to know, because you won't want to write it down in her file. So you won't ask."

"Am I going to be sorry?"

"Hold on."

Sorrel's voice sounded on the other end of the line. "Randy?" It didn't sound like her at all. "Randy, please, let me do this. I really want to."

"Sorrel. I'm going out on a limb for you. So is Jeanie, big time. You hear me?"

"I hear you. I know it." She sounded strange, a little hoarse.

"Are you going to let us down?"

"No. I'm not."

Randy closed his eyes. Past experience argued fiercely against it.

"I swear to you, it's for Tiffany. It's so I can be with my family again. Randy, am I going to screw that up? I love my grandma. These people at the old age home, they're like my grandma, and they need help. I know I've lied to you before. But I'm not going to hurt my chances of going home. Am I?"

"Not if you realize that you're doing it, no."

"If I louse this up, if I run away, or take stupid chances, I'm back in Corrections until I'm twenty-one. Right? I'm not going to risk that."

In spite of his better judgment, Randy found that he agreed. "Well. I'll put through the paperwork, and Jeanie's going to have to sign her name in blood about a dozen times."

"I will too."

Sorrel's signature wasn't worth a piece of scrap paper. She loved her daughter, though. He trusted her love for Tiffany, but that was about it. "Okay, girl. Put Jeanie back on. And don't louse it up."

ELEVEN

"She'll be glad to see you," the nurse said. "She hasn't had many visitors."

"No?" Jeanie said.

"None at all, in fact, except for policemen. Not even phone calls." Suppressed satisfaction lurked in the nurse's voice. Estelle had made her usual saintly impression.

"Oh." Jeanie considered the paperbacks in her hand. It was just a thought she'd had, to drop off some books, whiz in, and whiz out. Books were better than flowers. *Here, Estelle, something to read, get better soon, bye.*

"You can go right in."

"Thank you." Jeanie walked slowly down the hall.

"You've missed it," the nurse called, "it's just behind you."

"I know. I mean, I have something to do first." Jeanie scuttled to the small waiting area at the end of the hall, and looked blindly out the window. Estelle had been here for three days. She had no friends. If she had family, they didn't want to visit her. Jeanie fingered the paperbacks in her hands. Books had always been friends to her, but they hardly compared to someone who actually cared if you hurt. Jeanie could have fed pets with a willing heart, watered flowers, or brought books. The wisp of a notion to question Estelle vanished at the thought of Estelle's trauma. Questioning Estelle was a minefield better left untrodden. And apart from thorny subjects of students and pipe bombs, what on earth could she say?

Jeanie found her feet leading her down the hall. Oh God, not again. Her feet had minds of their own, and dragged her into countless problems. There was no point in fighting them. Feet were stubborn, and they hurt a lot when they were mad at you. Jeanie paused at the doorway. *Here goes nothing.*

"Hello, Estelle. It's Jeanie McCoy. We met at Bright Futures."

Blankets covered a metal framework over Estelle's body, and hid most of the damage. A white shield of gauze covered one side of her face, the rest of it prickled and swollen, as though she'd run into a cactus. Bandages swathed her right arm, elbow to wrist. The bomb, Jeanie remembered, was behind the accelerator. The floor took the greatest force of the explosion. Like Bryce Wogan, either she'd been lucky, or the bomb was deliberately nonlethal.

Estelle didn't seem to feel lucky. Her eyes, silver-gray in the mangled face, radiated suspicion, defense, and resentment. In fact, she looked a lot like Sorrel. Jeanie caught the back of the armchair to steady herself. "I brought you some books."

Estelle stared at her in silence.

"I'm Sorrel's teacher. And Brynna's. I thought you'd want some books to read. Unless your hands hurt too much to hold them."

"Thank you." The voice sounded like a hunk of granite hauled over gravel, hoarse and grating.

"I just thought, to pass the time, you know. Mysteries, different styles. I've always liked them."

Estelle's lips tightened. "I said thanks. You've brought them. You can go."

She sounded like Sorrel, too, or like Brynna. The parallel piqued her interest. Reject others before they reject

At Risk of Being a Fool

you. Jeanie's urge to run evaporated, and her pixyish recalcitrance came to the fore. She slid into the chair, putting the books on the side table.

"I notice you don't have the TV on," said Jeanie. Mentally, she replaced Estelle Torrez with an angry student. She'd often played the part of a rubber wall or a punching bag, something safe for the lunatic to pound or claw.

"Television is tedious in the extreme."

"Perhaps some conversation, then?"

"I think not," said Estelle, with a jab of disdain. "I don't require the charity of your time or conversation, thank you much." The lines of her face deepened, as she added with an effort at civility, "I do appreciate your effort, but I hardly think we have anything in common."

"Kids?"

"Delinquents, you mean." Estelle corrected.

"Now, now, Estelle," Jeanie mocked gently. "They're not delinquents any more. They're juvenile offenders. I know, because I read the research. Including a paper written recently by one Estelle Torrez, extolling the use of the justice model in the juvenile system."

The shot went home. Estelle flushed and her mouth opened. She shut it and looked out the window. She said nothing.

"An interesting paper, Estelle. A prestigious magazine in the corrections world, or so I'm told."

There was no response.

"Personally," said Jeanie provocatively, "I've always preferred the rehabilitative model in juvenile corrections." This was a dagger thrown. It hit its target, bulls-eye.

"Rubbish," snapped Estelle, glaring at Jeanie. "The rehabilitative model has been outmoded since nineteen seventy-five. The recidivism is horrific."

Jeanie raised her eyebrows. Very few people could use the word recidivism correctly, let alone say it without stammering. "Hardly horrific. Statistics are one thing, but anecdotal research displays the folly of ignoring the human side of crime. Just last year—"

Estelle's face lost its slackness. The joy of battle gleamed as she marshaled arguments. Jeanie crossed her fingers behind her back and settled in for the long haul.

Her good deed for the day: fight with Estelle.

"Three oranges go south at thirty miles an hour," said Kherra gravely, "and there's about seven apples goin' northeast at fifty miles an hour. What are you goin' to get when they crash in Silverton?"

Sorrel looked up into the concerned face overhead. Kherra's cornrowed hair descended into beaded braids that shook as she broke into a chuckle. "I'm sorry, girl, here you're tryin' to concentrate, and I'm messin' with you. The girls said I had to take a break. I figured I'd wander back here. I wondered where you'd got to."

Sorrel's muscles ached with tension. She closed her eyes. It could have been worse. She could have been stuck at Bright Futures, instead of here with a nosy fat woman. Saturdays were bathroom cleaning day, scrubbing the shower stalls. Getting wet wasn't a good idea. Hiding the small bulge would have been torture. So she'd traded a day at Bright Futures for a day with flaked-out old ladies and nosy nurses, a whole day spent watching her tongue.

"Hidin' out?"

"Gotta study my math," Sorrel muttered. "GED test coming up."

"Smart thinkin'. This place is probably gettin' to you. It gets to a lot of people. Sad."

At Risk of Being a Fool

"I'm glad to be here," said Sorrel.

"Uh huh."

What did she mean by that? She'd done her best with all these old people, with their damned walkers, and wobbly voices, and stubbornness, of I-will-do-this-my-way, when dressing would be so much faster if they'd just stand there, for God's sake. She hadn't lost her temper once, and she was proud of it. But it struck her as a little funny. When a math book started to look good, it was a bad sign.

"Sorry," Kherra said, with a sidelong glance. "It's just, you're thinkin' one thing, and sayin' another. Take it easy, girl. Say what you want to me. I don't tell on anybody. It's my biggest vice, bein' curious. If I was a cat, I'd have died a hundred times already."

Effortlessly, Kherra transformed the pile of laundry into neat stacks of towels and sheets, each folded with machine-like precision. She wore a large T-shirt that read: Please, God, if you can't make me skinny, make my friends fat.

"You got any questions? You could bug me, instead of me buggin' you."

Actually, she did. It had bugged her since the first afternoon Jeanie'd hauled her over here. "Yeah. How come you guys named an old folks home after a baseball team? It's stupid."

"Oriole's Nest? Girl, you're one after my own heart. Just what I said! It's not even like we're on the right coast. Baltimore, I ask you. But it turns out, an oriole's a bird, little thing with yellow spots. You learn something new every day, that's what I say. And now you're thinkin'," said Kherra easily, "that I'm makin' fun of you. Well, I'm not. Can't prove it, though. Tell me, what do you think's behind all this bomb stuff?"

"Huh?" Sorrel said, baffled.

Kherra's mouth quirked and she burst out laughing. "I'm sorry. Workin' here, I've learned to break the ice hard and fast, but sometimes I forget and use a sledgehammer. My word, the look on your face! Forget I asked. It's just, we've got our own idea, Jeanie and me. I just thought I try bouncin' it off you, see what you think."

"What's that?" Sorrel said.

Kherra sobered. "Well, first there's the construction site, one of those government recreation places for low-income families, right? I remember when it first went in, there was a lot of vandalism from the gangs. Don't look at me like that. There's gangs in Salem, and only a possum doesn't know it. The thing is, when there's free entertainment kids could be going to, the gang membership drops off. So, they weren't any too happy about that place going in, in the first place. So now, there's an expansion, and somebody plants a bomb. Anybody could've picked it up. Might have been Bryce, Danny, or even Quinto. Right? So, that's the first one. Once you start looking at gang involvement, the bomb at the courthouse makes a lot more sense, don't it?"

"You mean, there's a girl in Futures who belongs to a local gang? But hurting Torrez just causes trouble."

Kherra slapped the desk. "Exactly. There's no motive for any one livin' there right now. If the woman's such poison, you can bet her neighbors aren't fond of her, or anybody else she meets. It's likely she's tangled with some gang members, or even more likely, some are related to girls she booted out of the program. Ones that aren't there anymore. Well? Doesn't that make sense to you?"

"Some," said Sorrel. She put the pencil down carefully. "You figured that out on your own?"

"Nope, Jeanie and me, we've been talkin'. She badgered Mrs. Torrez's building manager. And some of the people at

At Risk of Being a Fool

the recreation facility, too. You put bits of information together, it's amazin' what you find. She wasn't sure it all went together, so I thought I'd try it out on you. Think it over, huh?"

A thready voice sounded in the hallway. "Bernie? Where are you, Bernie?"

Kherra bounded into the hall. "Leda, honey, what's the trouble? You lookin' for Bernie? Isn't he around here? Maybe he's gone home, what do you think, hmm?"

"He said he'd be here," fretted Leda. One hand clawed at Kherra's sleeve.

Kherra set a gentle arm around her shoulders and walked her down the hall. "I know he did. He loves you something fierce, I know that. Bernie was braggin' on your cookin' just last week. He was talkin' about Thanksgivin' one year, said you made about eighteen kinds of pie, best turkey a man ever threw a lip over, hmm hmm. I tell you, I about died listenin' to him. My mama couldn't cook worth nothin'." Kherra's voice faded, the words floating behind her. "If it didn't come straight out of a cracker box, she wouldn't have nothin' to do with it."

Sorrel's heart slowed to normal. The tension flowed out through her fingertips and spilled on the floor, leaving her limp, exhausted, and at peace. The bombs were just local gang stuff, all of it. It had nothing to do with that shithead. Or even Brynna's antics, because Brynna was from Portland. In fact, all the class except Rosalie came from Portland. It wasn't anybody from the class at all.

She watched Kherra, and noticed the hallway as if for the first time.

A big oval walking track with a rubberized floor ringed the inside of the building. A dining room sat on each end, outside the track. The residents' rooms were in little cul-desacs off the dining rooms. Inside the ring were small living room areas. One was formal with paintings and high-backed sofas. Another was light-hearted with animal wallpaper, a huge birdcage with finches, and an aquarium. There was even a place set up like an ice cream parlor. The garden out back had benches, a gazebo, and big raised flowerbeds.

Sometimes it seemed like a nice hotel, the fancy kind. Then Sorrel would come to an exit door and realize she needed a keypad combination to leave. She knew the combination. She'd tested it over and over again.

Halfway down the hall, she saw the back of Jeanie's head. She was sitting with Edward, talking, showing him pictures of the grandkids. He didn't have a clue. All through dinnertime he kept going on and on about some kind of mess-up in the CIA, something about submarines.

A nurse named Marlo intercepted Kherra and Leda. Marlo shook a finger at Kherra and headed off with Leda. Kherra returned to the office.

"They won't let me do anythin' around here. They figure since I'm doin' a double shift I should take it easy. Excuse me." Kherra extracted several patient charts from a stack on the desk, and flipped the top one open, making notations in a quick, neat hand. "So, what do you think of our—scenario." Kherra winked, drawing out the word dramatically.

"Sounds okay to me. What's your accent from?" said Sorrel, hoping to change the subject to something less dangerous.

"A touch of the Virginia Reel, with some of the islands thrown in. Mama was from Jamaica. Daddy was a Southern boy."

"That's your Mama who cooks out of a cracker box."

"There's a lot you can do with a cracker box. My Mama

At Risk of Being a Fool

makes the best pan-fried oysters you ever ate. So, okay, I've got another question for you. Is Jeanie doing okay, or is that outside the scope of this little talk?"

"Like what? I guess she's okay. She's just a teacher."

"Hmm. Teachers are people, too. Jeanie have any friends, that you know about?"

"There's Mackie. And you."

Kherra shook her head, dissatisfied. "Dang it."

"She did something funny at the park. She was picking up things under the trees. Then later, when we dropped Corrigan at the house, she went and planted them."

"She's plantin' acorns." Kherra chuckled. "Don't look like that, girl, she's not out of her mind yet. She's got this thing about oak trees. They take hundreds of years to grow up to any size, so she's took to plantin' 'em herself. Says you can't trust the squirrels to do it."

"Why bother, if they take that long to grow?"

"Somebody's got to bother. I've planted a few myself, since she told me."

Kherra bolted out of her seat and ran into the hallway. Belatedly, Sorrel heard a high-pitched screaming. She followed, but Kherra was halfway down the hallway, moving at a speed Sorrel couldn't believe. Kherra disappeared into a bedroom as a frizzy-haired woman in a pink bathrobe emerged. Phyllis, that was her name. Marlo ran up and tucked an arm around Phyllis' waist.

"What is it?" Sorrel panted, skidding up behind them.

Phyllis stood trembling in her bedroom doorway. "A man," she quavered. She pointed a shaking finger into her room.

"Has Bill gone to sleep in your bed again?" Marlo said. "I'll go chase him out, Phyllis, don't you worry."

Kherra shot out the door, and passed them. "Not Bill," she said, running for the back door into the yard. She unlatched the top of the door, threw it open, and darted through. "You get the hell out of here, you hoodlum," she shrieked. "If I catch you, I'm goin' to wring your neck."

Oh my God. The fear crushed Sorrel back against the wall.

Marlo's hand shook as she picked up the emergency phone from the wall, and punched a single number. "Prowler," she said, "tell Nate. Back side of the building." Marlo dashed down the halls, glancing into each bedroom.

It was *him.* How had he found her? Through her terror, she discovered Phyllis clinging to her arm. She throttled an urge to shake the woman off. Where should she go? Where was safe? Lights, she needed to be in the lights, away from the windows, away from where he could see her. If he saw her, he'd know— Know what? Where to throw the bomb? Where to shoot? *Oh my God, oh my God. And all these old people, they could get hurt, too.*

"Come on," she said. She took Phyllis by the arm, and pulled her through the dining room, and across the walking track. There were no windows in the inner rooms, though they were open to the track. Phyllis pulled back. Sorrel fought the urge to hit her, to leave her, and through her panic, the words came. "Phyllis, it's okay. Don't worry now. Look, it's, uh, time for dress-up, for a performance, all right? You're going to be, I don't know, um—"

"The Queen?" said Phyllis, with a tremulous smile.

"That's right, the Queen. So we need to get you made up, all right?"

"All right," said Phyllis.

"It's too late for a play," said Marian.

Where had Marian come from? All around her, suddenly, were old ladies, four or five of them. What the hell was she going to do?

At Risk of Being a Fool

"It's almost bedtime," said Marian, frowning. "It's dark outside."

"Yes, well," said Sorrel, "but there's going to be a play tomorrow, and this is the best time to figure out your costumes, right? So, uh, I can find the right makeup for you for tomorrow."

Marlo trotted back to them, in time to hear the tail end of the explanation. "Great idea, Sorrel," said Marlo. "You're absolutely right. Come on, ladies."

Jeanie arrived, holding onto Edward's arm.

"We have to get everyone away from the windows," said Sorrel. Oh God, the windows, all her old ladies. He couldn't do it. He couldn't loose off a bomb and hurt all these old people. Could he? She wanted to run, to get the hell out of here, but something held her. "Come on, Jeanie. Help me get the others."

There was a bustle of confusion, as activities began in the middle of the evening. Kherra reappeared and organized balloon volleyball, which involved a dozen people sitting in the ice cream parlor chairs, hitting balloons at each other. In the dress-up room, Marlo fitted feather boas and fancy dresses to residents. Jeanie sat at the piano, picking out a tune, singing "She'll be Comin' 'Round the Mountain When She Comes." An aide, a housekeeper, and two nurses appeared with stragglers. Nate and another guy came in, both of them with friendly smiles, and checked all the bedrooms.

It was bizarre.

Sorrel retrieved a balloon and gave it to Bill. She wouldn't think about it. She wouldn't. Nate would take care of it, and the guy must be long gone, with Kherra bellowing at him like that.

God, Kherra. Who'd have believed it? Running out

there, yelling obscenities at a running shadow, protecting her old people. Kherra, she saw, was looking at her, a warm look in her eyes. Sorrel flushed and managed a smile at Leda.

After half an hour, Nate and the other guy left, waving casually. The nurses began winding up activities and corralling their charges towards their bedrooms. Jeanie took Edward to his room.

"I'll be with you in twenty minutes, Sorrel," she said.

Sorrel nodded and collapsed into a chair against the wall.

"You did a good job," Kherra said. Sorrel looked at her gratefully. "It scared you a lot more than I figured. Did you think he was lookin' for you?" She waited for a beat, and continued. "It was probably the same guy that showed up last week. That was before you came. He was likely hopin' to see where the drug cabinet was. Didn't have a thing to do with you." Kherra seemed to read Sorrel's relief. "Take it easy, girl. There's a whole lot of things that go on, that don't have nothin' to do with you. Or your family. It's okay, honey. You did fine."

She touched Sorrel lightly on the shoulder as she left. Bewildered, Sorrel discovered that she didn't mind the touch. A rare moment of pleasure lightened her heart.

TWELVE

... *Estelle won't discuss the bomb, or anything else. Not even the license plate list. Drat. She likes to argue, and that's about it. I'm making a list of topics to fight about. If you think of any, let me know. Yesterday, I got her going on sealing court records of juveniles. I ask you, Shelley, how boring!*

She insists the girls at Bright Futures are safe from temptation, "and not for any of your sentimental reasons, either, but because they simply haven't the opportunity. I know where they are every minute. I get a history on every phone call, and they know it. Number called, time, date, duration, and so on. There are few." Well, I'd guess so. Sounds like a police state, if you ask me.

Of course, she's wrong. I know Sorrel's little trip to the health clinic was after Estelle was in the hospital, but she called Randy from work before the bomb, and Estelle didn't know. I wonder if Sorrel or Brynna has access to explosives. Rosalie does. Her Dad's a hunter. Uses a rifle, she says. He's a plumber too, so there's the pipe for the bombs. If this were a murder mystery, I'd be all over him. But he sounds like he's death on drugs and crime, since that's why he kicked Rosalie out in the first place. That girl really worries me. Today I saw her heading upstairs again, to talk to Mr. Kemmerich, her so-called friend. I half expected him to come down and complain about her, but he didn't. And that worries me, too. That's the third time that I know of that she's wandered upstairs to talk to him. He's not the sort to give free legal advice, so it couldn't be about Dominic. Or maybe it could, and she's paying him somehow. Only, where would she get the money?

It's scary, Shell. My kids connect with all three explosives. I like all of my kids. Of course, I liked Robert five years ago, and you know how that worked out. My major failing. I like everybody, but that thing about his sister was too much, even for me. He's in the Corrections system, somewhere, but he won't go through my program. He must be over twenty-one by now.

Thanks for listening, sister mine. I hear the train rumbling. Time to go stand at the window, do a little dreaming, and try to catch some sleep. The trick, I find, is keeping Rita's tail out of my mouth.

Love you always, Jeanie

Jeanie hit Send, and shut down the computer. She leaned against the windowsill as the screen went blank behind her. The train passed by, its comforting rumble carrying her niggling worries with it.

Rosalie, whose love for her father was more constant than her love for a wailing baby.

Quinto and his math, still not up to the blueprint level, but getting there.

Tonio, hungry, living in his car, but still getting to school and work.

Sorrel, who might lose Tiffany by trying to save the new baby.

Brynna, plain, sour, malicious, but so wistful, like a child looking into a neighbor's house on Christmas Day.

Dillon and his grandmother, and the cat.

Corrigan, who steered clear of Dillon and Sorrel, and

At Risk of Being a Fool

loved the other four. Shelley said she hadn't named him Wrong-Way Corrigan for nothing. So maybe the two were all right, and the other four were major trouble.

The end of the train grumbled its way past the window, like a fat dog waddling its weary way to the doghouse. Jeanie flicked off the light and got into bed. It was so cold, without Edward's warmth to snuggle. Rita's purrs picked up the comforting rhythm of the train in the distance. Jeanie slept.

He stood in the shadow of the apartment building and studied the street. A light breeze lifted a scrap of newspaper. It skittered down the asphalt, and stuck under the front tire of a Ford Taurus. There was a streetlight behind him, past the bushes, and another at the end of the street. All the houses and apartments were dark.

He straightened with an easy grace and moved soundlessly down the street. His car was at the park, a couple of blocks back. There wasn't a lot of traffic around here. He didn't want to stand out, driving around in the quiet.

It was too quiet, almost spooky. How could they stand it, living here? Were they all old, and gray-haired, tottering along the sidewalks with their canes? Still, old folks had young ones coming around, taking care of them. There was a playground too, so there must be kids.

He scanned the road. Two small apartment buildings faced each other, two stories each, end-on to the street. Tiny things, couldn't hold more than six families each. Then came a house, maybe the manager's, and another building, facing the street. Eight units in that one, it looked like. A little playground took up the front, but there was no graffiti, no rusting appliances, no beer cans, or Burger King wrappers, and not a single TV light in any window.

He passed the apartments and came to a line of four little houses. He paused, counted them, and checked the cars. Third one. Yeah, that was it. He circled the car, glanced around, and peered inside for the dog harness. He checked the license plate, but he already knew. There were no lights on in the front of her house. Early to bed, early to rise, made a guy something, something, something.

He leaned against the car, looking at the house.

First, it was the construction site, Rivera and Wogan getting their noses in where they didn't belong. That one was chancy. There were too many people around. He liked things to be precise, exactly on target. Even after Wogan went down, Rivera didn't get the idea. Now there was a rent-a-cop coming around nights, just dropping by.

He hadn't worried about that at first. "Random basis," that was a laugh, like "random surveillance." Like a guy didn't figure out when the cops were going to show up, or drop by. The longer you were out of good old D-Home—Juvenile Detention Home, the judge called it—or wherever, the less "random" the checkups were. There were always a couple hours here or there, if you timed it right. Being under house arrest, with that thing strapped around your ankle, that was more trouble. Still, there were ways around it, when it mattered. Even getting out of the transition houses wasn't that much trouble, if you went at it right.

But he couldn't get the schedule figured out for this rent-a-cop. Whether the guard planned it that way, had crummy digestion, or was just a pal of Rivera's taking a personal interest, he didn't know. The guy nearly caught him last night. He'd skipped out quick, scaling the back fence as the guard rattled the front gate.

He'd had to look things over. It made him edgy, not knowing exactly when the roof was going up, afraid he'd miss by a couple of days. It was the best way though, the most likely way to work it. Rivera always checked the supports himself, first thing every morning. Rivera was predictable. It was something a guy could count on.

The only thing was, that security guy was a pain.

The courthouse bomb had got a little whacked out, with Sorrel working right there. Maybe he should combine the problems. He'd have to think it through. This one, though, was no trouble. There was the house itself, but that wasn't good. The dog or cat might trip it when she wasn't around. Daytimes were no good. Too many people noticed what he did. He'd cut it way too fine that last time, when he'd been watching in the park. Besides, she was never home in the daytime.

And then a few hours ago, that black woman nearly caught him at the old folks' home. It had surprised the hell out of him, too. He'd kept track of the security guard, and timed his little expedition for when everybody was watching TV in the main rooms. But the one old lady saw him, and then that woman came shooting out of there yelling at him. What had she thought she'd do, if she'd caught him? She was wide-awake, though, he had to give her that. His grandma was like that, up to everything. He'd never been able to pull a thing on her.

The only people who ever saw him were the brain donors in the old folks' home, first Jeanie's old man, and now the old lady. It was like, you had to be crazy to see a guy who was invisible. There'd been too many close calls, though. He was taking too many chances. He wasn't sure why, but something about the whole deal got under his skin.

So if he couldn't use the house, and he couldn't use the old folks' home, that left the car. He turned, looking at the dog harness. Shit.

It bothered him some, this one did, not just because of the dog. But she wouldn't learn, wouldn't stop trying to get her little hooks into people. Now she was in everybody's face, talked to his parole officer, even talked to his neighbors, for God's sake. The worst of it was, she was pulling the girls in with her, and they should know better. Especially Brynna. He studied the windows, automatically looking for a way in. *Don't let the cat out.* She was always saying that. A small smile twisted his mouth.

A small rumbling vibration ran through his feet. His body stilled. What the hell? The vibration became a sound, a distant rattling, coming nearer. A train whistle sounded, breaking the stillness of the quiet street.

The hood of the car rattled under his butt. He straightened as a new thought arose. Trains. Some of the gangs damn near owned 'em, or thought they did. Better check.

He moved up next to the house. There was the track, right through her back yard. Don't let the cat out, for damned sure. It was a stupid little cat, with no sense at all. She'd jump right onto a train track to see what that big thing was, get run down, and squashed into a cat burrito in three seconds. Flat.

Light glowed on the scraggly weeds near the rails. The only light in whole street, and it was in *her* house. Wouldn't you know it?

He moved down the track a ways, and checked the crossing sign. Sure enough, not only gang-owned, but *them*. Shit, just when he was doing his damnedest to stay clear. That was the end of *that* plan. Just as well, maybe. No telling how many trains went through here, maybe some of them at high enough speed to set off a pipe bomb with the vibrations. You just couldn't tell with those damned things. Between gang involvement and train activity, it was just too risky.

At Risk of Being a Fool

He slipped back to her house, ducking into the shadows as the train rumbled past on its trip to nowhere. As the cars clanked on, he moved where he could see her face in the window. Had she seen him? No, it didn't look like it. She was watching the train, talking to herself, or maybe to the dog or cat.

He lost track of time, watching her, watching the train. He didn't know why he hung around, looking at her face, the lines in it, and the streaks of brown running through the frazzled white hair. She was a strange woman, didn't seem to care what she looked like. Half the time she looked like she'd stuck her finger in an electric socket.

The last car on the train crawled past, trailed on to the next house, and the next, to the apartments. It rounded a corner and was gone. The face left the window and the light turned out.

He stood there, staring at the blank window. He left, not quite as soundlessly as before. He went back to his car, back to a neighborhood that looked like home, cluttered and friendly, marks on the walls proving gangs were alive and well, not sneaking their signs so a fellow had to hunt for 'em. Back to a place where dogs were skinny and looked like dogs, not wieners.

Life is a potato. Mashed, baked, or fried.

Or boiled, or sliced thin, or peeled, and chopped into little tiny bits. What the hell did she know about it anyway?

His mouth twisted.

THIRTEEN

"Fluff, Mrs. McCoy. I'm sorry to say it, but they're fluff."

"And this isn't fluff?" Jeanie picked up the book on the bedside table and turned the pages. "No, it's not, is it? Blood and guts strewn all over everything."

"Well, it's not my chosen reading material," said Estelle Torrez, looking a little embarrassed. "I was limited to the availability on the library cart. Other people's castoffs."

"Romances, westerns, science fiction? I read those too, I'll admit it."

Estelle snorted. "Well I don't."

"Give me a list of authors. I'll pick up some library books for you." Estelle flinched as though struck. It was such a small thing, but the notion seemed revolutionary to Estelle. "Who do you like?"

"I don't read much fiction. Biographies, histories." Her voice was stiff. The subject was too personal.

"So," Jeanie ventured, "how are you doing?"

"I'll be fine. I'll be back on the job in a couple of weeks."

Jeanie held her tongue. Yesterday, which was Sunday, Jeanie had walked onto the hospital floor as a doctor stomped out of Estelle's room. Jeanie retreated to an elevator, but a nurse pointed to her. The doctor collared her, and insisted on talking in the unused waiting room.

"Are you a relative?"

"No, I'm—"

"A good friend?"

"Well, not really."

At Risk of Being a Fool

"Hah. Well, you're what I've got to work with, anyway. You need to know some things."

"I hardly think I'm the appropriate—"

"She's never thrown anything at you, right? You're about the only one, let me tell you. She hasn't had a single visitor except for a lawyer hunting business for personal injury claims. She gets flowers by the keg, cards by the million, but not a single phone call or visitor. She's in complete denial. She won't look at the surgery site; she denies there was an amputation— What? You didn't know? God, seems like half the world knows. Sorry, sit down, you're looking faint. We amputated her right leg just below the knee. She's got most of her left foot and ankle left. All the other damage is repairable, given time. But she won't listen when we talk about prosthetics, or wheelchairs, or occupational therapy."

"Estelle's not stupid. She'll come to terms with it on her own time."

"Probably. But it would be easier on her if she had a friend, someone to discuss the matter. Don't look so horrified. I'm not asking you to break the news to her. She knows. All I'm asking is, if she gives you any opening at all, encourage her to talk about it. But first, move any portable items out of arm's reach. I don't want to treat you for head injuries."

Jeanie had visited Estelle five days in a row, since the first visit last Thursday. Estelle never gave her the slightest opening, or even an indication that there were personal problems to discuss. Perhaps this was an opening.

"I'd think it'll be longer than a couple of weeks," Jeanie said. "Mackie indicated closer to six weeks."

"Miss Sandoval is not apprised of my medical situation. Informing total strangers of one's most intimate problems has always seemed to me the height of crassness."

It was hard to envision a statement that said more clearly: "Keep Out." Jeanie gasped melodramatically and threw a hand to her heart. "Oh my God."

"What?"

"I can't believe it, can it be true? We actually agree on a subject?"

Estelle wore the look of someone who had opened a can of tuna fish and found a live mouse inside.

"Well," said Jeanie, "let's get off this dismal topic, and talk about something really important."

"And that would be?" Estelle's tone was less confident than it had been.

"The death penalty. Now there's a real life application of the justice model versus rehabilitation."

"Capital punishment is the ultimate response of society for ensuring the safety of its members. Naturally, the softhearted are unable to appreciate the true deterrent effect on criminals. I assure you, Jeanie, measured consequences are the cornerstone of society's foundation."

"Hardly, Estelle. Capital punishment is an outmoded, barbaric exercise in futility. In fact, it is reminiscent of the child-sacrifices to the ancient god Baal . . ."

Jeanie's courage failed her. Tackling the amputation issue would only set her dodging vases of flowers, at this point. However, Estelle had called her Jeanie instead of Mrs. McCoy.

A teacher measures progress by inches.

A small bundle of gray fur squirmed in Dillon's lap. The beat of his music escaped the headphones and punched its way into the room. Dillon scored his paper with black wedges. As Jeanie watched covertly, the pencil slowed, curving into arches and swirls.

At Risk of Being a Fool

Rita had attached herself to a favorite lap. The hands belonging to it were untrained, but she had hopes. Rita stood and set one paw on the edge of the table. She peered over the book, and spotted the moving hand. She wriggled her rear end, and pounced. Jeanie ducked her head and pretended great concentration on Rosalie's essay. She felt Dillon's eyes on her.

"Much better, Rosalie," she said, lying her head off. "Complete sentences, on topic, nice." Complete sentences, yes. Strung together haphazardly, rather like the pencil marks on Dillon's paper. "TV with vilance is no good. This kid took a gun to schol. Poor kid, nobdy took care. If his Daddy took care him guns locked up . . ." No matter what the topic of the GED test, Jeanie suspected the examiners would be reading a story about Rosalie's Dad.

Jeanie snuck a look at Dillon. He cupped the small cat against his chest, one large hand engulfing her with each stroke. A small glow of satisfaction kindled in her chest. At last, she'd done something right for Dillon.

Reluctantly, she checked her watch. "Well, sorry, guys. I'm sure you'd be happy to go for another hour, but we've got to quit. Corrigan wants his dinner."

Without a word, Dillon penned the cat in Mackie's office before grabbing his coat and radio. Tonio followed.

"Bye, Jeanie," said Quinto, crouching by Corrigan.

"Bye, Quinto. You need to leave now, Quinto. Mr. Matthews will be upset if you're late." She'd spoken to Mr. Matthews twice, in her abortive attempts at gathering alibi information. Perhaps he was an android, incapable of independent thought. He counted heads, drove, dropped off, picked up, counted heads, and went back to Dandridge. If the "heads" had faces and personalities attached, it was news to him.

"Gotta go to the bus stop, now," Rosalie cooed to Corrigan. "Bye, baby. Bye, Jeanie."

"Rosalie, do you want a ride home? You're not looking good."

"Nah, I'm fine."

Rosalie moved towards the door. Jeanie spotted the deep purplish circles under her eyes, now that fluorescent light didn't wash out the contrasts.

"Rosalie, are you sleeping all right?"

"Huh? Oh sure."

Rosalie's mouth quivered. Still fretting about her father, no doubt. "Look, Rosalie, do you want me to call your father? Maybe if he knows you're studying every day, he'll realize you're changing yourself." Jeanie had left several messages for Mr. Perea. She'd never told Rosalie. No one ever answered Mr. Perea's phone. The message machine always picked up, and no one ever responded.

Rosalie's eyes clung to her. "Yeah, maybe, would you?"

"Sure, no problem." She'd call his workplace this time. Mackie must have the number.

"Okay, thanks."

Jeanie waited for one of Rosalie's blinding smiles, but it didn't come. She'd lost more weight. Her head looked too big for that scrawny neck; the emaciated body too heavy for the tired feet. "Rosalie, just wait for me. I've got a little work to do here, and then I'll run you home, okay?"

"No, no," said Rosalie, vaguely. "I'll just . . ." The words faded as she walked through the door.

". . . Lucky bitch—"

Jeanie swiveled. "Good-bye, Brynna, see you tomorrow."

Brynna gave Sorrel a dirty look. "Community service, my fuckin' ass. How come she gets so lucky, get out from under Cuthbert's thumb every goddamn night . . ."

At Risk of Being a Fool

"Did you want a ride back to Bright Futures, Brynna?" Of course she didn't. Like Sorrel, she prized the luxury of taking the bus, but the mild threat got Brynna out of the door. Jeanie sighed with relief.

While Sorrel plugged away at fractions, Jeanie spent half an hour on paperwork, generating the paper trail demanded by the feds and the charitable organizations that funded the program. At last, she stuffed it all in a folder, and set it in Mackie Sandoval's inbox. With Sorrel, a boxed cat, and a harnessed dog, she set the car on the road towards Oriole's Nest. She'd gone barely three blocks when Sorrel grabbed her arm.

"Hey, stop the car," Sorrel commanded. She jumped to the sidewalk, and raced between two dilapidated houses.

"Sorrel," yelled Jeanie, belatedly climbing out of the car. "What the—"

Sorrel came back, talking a blue streak, shoving a girl in front of her. "What the hell you think you're doing? Damned lucky we were coming this way. Get in the car, you." She yanked the back door open, and shoved Rosalie inside. Long tangled black hair hid her face. "Sorry, puppy," Sorrel said to Corrigan. "Jeanie, he's going to have to sit on the floor."

"No," said the girl. She clutched the dog to her chest, and with the motion, Jeanie's mind slipped back into gear.

"Rosalie? Why—"

"Shut up a minute," Sorrel said. "Look, girl, you're not gonna jump out of this car, you hear me? You do, and Jeanie's calling the cops, got it? God, you got no more fuckin' sense than Donald Duck." She slammed the back door, and got in the front.

Jeanie got back in the car. "Why—"

"This ain't a good place to park," Sorrel said, her eyes

snapping with anger. "You gotta stop somewhere, go find a Wal-Mart parking lot or something, huh? Our stupid little Rosalie decided to buy herself something, didn't you, dumbass?"

Jeanie drove obediently, casting the occasional glance in the mirror. She saw Rosalie nod, tears streaking her face. Corrigan licked her face. Rosalie clutched him tighter, and her sobs filled the car.

"God, of all the dipshit things to pull. Who'd you go to? Oh God, who was it? Couldn't have been Silvio, he's in jail, and I know he can't raise the bail, not this time. His Mama's sick of bailing him out. Talk! Who was it?"

"Corky," whispered Rosalie.

"That shit? What the hell's he doing down here? Isn't he one of Silvio's men, up in Portland? God, everybody in the world's gotta move to Salem."

"Must be because you're here," Jeanie suggested, trying to inject a lighter note into the proceedings.

Sorrel gave her a sharp look, and grimaced. "Feels like it. Don't say it."

"Don't say what?"

" 'Let's all calm down,' stuff like that. I'm so *sick* of calming down."

"I agree, it's never been your strong point. Nevertheless, I think Rosalie could talk better if she weren't crying, and that's hard to do when you're yelling at her."

Sorrel rolled her eyes and bit her lip, gouging the lipstick. She faced forward, leaving Rosalie a measure of privacy. "Right."

"Right?" said Jeanie, involuntarily.

"Don't rub it in. Okay, Rosalie, listen up. You may have bought the stuff—"

"—What stuff?" Jeanie interjected.

At Risk of Being a Fool

"Crack. It's about all Corky does, fast and cheap. Rotten stuff, too. Good way to kill yourself, Rosalie." She looked over her shoulder. "Or was that the plan? It's a nasty way to go, girl." She waited a moment. "Anyway, you may have bought it, but you didn't use it yet. Give it to Jeanie. She'll get rid of it. No one's gotta know nothing. Not the cops, not Esperanza, nobody, okay? Like it never happened. You don't want to do it, Rosalie. You'll never get your kid back."

"She filed the papers," said Rosalie, tear-choked. "She did this morning."

"Who filed what papers?" Jeanie said.

"Her. Her and that social worker. So's I don't get Dominic no more."

The foster mother, Jeanie realized, had pressured social services into filing for termination of parental rights. She pulled into a grocery store parking lot, parking in an unused section under a tree. She lifted the cat carrier into the front seat, and got into the back next to Rosalie. "Honey, listen to me. Mackie told me that she didn't have a case. You didn't abuse him, or abandon him. You're under treatment, and doing well. The fact that she filed them doesn't mean she'll win."

"The judge, he don't like me." She curled over Corrigan, rocking him up and down. "Never no more. My baby, my little doll, I'll never get him back."

"Rosalie—" Rosalie wasn't listening. She tilted sideways, as if accidentally. After a moment, Jeanie opened her arms, and Rosalie fell into them, Corrigan and all. Jeanie tucked Rosalie's head under her chin, and rocked her back and forth, murmuring nonsense words, as she had with her small sons, countless times. She opened her eyes and found Sorrel staring at her, expressionless.

★ ★ ★ ★ ★

Jeanie dropped Rosalie off at Esperanza, with a brief explanation to Linda. The crack, in an innocuous prescription bottle, rested in her glove compartment. Kherra would know what to do with it.

Sorrel, who'd been silent for the last half hour, finally spoke. "Don't speed or nothing. If the cops catch you with that, we're gonna be in deep shit."

"Okay." She didn't explain that no police officer would ask if Jeanie had crack in her glove compartment, much less search her car. Jeanie had gotten half a dozen traffic warnings in the last ten years, but never a single ticket.

"Where we going? You gotta go south on Commercial, don't you?"

"Not yet. We're doubling back to the school." She checked her watch. Four thirty. "I hope we get there before he leaves."

"Who? If you're going looking for Corky, that's a shitty idea."

"Not Corky. But you said he was Silvio's man, down from Portland, right? Rosalie's local. She's the only one of you who's lived here most of her life. How would she know to find a newly-arrived drug dealer unless someone told her? And if he happened to be right here in this neighborhood, that sort of narrows down our likely informants, doesn't it? Especially since I saw Silvio's phone number on a certain business card. Oh good, he's still here."

"Who—" Sorrel saw the motorcycle, and her eyes flamed. She jumped out of the car and ran after Jeanie. She caught up to her on the stairs. "That son-of-a-bitch—"

Jeanie held up one finger. Sorrel glanced at her. "What—"

Jeanie opened the office door, and shoved it back with a

At Risk of Being a Fool

bang. "Mr. Kemmerich," she sang. "Oh there you are, how opportune."

Oscar Kemmerich looked up from his computer keyboard, leaving two fingers poised in the air. His jaw dropped. His office was a one-room affair. Sorrel figured he'd gotten the furniture at thrift shops. It had that look about it, surface pretty, but wedged up with cardboard. Framed certificates lined the wall. Sorrel squinted her eyes at one. "Future Farmers of America gratefully acknowledges your gift of $25." Probably had his third-grade citizenship award up here somewhere.

Jeanie smiled as she leaned on the edge of his desk.

"I believe you have an acquaintance with a gentleman by the name of Corky. A recent transplant from Portland. Perhaps you represent him. Is that so? No, no, forgive me; he's still out and about. You must represent his Salem partner. Now who could *he* be, I wonder? Possibly someone named Silvio, whose phone number I coincidentally managed to acquire. Now, I have a small legal question for you, Mr. Kemmerich. Let us suppose that a lawyer with a drug dealer as a client was in the habit of passing the names of alternate suppliers to young girls. Do you suppose that might be inappropriate? Possibly even illegal?"

Mr. Kemmerich shut his mouth and rose to his feet, facing Jeanie across the table. A vein stood out in his forehead, pulsing rapidly. With a visible effort, he leaned over the desk, nearly nose to nose with Jeanie. Sorrel bristled at the aggression, and stepped forward, only to find Jeanie's outstretched arm blocking her. She stopped, mesmerized by Jeanie's fixed smile.

"Let the man talk, dear. It's not polite of me to hog the conversation."

"You, madam, are committing slander—"

"Hardly. This is a private conversation. I suggest you refer to your law books."

"The young lady in question is a liar. I did no such thing. I merely offered her a little private advice, since she obviously needs guidance."

"Which young lady is that? How do you know who I'm talking about?"

He flushed. "My client records are confidential. I'm sure you know that much from Court TV," he sneered. "You have no evidence—"

"Imitating Bill Clinton, are you?"

"You," he snarled, pointing his finger at her chest, "had damn well better watch your tongue. I don't appreciate your aspersions on my character, and neither, let me tell you, will my clients. You try sharing these little opinions, and it will be slander. Publish them, and it's libel, too. Won't be much of your retirement savings left then, will there? So watch yourself."

Jeanie sighed. To Sorrel's amazement, her anger seemed to have evaporated, replaced with a vast exasperation. She raised her hand, put the palm of her hand on Mr. Kemmerich's forehead, and shoved him back.

"Sit down, you dimwit. Now listen to me. If you tell Silvio what I said, odds are high that his first rage will be with you. No doubt, he'd get around to me, but you'd be first on his list for involving him in a situation that is larger than you know. My little Rosalie has a wide range of affectionate supporters, and some of them likely resemble, in character, your mythical Silvio. While Rosalie is easily tempted, the results of her temptation may be considerably more than you are willing to live with. Certainly, it would give your client headaches he doesn't need. Do you understand me?"

Mr. Kemmerich sank into his seat.

At Risk of Being a Fool

Jeanie's face softened. "You're young, Mr. Kemmerich. You need to find an experienced lawyer to take you under his wing, and teach you wisdom. I doubt you'll do it, because you're not the type to heed advice. I want you to realize one thing. I am the perfect enraged protective mother, and the fact that Rosalie is not my daughter is irrelevant. I've no doubt I could interest the press, and publish my story on the Internet well before you could get a court date. You will keep your hands, mouth, eyes, actions, and influence well away from my students. Every single one of them."

Jeanie straightened. "Do we understand each other?" Silence. "I'll take that as an affirmative. Good day to you, Mr. Kemmerich."

Sorrel followed her out to the car. She watched Jeanie as she put the car in motion. "Are you okay?" she asked, finally.

"I guess so. I don't know that I accomplished anything. If he was more experienced, I'd never have gotten away with that. On the other hand, if he was more experienced, he'd never have contacted Rosalie directly. It was stupid. I just hope he knows it, now."

"You're not going to tell anybody on him?"

"Of course I am. If he'd do that to Rosalie, he would to anyone else who looked susceptible. I suspect Silvio has a considerable client list. I'll tell the police about Corky, too, but they probably already know. They're a lot sharper than you think."

"I won't talk to the cops," said Sorrel.

Jeanie smiled. "Did you think I'd involve you?"

"No. What's going to happen to the lawyer when you tell on him?"

"Nothing at all. There's no evidence. He'll know that when he recovers. Mackie might be able to shame him into giving free legal services, but actually, I don't think he'd mind that. It would give him access to a wider client base."

"Could he really put you in jail for writing stuff about him on the Internet?"

Jeanie cocked her head. "I don't know. That's an interesting question."

"Don't get stuck in corrections," Sorrel said, her voice low and intense. "It's the pits."

Jeanie grinned at her. "I don't know. It might be interesting. I might make a few friends there. What do you think?"

Sorrel was quiet for several miles. As Jeanie parked at Oriole's Nest, she spoke.

"You probably would."

FOURTEEN

Vic Dunlap settled his ample posterior into the driver's seat and turned on the overhead light. He reached in the glove box, put on his reading glasses, and pulled over the clipboard with its list of addresses. He checked his watch, noting the time next to the convenience store's address. Right, time to see what was next. He ran his finger down the unmarked lines. Six left, and then Danny's site; that made seven.

He opened the lunch pail and pulled out his grandson's collection of many-sided dice. His visits were supposed to be random, and random they would be, with a little edge for his good friend Danny Rivera. So what if it chewed up a little more gas, getting from this spot to that one across town? If he drove a little faster and made forty visits instead of thirty, who was he hurting? It put a little interest in a boring job. Let's see, here it was. He'd kind of thought Brad had a seven-sided die. Okay, so what was the roll? Hmm, well, by golly, looked like Danny hit it lucky again.

Vic turned the paper back to the one underneath. *Call Ernie,* he wrote with careful jabs of his pencil. He underlined it twice, flipped the paper, and set the pencil under the clip.

He double-checked the door locks and threw the car into gear. This was a nice job, as long as it was only for a month or two. He liked being an on-call security guard. "On call." It made him feel useful. The extra money would be handy, too. He could finally afford to take Debbie to Hawaii. She was fussing some, said she had no figure for a bathing suit. *No problem,* he'd deadpanned, *you won't be wearing it for long.* After all these years, he still loved her smile.

He'd have to remember to call Ernie, though. Working the extra shift three nights one week, four the other, was a bit tiring for a man his age. He'd just slide Ernie to Saturday afternoon, so he could catch a little more sleep. He nodded to himself cheerfully. The kid was working out fine, Ernie was. They mostly did. It was a good idea of Debbie's. He was glad he'd taken it up. Boys liked cars.

For thirty years now, he'd generally had an old car in the garage in some state of disaster. He relished tinkering with engines, new filters, studying how they worked, and fixing up the dents. Over the years, the cars had changed and he'd had to get a bunch more tools, all that electronic stuff. He'd buy a wreck, fix it up, and sell it. He tried to cover his costs and tools, and he managed it mostly.

Back when Debbie was in that social service job, she'd run into boys who got into a lot of trouble. This one boy, Hiroshi, she'd took a liking to, and she brought him home for a few hours. In no time at all, the kid had his head under the hood of Vic's old Chevy sedan, asking questions, poking around. They'd pulled the whole engine block that day, and made a hell of a mess. Vic had a blast. Hiroshi grew up, moved on, and Debbie found another one. After that, it was a habit, having a kid around every Saturday, some weekday evenings, working on cars. He never paid 'em anything, but they didn't care. Well, a few of 'em did, but those didn't stick around long. The ones that just loved cars, like him, they'd come by for months, even years. He'd had about a dozen of them, he figured, who'd stuck with him. He'd learned as much as he'd taught.

A few still kept in touch, called him, or stopped by to see

At Risk of Being a Fool

what he had in the garage. A couple of them were in prison. He regretted that. A few had turned out well, like Danny Rivera. Old Danny, now there was a success story. He'd had real trouble—Dad gone, mother a drunk, fights in the gangs. Several of Vic's boys had had records, but he didn't care. They had their problems and he had his, and they never talked about personal stuff, just cars. God knew, there was plenty to say.

Danny'd been with him, off and on, for two or three years. Then he went to the trade school and got some kind of a certificate. It wasn't in cars, though. It was in construction. He was deputy foreman on some nice jobs now, and always had a kid in tow. *Mentoring,* they called it now, *job experience.* Danny was following in Vic's footsteps. It filled Vic with a sort of astonished pleasure. A man couldn't hope for a better thank you.

Vic and Danny talked about the kids sometimes. Danny got into their home lives more than he did. Danny was some worried about this new one, Quinto his name was. Funny name. When all the kids wanted to be Numero Uno, it struck him odd hearing a boy called the Fifth One. Short for Joaquin, Danny said, but he frowned about it. Then Bryce got hurt, and Danny got discouraged. Damned pipe bomb. It was hell, what people got up to nowadays.

Vic couldn't stand seeing Danny so down on himself. *Get back in there,* he'd urged. *Get your boy back, or find a new one. It makes you feel good, don't it?* He'd stopped there, and they grinned at each other, embarrassed as all hell. It wasn't the kind of thing you talked about.

But boy, it made you feel good, it really did.

So, Danny'd talked the new foreman into it. Vic had half-expected him to get a new boy, but Danny'd shuffled his feet and finally said no, he'd give it another try with this

Quinto. Danny liked Quinto, he just felt uneasy about him. Danny'd had a couple bad experiences with boys. There was one, kept slipping out of that detention home, whatever they called it. One of the other boys finally snitched. They'd moved him somewhere, Eugene maybe. Sheridan? No, that was the main prison. Wherever.

Still, this Quinto, he didn't seem bright enough to get past those alarms.

The street opened out, filled on both sides with those rectangular buildings that seemed to trumpet their use. These were the government and non-profit places, with a few warehouses shoved in. Vic approved of Danny's expansion on the recreation center. Put in a few pool tables, air hockey, and basketball hoops, and you could change young people's lives for good.

Vic slowed, threw up his brights, and took a pass in front of the building. Everything looked peaceful, like the last time. He parked the car and got out, automatically checking shadows.

One thing puzzled him about that pipe bomb. With the bomb sitting there at closing time, it seemed like it must have been stuck there during the day. But they'd notice strangers on the site, wouldn't they?

His footsteps slowed. Was that it?

Did Danny think Quinto planted it? Or that he knew who did? He'd be some upset if Quinto knew who did it, and wasn't saying.

He checked the lock on the south gate and rattled it. All secure. He flashed his spotlight into the yard, lighting up dark corners. He moved down the fence, walking the perimeter of the yard. It wasn't strictly part of the job, but it was the least he could do for Danny.

It couldn't be Quinto. How could the kid carry it in? In a

At Risk of Being a Fool

backpack? In the van from the home? Maybe somebody passed it to him while he was on the site.

Vic threw more light on the spot where Bryce took the blast. Bryce was the target. He had to be. He could be a right son-of-a-gun when he wanted. A bit of a loose cannon since the cops arrested his daughter. And with Bryce gone, the danger here was gone too, wasn't it? Still, Vic felt better, checking the yard himself at nights.

Vic got to the north gate and stopped, taking a last look around. He nodded judiciously, holding his spotlight higher, double-checking. There were no problems here either. He reached for the lock on the gate. It was secure. He grabbed the gate, gave it a sharp tug, checking hinges.

The blast caught him in the gut.

The blackened spotlight spun out of a mangled hand, and landed hard on the pavement. It rolled a short way and lay there, undisturbed.

"Jeanie?" Mackie's voice was almost unrecognizable.

"Yes?" Jeanie backed up and sank into a chair.

"There was another bomb at Danny Rivera's work site. The watchman was killed."

"Oh, Mackie, no."

"The police figure he'd been dead for an hour or so before they got there. He didn't check in on time, so the security company sent someone to look for him. There aren't any houses around there. Just a warehouse guard, who thought he heard a car backfire."

"That's dreadful."

"Yeah. There's more. Our powers-that-be are closing the school."

"No, Mackie." Her hand clenched on the phone.

"Jeanie, think about the connections: Bright Futures, the courthouse, and the work site. Our program is the only obvious link. So, Ben decided to close down the school. It's not," Mackie argued, "that anyone thinks you could have prevented anything. It's not like that. It's just that if it turns out there is a link, and there's another death—"

"That's not fair. It's punishing all of them for something one person did."

"It's not safe, Jeanie. You're not thinking clearly. Whichever one it is—"

"It isn't *any* of them. They wouldn't do that."

"It's someone connected with the program," said Mackie doggedly. "It has to be. It's beyond coincidence. I've been talking to the police for the last half-hour."

Sorrel, Quinto, Brynna, Tonio, Rosalie, even Dillon. They wouldn't do it. Would they? "What about the work experience? Is that closing too?"

"No. The kids don't meet there. There's no place for them to talk to each other, so that's going forward."

"So now you're saying it's several of them. That there's a conspiracy going on."

"I don't know," Mackie said sharply. "Jeanie, this isn't like you."

"I'm a teacher, Mackie. I fight for my kids, just as you do. You can't tell me you didn't have a heck of fight with Ben over this."

"Yeah," she said, defeated.

"I thought our funding was based on education and work experience, the two of them together."

"I know, it is. We'll have to figure out something, maybe merge it with another program."

"Then they'll be linked in that program too. You'd have the same problem."

At Risk of Being a Fool

"The college has night classes. Maybe I can put a couple there in different sessions."

"Or?"

"Or what? Jeanie, please, don't give me a hard time here, okay? I feel awful about it. Look, if you need the money, maybe—"

"I can make home visits."

"To all of them? Jeanie, you can't possibly—"

"For a while, until things sort out. I'll start today. Can you fax the address list here to the Nest? You've got the number. Thanks. They're all working this morning?"

"I don't know. I guess I'd better tell them not to go today. It's not good for police to show up at the work sites. Quinto can't work until I line up another site. Delancey Brothers nixed the mentorship. Jeanie, the program can't cover your extra hours or the mileage. I can't ask you to do this."

"You're not asking, I am. No, I'm not, I'm telling you. There's just one thing. Let them come to school on Thursday. That's testing day, and four of them have to go in."

"Jeanie, I can't. They can get rides to the testing center."

"But they won't, you know it. You told me yourself, if you don't take them directly to the testing center, half of them won't bother going. Do you want me to go around and pick them up? They'd still be in the car together."

"No, no, I'll do it. No, wait a minute. I can't. Hills of Glory has a re-inspection coming up and I promised I'd be there. Well, I'll clear it with Dan just for Thursday. It's only an hour. I've got time to haul them to the Testing Center as long as they're all there. As soon as the police figure things out, we'll start up again. It can't take too long, can it? Whoever this is, he's crazy. They've got to catch him soon."

Jeanie hung up the phone. She said a prayer for the watchman and his family. They'd be grieving, just as she would if it were Edward or one of the boys. Tears stung her eyes.

As the tears passed, anger flared. It was intolerable that anyone could do such a thing. And if, God forbid, it was one of her students, the police shouldn't tar the others with the same brush. Tonio was doing well at the yard and Dillon at the cannery. But how long could they work there, if their employers saw the notices in the papers, added two and two, and connected them with the ill-fated GED program?

There was Sorrel, too. If Jeanie let the matter go and the school closed, Sorrel's time at Oriole's Nest would end too. Dolores Cuthbert resented the community service idea already, and all the house chores that Sorrel was "escaping." The nets would close in on Sorrel, the pregnancy officially discovered, and Sorrel would be back in Corrections until the end of her sentence. The baby, at best, would go to Sorrel's mother with Tiffany, but foster care was more likely.

Jeanie retrieved the address list from the fax machine, and began planning her route. She didn't want to wind up on Lancaster or Commercial during the evening rush hour. Highway 22 wasn't bad though, at that time of day. Unless it was Friday afternoon, when half of the valley drove to the coast for the weekend.

She frowned, running her mind back over the days. First, there'd been Bryce Wogan, on that Saturday. Then it was the courthouse, early on the next Tuesday. Next came Estelle, also early on a Tuesday.

Early this morning, a bomb killed a night watchman. Today was Tuesday. Except for the first one, every bomb had been set on a Monday night.

At Risk of Being a Fool

★ ★ ★ ★ ★

"Thank you, Mrs. Otero. It's so kind of you to let me bother you like this."

"It is not a problem, Mrs. McCoy," said Mrs. Otero. The delightful smile crinkled her eyes, warming the carefully spoken words. "My Dillon, he was not to go to work today. He has appointments, because of this terrible thing. He has every wish to help the police, of course." She spoke without sarcasm, pitching her voice to reach beyond the doorway. Mrs. Otero was educating her grandson, telling him by her manner: *This is how it should be, in a good family. We want to help the police. The police are our friends.*

A good lesson, but a dozen years too late.

"This bad man, he must be caught. Poor Daniel," murmured Mrs. Otero. "Such a terrible thing."

"Daniel?"

"Daniel Rivera. So sad for him, two of his friends attacked with the bombs." She read Jeanie's confusion. "You know Daniel Rivera? The builder."

"Danny Rivera? Yes, I've met him. One of my students works with him."

"I have known him since he was small." She measured a distance waist-high. "Such a nice boy. This is so sad for him. His mother and I attend the same church. I saw her last night at choir practice. I thought perhaps my Dillon could work with him, and Miss Sandoval arranged it, but after all, it did not work out. Dillon did not care for the construction work. He likes the machinery at his new job."

Mrs. Otero knew Danny. Dillon then, knew Danny Rivera before the abortive job attempt last summer. Although perhaps he didn't, since he'd lived in Portland. Did Dillon go to choir practice on Mondays? It seemed improbable.

Dillon sat at the small table, regarding the remains of a

mountain of pancakes. A platter sat in front of him, holding a couple of scraps of bacon, half a sausage, and a few shreds of hash browns.

"My Dillon," said Mrs. Otero affectionately, "only now does he wake up. I tell him an hour ago, Dillon, if you want the pancakes, you get up now. Or the cook, she goes shopping with friends." A quick look of concern crossed her face. "*Hijo mio, quieres más?* More pancakes, bacon?"

Dillon gave a half-smile, looked at Jeanie, and let it slip. "No, Grandma, I'm ready to bust."

"Perhaps some coffee, little one?" Mrs. Otero bustled towards the kitchen. She paused behind Dillon, and rested the palm of her hand against his cheek. He leaned into her hand, rubbing his cheek against it. The fleeting affection took Jeanie's breath away. Mrs. Otero moved into the kitchen.

"Ah yes, I know it. You are after my *chocolada* again, bad boy. Whipped cream? Mrs. McCoy, could I get you some hot chocolate? Coffee?"

"No, thank you." Dillon looked at her, sidelong. Her heart skipped a beat.

"Hot tea?"

The look intensified. "Ah, yes, thank you, that would be kind." Dillon's eyes slid to the cat carrier. Jeanie reached to unlatch it. Dillon crouched on the floor, fingers wriggling coaxingly. He'd left the dishes, she noticed, and the napkins wadded into a mass next to it. A gooey syrup spill on the table engulfed a clean spoon.

Rita nosed her way out of the crate and pounced on Dillon's hand. He cupped her in his hands as he sat down in the only armchair. Jeanie sat on the small sofa. The boy's huge hands moved with a delicacy that argued against his case file. He'd been convicted of robbery, Randy said, and

At Risk of Being a Fool

carjacking with only his fists. The police had never tied him to a weapon.

Mrs. Otero presented Jeanie with hot tea, a sugar bowl, and small cup with milk in it. Dillon's hot chocolate sported whipped cream and chocolate chips.

"Oh, *la gatita pequeña. Que linda.*" Mrs. Otero passed a gentle hand over Rita's ears, and directed a covert glance at her grandson. "So nice, you bring the little Rita with you. Is Corry-gan here as well, in the car perhaps?"

Jeanie's eyes widened. Dillon talked with his grandmother a lot, it seemed. "No, actually, he's at home. Bringing two pets in a single visit seemed a bit rude."

"Dillon tells me has the next test Thursday. So exciting. He is the first in our family to finish school, did you know? I went to eighth grade in Puerto Rico. Dillon's mother," her voice broke, then recovered, "she stopped at tenth grade." Mrs. Otero cleaned the table with quick, competent hands. "I am so proud of my Dillon. Thank you so much for this opportunity."

"We're delighted to have Dillon. He's a good worker." Stock answer number 342, straight from the teacher's manual. It was the things you didn't say that gave the true picture, but few relatives realized it. "Thank you for letting me interrupt you this morning. Dillon, I thought we'd review some percentages today, since you're taking the math test on Thursday. And I'll leave you a book with some lessons. You can look at them between appointments."

Dillon was glaring at her again, she realized. "Very nice tea, Mrs. Otero, thank you much." Dillon relaxed, rolled Rita over, and scratched her stomach. Rita wrapped herself in a ball around his hand, chewed on his finger, and batted him with soft hind paws.

Mrs. Otero looked at the back of her grandson's head,

raising her hand to the silver cross she wore. Many parents denied their children's misdoings; defended them with misguided lies; attacked those who bore the messages of guilt. Mrs. Otero loved Dillon with warmth, tenderness, and a hard-edged honest eye. It reminded Jeanie of a particular serial killer, whose mother came to his execution, not to watch, but to remain in the next room and pray. *Please tell my son,* she had said, *that I love him.* Mrs. Otero would have understood.

"Dillon, you talk now with Mrs. McCoy," Mrs. Otero insisted. "It is kind of her to bring your books to you, isn't it?"

"Yeah," said Dillon unwillingly. Mrs. Otero stroked his hair. "Thanks," he added.

Half an hour of review on percentages stretched Dillon's tolerance to the limit. He stretched and set Rita on the floor. He didn't put the books and papers together, which probably meant he'd work on it later. Or perhaps he'd wait for his grandmother to pick them up. Now what? Should she just come out with it? *Where were you last night?* As if the answer would be enlightening?

"Dillon, you give her some flowers from the garden." Mrs. Otero handed him some small scissors. "She has been so kind to you, of course you will want to do something for her."

Of course, he would. For a moment, Jeanie saw her own amusement echoed in Dillon's face.

Mrs. Otero's front yard was ablaze with color, the mild breeze heavy with the sleepy scent of roses. In the midst of the small, rundown houses on her block, Mrs. Otero's stood out like a tropical fish among guppies. A mass of rose bushes—red, orange, yellow, and cascades of pink variegated blossoms—smothered the four-foot chain link fence.

At Risk of Being a Fool

Briskly efficient, Dillon clipped off a bunch of flowers and stuffed them into her hands.

"Hang on," he said, moving to a healthy orange-pink rose bush, set apart from the others. "She'll ask if I gave you this."

"It's a Peace rose," said Jeanie, in pleased discovery. "An award winner from decades ago. I used to have one, at my old house."

Dillon shot her a glance, stone-faced. "She likes it." He was more careful with this plant than with the others. He handed her two buds, one of them half-open.

"Your grandmother is an artist in the garden."

His scowl lessened perceptibly. He selected a third flower, nipping it off further down the stem. He rotated it, carefully clipping off the thorns.

"Ah, that one's for your grandmother," Jeanie teased.

The rose stilled in his hands. Their eyes met. Dillon cleared his throat. "She means a lot to me."

"I can tell."

"I wouldn't," he paused, doling out his thoughts, "do nothing to hurt her."

"Including slipping out at night?" asked Jeanie. "When she goes to Monday night choir practice?" A shot in the dark. But if he were slipping out at night, he'd time it so she wouldn't know. And except for Bryce's, the bombs were set on Monday nights.

"Church is right at the end of the block. I walk her to the church. And I walk her back home again." He directed a look at the front door. "They searched the house. You know that."

"Yes." If he walked her to the church, then her car was available. She wondered if he'd implied that on purpose.

"They shoved her roses all over the place, looking under

'em." His foot mounded the bark mulch around the Peace rose.

"They didn't dig them up, though. At least there's that."

"Metal detector," he said meditatively.

"A metal detector wouldn't have caught some of those ingredients. The police knew that, and they still didn't dig up her roses. They weren't being destructive."

"I knew they'd tear the place up, if I did something. You think I'd put her through that?"

"Not on purpose. So you didn't slip out last night."

"I didn't set any bombs, and I didn't arrange for 'em either." It was a simple statement, not urging her to believe or disbelieve. "Wait here, I'll get your cat." Holding the perfectly trimmed rose, he vaulted the three steps and entered the house.

Nine-month-old Dominic grabbed the edge of the sofa and pulled himself onto his feet. He flashed a gap-toothed grin of triumph at his audience. He glanced at the floor by his feet. With a ludicrous change of expression, he measured the distance from his face to the carpet. The floor was much further away than he had expected.

Rosalie swooped on him, grabbed him in both arms, and gave him a throttling hug, like a small girl with a brand-new doll. "Oh he's so big, isn't he big, Jeanie? Maria, see how strong he is?" Rosalie was instantly engrossed in a conversation with Maria, comparing Dominic to Maria's Nikki, who had visited yesterday. Dominic struggled to free himself. Rosalie didn't notice.

Jeanie was glad she'd left Rita in Linda's office. Esperanza had too much hustle and bustle, and not enough doors that closed, to prevent small cats from straying.

"I'm amazed you arranged visitation," she told Linda. "I

thought Mrs. Thatcher filed for termination of parental rights."

"She's filed, but visitation goes on unless and until she wins. Since you cancelled school, I thought I'd arrange it this afternoon. The whole thing's a shame, really. Mrs. Thatcher is wonderful with Dominic, but she gets tight-lipped about Rosalie."

A huge whiteboard hung in the hallway. Down one side were the hours of the day, marked in half-hour increments. Printed neatly across the top were the names of the twelve residents. Rosalie was fourth. In the midst of notations for group therapy, GED, work, morning chores, and KP were specific times and bus numbers indicating when each girl was supposed to leave and return. A second whiteboard displayed tomorrow's schedule. A clipboard dangled nearby, holding phone numbers for every person in official contact with each girl. Jeanie spotted her work number, her home number, and even Oriole's Nest's number, with Kherra's name printed next to it.

Dominic squawked. Rosalie covered his face with kisses. He wriggled determinedly. Rosalie growled and snapped at his nose. He dissolved into giggles and wound himself around her arm, grabbing her hair to keep his balance.

"I brought a textbook for her. She has the reading test Thursday. Will she have some time to go over it? A couple of hours?"

"Hours?"

"Well, let's say several ten-minute tries?"

"Sure. Dominic goes back at five." Linda crossed to the whiteboard, marked out the evening's scheduled visitation, and replaced it with the word *Study*. "You think she can sit still through the test?" She added notations to the clipboard, and the next day's schedule.

"I hope so. It's her second try at this one." If they'd let Jeanie into the testing center, she'd gladly sit on Rosalie for the duration, but it wasn't permitted. Rosalie could know every answer and still be incapable of sitting still to write them down. A thought came to her. "Linda? How do you keep the girls in at night? I didn't see any bars on the windows. They could just sneak out, if they wanted to."

"They could and they do sometimes. This is a transition facility, not a prison. They have to get used to temptation, and making good choices." Linda made a face. "Like not sneaking out windows at night. We do have bed checks, but I'm sure we miss some. Generally, I think, if they keep it up, we catch them." A spark of humor lit her eye. "Sorrel Quintana is one of your students, isn't she?"

"Yes."

"Enough said."

"Does Rosalie slip out?"

"She did once that I know of, but that was early on. And of course, we're a bit more vigilant just now, after the drug incident."

"At the child care, they told me that a man came by to visit her on the sly."

"I know. I asked her about him. Cousin Arturo, she said, came to give her a message from her father." Linda's voice was heavy with disbelief.

"I thought her father didn't talk to her any more. She's always crying about it."

"I don't think it was her cousin. She talked to somebody on the phone yesterday. They get five-minute local calls, and we can track the numbers if it's important. She does have to talk out here where everyone can hear her. It sounded innocuous."

Rosalie put Dominic down, held his tiny hands, and

At Risk of Being a Fool

walked him in front of her, crooning encouragement.

"She's quite fond of Dominic," said Jeanie.

"Oh, definitely."

A breeze moved one of the drapes. Rosalie's eye caught it. She let Dominic's hands fall, wandered to the window, and peered outside.

Linda looked tired.

Tonio's uncle opened the door and looked at Jeanie blankly. He scratched his bare chest and tilted his beer can. A small but steady stream missed his mouth, dribbling down his hairy chest. He shrugged at her question and shut the door in her face.

Yes, well.

Come to think of it, why was Tonio living with his uncle in Salem? If he was in the same gang as Quinto, he should have moved back to Portland as soon as he got out of the transition facility. Usually kids moved back home and transferred their files to the local probation officers.

So many worries, so many questions. Life had a frantic feel. She got in the car, double-checked the windows, and released Rita from her carrier. Rita remarked on every hidey-hole, discovered a dropped pencil, and chewed on it.

The web of violence tightened, and her world was its center. Bryce Wogan had given Quinto a hard time, and accused Dillon of theft. Sorrel and Brynna hated Estelle Torrez. Sorrel worked at the courthouse. The bomb at the courthouse was in front of Judge Hodges' window, and Judge Hodges dealt with juvenile criminal cases, including Rosalie's and, she'd found, Quinto's. And now this new victim, Vic Dunlap, security guard, apparently set off a bomb taped to the inside of the chain-link fence at Quinto's work site.

Why these particular people? Every rationale she considered seemed paranoid, and did battle with her instinctive affection for "her" kids. *Remember Robert,* she told herself firmly. A person could be engaging and likeable, and still be a villain. She shied away from the word "villain," and forced her way back to it. What else would you call a boy who slipped his sister a date-rape drug at the request of his friend? The dizzying unreality swept over her, as it had when she'd first heard the story. Robert couldn't have done such a thing, she'd protested. He wasn't like that. He'd put in countless happy hours studying computer programming with her, and wasn't that proof of something? Yes. It was proof that there were multiple facets, even to a villain. Just think about Dillon, the quiescent volcano, and his sweetness with his grandmother.

Shelley had weighed in on the matter, in last night's e-mail:

We're all bleeding hearts and totally blind when it comes to our own. Look at me, Jeanie. How many years did it take before I saw Sam clearly? Looked past the sweet, muzzy smile he gave me before passing out again on the sofa? Much as I love him, no matter how many excuses I find, he simply can't stay sober . . .

She had hit the end of her rope and end of her thirty years of civil service at the same time. Shelley retired, collected her pension, got a legal separation, and found a job in Germany, assisting American tourists with their problems. It was a low-level job, but she didn't care. She could get by while she undertook an adventure in living alone.

Christy says he's in a treatment center. What is this,

At Risk of Being a Fool

the fifth time? I hope she won't take him in the next time he falls apart. She's stronger than I am, and Al-Anon has helped her a lot. Patricia is out of his reach. I doubt he'd go all the way to Arizona to collapse on her doorstep. I keep thinking I'm over him, but I'm not . . .

Every person was prey to his own delusions. She was deluded into thinking that her students were good at heart. She hoped it was her only delusion. An image of Kherra's concerned face rose in her mind, and was banished.

Her students were at risk of permanently scarring themselves through their own terrible judgment. What did she risk? Nothing at all.

She was only at risk of being a fool.

FIFTEEN

Castellano's Plumbing and Supplies. The words shone bold and bright from the side of the service truck. Jeanie's footsteps crunched through the graveled parking lot as she passed the cab and rounded the end. Inside, Horacio Perea stood making the weekly inventory on the mobile repair shop.

The middle-aged face didn't fit the powerful body. Rock-like shoulders surmounted a back as straight as a pillar of marble, and just as unyielding. He ran a precise hand down the racks of pipes, and turned to the tool chest fastened into one side of the truck's wall. The top of the chest formed a compact workbench. He examined the tools, with a desultory look at the paper in his other hand.

Jeanie felt smaller than usual. "Mr. Perea?"

Horacio Perea turned, showing only a mild surprise. "Yes, ma'am? Can I help you with something?"

"Um . . ."

He seemed to read her discomfort. He jumped to the ground. The truck shook. Facing her squarely, he said again, "Help you with something?"

"I'm Jeanie McCoy, Mr. Perea. I'm glad to meet you."

Mr. Perea's eyebrows rose. He shook her hand and waited.

"I'm a teacher. I work with your daughter." She watched him closely, but his face remained bemused. "Your daughter, Rosalie."

His eyes blazed at her. His shoulders lifted, and he bulked

a little larger. Involuntarily, Jeanie took a step backwards.

"I'm quite fond of Rosalie," she said. "She's a loving child." That was a mistake, she realized, seeing the curl of his lip. She hurried on. "What I mean to say is, she's affectionate with cats and dogs, and that's been a great help to her. Mackie Sandoval found her a job at a kennel, walking dogs, feeding the animals. She's moving along with her GED studies, too."

Hostility radiated from every line of his body.

"Esperanza, her transition facility, is pleased with her. They had a little celebration for her, sixty days clean and sober. She's putting forth tremendous effort." Jeanie's hopes died. It was obvious that Mr. Perea had not contacted his daughter, through Arturo or directly. "I'm sorry, Mr. Perea. I know you've had a lot of pain with Rosalie. I shouldn't have bothered you."

"They should have told you." His words were clipped and even. "She's not our daughter, not any more."

Her mind slipped a gear. The girl's life was like a huge game board, tilted incxorably towards one corner, one outcome. The only piece on the board was Rosalie, and the outcome was prostitution, drug addiction, and death. Take a host of well-meaning teachers, social workers, and counselors, and they tilted the board out of shape, temporarily creating a new path for Rosalie on a more level playing field. But probation would cease, her time at Esperanza would end, and she'd be free. And as the benevolent fingers released it, the warped board would spring back to the old orientation. Step by sliding step, Rosalie would descend into hell on earth, dragging Dominic with her.

"She loves you."

"Huh." He loomed over her. "Her love means nothing. She steals money from her family, brings drugs into our home. We tried, we talked to her, went to a counselor, even that. Again and again, she promises. One day, she brings a man, *un cabrón*. To our home, an evil man." He swallowed hard, as though he were nauseated. "I find them in our bedroom, while the man handles my rifles. With her sisters there, she brings him, to look for guns. *Out,* I tell her. But still, her mother begs me, let the girl come home. I go to the courthouse, I talk to Judge Hodges. He listens to me. I make promises, Rosalie makes promises, we all promise each other, never again. But again, it all happens, all over. Is this the life for my younger daughters to see? To break the law, to break their mother's heart?" His fists clenched. His voice was low, controlled. "No. I say it, no. It will not be so."

Fiery intelligence burned in his eyes; pain lay naked on his face. Hispanic, plumber, refugee from South America, she'd thought, and without knowing it, she'd pigeonholed him as under-educated, and had tailored her approach accordingly.

"I'm sorry, Mr. Perea," she said humbly.

"It is your job. I understand that."

"Mr. Perea, Rosalie's put your family through misery. And you're right; it's my job to teach Rosalie. But it hurts, teaching her, and knowing that she's got no real future. Because, with everything I know, still—" Unconsciously, Jeanie's hand went to her heart.

Horacio Perea glanced at her hand. With a visible effort, he calmed himself. "She has a job, you say. That is good."

"She's got the job, she's getting the education. What she hasn't got is any kind of anchor. And without an anchor, she'll drift right back into what she left."

"She would anyway."

"She talks about her family a lot. She talks about you most of all."

At Risk of Being a Fool

"Rosalie knows nothing of love." Horacio was still, watching his own thoughts unfold in the sky in front of him. "When I was a young man, I lived in Chile. The government there, it was not good. When my uncle disappeared, my father sent us away, my brothers, my sister, and I, each, to a different country. My father stayed, to sell the property. Who can fear him, he says, if his children are gone? He is just an old man. My brother went to Germany, another to Argentina, my sister to Brazil, and I to America.

"My friends and I, we had a small fishing boat. We went out to sea during a storm, so they will think the boat is lost. Two weeks we travel in the ocean. It does not sound dangerous, does it? But I remember. That boat, that boat." He gave a short laugh. "We landed in San Diego, claimed political asylum until the coup comes. Then, said America, we can go home again, yes? Repression is no more a factor. But I hear from my father in Chile. My brother from Argentina, he came back, and they killed him. Two cousins died also. I told my father I would come for him, but he said no. He was a stubborn man." Horacio's eyes met Jeanie's briefly, and turned back to the clouds. "I went back and got him. My father saved his family, and his family saved him. That is love." His eyes challenged her.

"I am a citizen now. I have a wife, and four daughters, all born here. All this they have: opportunity, education, freedom, the love of their family. An easy life. We made this chance for them, my father, my wife, and me. For love."

Jeanie asked quietly, "Were you a plumber in Chile?"

"Engineer, six years university. Teresa is at Western Oregon University now. Margarita and Alicia are in high school still. Rosalie was my second daughter."

"She *is* your second daughter," Jeanie said, stressing the second word.

"To bring drugs and gangsters into my home? To bring danger to her mother, her sisters? No."

"Rosalie is an engaging person," said Jeanie, trying a different tack. "Has she always been that way? So open and friendly?"

"She has her secrets, that one. Don't be fooled. But yes, always. From a little girl, always dancing, skipping, laughing. She was," he said sadly, "a candle-flame in our lives. Always the little joke with Rosalie, the pretty picture. Sparkling like fireworks."

"Dazzling light, glittering colors?"

"Yes, that. And as quickly gone again, leaving smoke and darkness behind her."

"She seems fond of her Cousin Arturo."

His eyes flashed. "She has no cousin named Arturo. Secrets. Always with Rosalie, the secrets, the lies." He blocked her speech with the palm of his hand. "Please, no. No more."

"Just one more thing? And please don't get angry with me. You're quite intimidating, you know."

"So my wife tells me." A hint of a smile touched his face.

"There's the baby, Dominic." Seeing the gathering thunder in his face, she plunged on hurriedly, "He has a foster mother who wants to adopt him. Rosalie won't give him up, because he's all she has left. Mr. Perea, what kind of life is he going to have with Rosalie as a mother, the way she is now? He'd be much better off with his foster mother. Couldn't you talk to Rosalie and ask her to give him up?"

"No more." Horacio Perea stood rigidly, rock-solid. "The child is nothing to me. Rosalie has chosen her life. She must live with it. Perhaps she will rise to the challenge."

"Mr. Perea—"

At Risk of Being a Fool

"Good bye." Mr. Perea slammed the rear door shut and strode to the cab. With a grinding of gears and a shudder, the truck took off, spitting pebbles from its tires.

The dust settled back into the gravel at Jeanie's feet.

The Dandridge Residential Transition Facility for Boys was a world away from Esperanza. Its supervisor, Mr. Maldonado, scorned sofas and wallpaper, magazines, and practical lessons like using a microwave or tape measure. The resulting regimented "I am the boss" atmosphere resembled a cross between a boot camp and slave quarters.

Jeanie's ID was insufficient, though she talked to staff members every week, and knew most of them by voice. Suspicious looks were directed at her, her purse, her thin pile of reading materials for Quinto, and last but not least, her cat carrier. Jeanie tired of the conversation, and embarked on the strategy her friend Annalisa had pegged as "vintage McCoy."

"Perhaps you should put my cat through a metal detector," she suggested helpfully, extracting the cat from the carrier. Rita hung limply over her hand, in boneless-cat mode.

The clerk looked at her sharply for signs of sarcasm. "That won't be necessary, Mrs., er . . ."

"Wonderful, I'm glad this is over. Now, if you'd just let me in—"

"I can't do that."

Jeanie opened her eyes wide. "Oh dear, you poor thing. You mean to say they've locked you in here, without a key?"

"Well, no—"

"No, of course not, how silly of me. You could simply go out the front door, and climb over a wall, couldn't you? Perhaps I could try that," she said, with an air of vague consideration. "Only I'm afraid I'll need you to come with me, to hand the cat over the fence. I could manage the chain link, I suppose, but I wouldn't want to hurt my little cat."

Variations on this gentle theme baffled the staff, apparent concessions on her part accidentally cornering people in locations of her choosing. The strategy worked as well with adults as on any batch of teenagers she'd taught. In theory, of course, she deplored such tactics, but there was a singular advantage to them: they worked. It was just too much work to eject the befuddled white-haired old lady carrying a cat under one arm.

Thus, with only mild surprise, she found herself in Dandridge's small study room with the doors closed and Quinto plopped in a chair. Rita refused to be a lap cat, feeling that a cat's job was to be in as many places as possible, as rapidly as possible. She pounced on Quinto's feet, leaped on the table, and skidded to the other end, executing 180-degree turns at the slightest rustle.

Despite the cat's distraction, Quinto looked dreadful. He'd developed a tic under his right eye. His hands flailed restlessly, picked at his clothes, roamed through his hair, and rattled the tabletop. He talked convulsively, his hands moving independently of his conversation. Jeanie pushed a tablet and a pencil under his hand. His speech never paused, but his hand picked up the pencil, and jabbed it at the tablet, in lines of fire and jagged glass.

"Mr. Rivera, but he says he ain't working now, and I understand it, 'cause, on account of, the guy was his friend, Mr. Dunlap was. They use to do stuff together, work on cars, and like that, like homeys, you know? And now he's dead. And right after Mr. Wogan was hurt, too. Two of his pals, it's real hard on Mr. Rivera, I know it's hard, like if somethin' happened to one of my buds, you know? But

At Risk of Being a Fool

what am I gonna do? Stay at this fuckin' place for the rest of my life?" Under his hand, layer after layer of rough cinder block coated the paper, each one sharply edged. Each block carried the rapid-fire sketch of a face. She recognized Danny Rivera, Bryce Wogan from the newspaper photo, and the new foreman with the clipboard. A fourth face looked oddly familiar. Oh yes, it was Mackie's friend, the security guard from the courthouse.

"Quinto, I'm sure Mackie will find you—"

"I don't want no other job," he exploded. "I don't. I like this stuff, building things, Jeanie, I can't tell you. It's like, you know . . . oh God, I can't explain it." He seemed lost in thought, as he began drawing bloody drips from the fourth face. Involuntarily, Jeanie put out a hand towards the paper. Quinto seemed to notice the tablet for the first time.

He started a fresh sheet, his face rapt. He sketched a rough piece of ground. "Like this, Jeanie, see? First there's just dirt and trash and stuff, and then you dig, and the foundation goes in, and the footings." As quickly as he spoke, the picture grew as a perfect reflection of his words. "And your rebar and stuff like that, all gotta be up to code. Then you throw up your braces." As he spoke, he erased lines, and added others, dirt fading away, replaced by clean lines, square corners, and foundations, quickly hidden. He was crying, the tears coursing down his face like a river, plopping onto the paper.

"Quinto." She put her hand between his eyes and the paper. "Quinto, I didn't know. I thought—" She'd thought he loved the job because he liked Danny, because he wanted out of the House for a few precious hours a day. But it wasn't like that at all. It was the frustrated need to create, to build, to see his creations blaze across the world. This was what graffiti had been for him, just the desire to create.

Danny Rivera had shown him the way. "I'll tell Mackie how important this is. Believe me, she'll try hard to get you into another crew. But it's going to be hard to replace someone like Mr. Rivera. You might wind up with someone not so understanding."

"I don't care." Quinto's breathing slowed. No one had listened to him when he'd gotten the news. They'd told him he wouldn't be working at the site, that Mr. Rivera was quitting, to shut up and be grateful, to talk to the police, and for-God's-sake to watch his step, take off his hat, and say-Sir-when-you-talk-to-me-boy. But no one had listened.

He looked her in the eye for the first time. His fleeting smile was touched with panic and despair. "Ricardo, my brother, he was on at me yesterday, says maybe I should give it up, you know? Go on with the art, learn graphic arts, the computer stuff. He says I'd be real good, go into the store with him, advertising, you know." He'd shifted back to the first drawing, placing Ricardo's face on a fifth block. "He says I'd be good, I'd make the big bucks in advertising."

"He may be right, Quinto. You have the most remarkable artistic gift I've ever seen in my life."

"Maybe," Quinto said doubtfully. "Only, I'd have to go back to Portland, 'cause that's where them schools are. Ricardo can get me in, he says. He knows somebody." Mackie Sandoval's face went on block six.

"You're so good at drawing faces, Quinto."

"Yeah, well," he muttered. Jeanie herself was on block seven. "I don't know what to do, no more. Maybe Ricky's right, huh?"

"I must have seen you draw dozens of people," she said, feeling her way. "But I've never seen you draw yourself."

"Me?"

At Risk of Being a Fool

"Your own face. Can you?"

Quinto's hand poised in midair. Jeanie turned the tablet to a new page.

"Draw your own face Quinto, when it's happy. When you're as happy as you can possibly be."

Slowly, indefinite lines formed a face, hesitant watery lines. Quinto frowned. "I don't know. I never done that."

"But you know what you look like, you know how you feel. Close your eyes, and draw."

Eyes closed, he sat there utterly still. Suddenly, his hand flew, and splashed his own face across the page, eyes alight with joy. He looked at it wonderingly. "Is that what I look like, for real?"

"Exactly. Every detail." There'd been a breakthrough of some kind. She wasn't sure what it was. "I've seen you look just that way. Now tell me, what are your hands doing when you look like this?"

"I'm making things," he said. Around the face went small pictures of houses, cars, and paintings. And then, in large sweeping strokes, he was drawing houses, large and beautiful, people walking up the steps, ready to open a door with dreams alive behind it. "That's it, Jeanie!" He dropped the pencil, threw his arms around her, and then jumped to his feet. "I'm building houses, and then I'm drawing them. I can do *both*, Jeanie. There ain't nothing in the world says I can't do *both*."

His grin nearly split his face in two. He dropped into his seat, grabbed her hand, and shook it. "So you tell Mackie, okay? You'll tell her. Get me on a job, I'll work my butt off, I'll get that math down, and learn all about construction."

"I'll tell her." He needed a little space to himself. Jeanie set about gathering Rita, a matter that took a certain amount of attention. Cats had more tentacles than an octopus when it was time to go in a carrier. She latched the door shut, and found Quinto regarding the picture of Ricardo ruefully.

"He's gonna be some mad at me, Ricky is. He really wanted me to go into the store with him, but it ain't right for me. He'll understand, won't he?"

"I'm sure he will. He only wants what's best for you." Quinto was back to drawing drip marks under the picture of Mackie's friend. "Why are you putting blood on his face?"

Quinto looked at her, startled. "On account of he's dead, Jeanie. Mr. Rivera's friend, Mr. Dunlap? He's the one what got killed by the bomb."

"At the construction site?"

"Yeah. What's up? You knew about that, I know you did."

"I didn't realize," she said numbly, "who he was." Vic Dunlap, Mackie's friend at the courthouse, was the security guard who'd triggered the pipe bomb at Danny Rivera's site. No one had set the courthouse bomb for Judge Hodges. Vic Dunlap was the true target. When it missed, another had awaited him. And that one worked.

SIXTEEN

"Do you miss Bright Futures?"

Jeanie parked Estelle's wheelchair in front of the sunroom's window. The sparse furnishings left ample room for wheelchairs and gurneys. From the presence of a dusty jigsaw puzzle open on the table, Jeanie deduced that it served patients who were sick of their own rooms. No one demurred as Jeanie pushed Estelle into it, and closed the door. There was no way to lock it. With a mental shrug, she opened the cat carrier.

"This is Rita. She's tired of being in the carrier. I don't know what she'll make of your wheelchair." Rita had never met a wheelchair before. Walkers and canes, yes, but not wheelchairs. Oriole's Nest only tended people who were ambulatory.

The nurses didn't seem to have noticed the cat. They didn't, in fact, seem to have noticed Estelle in quite some time. Jeanie had found Estelle in a wheelchair, parked in front of a blank television in her room. In the past week, Estelle had spared no effort to reject the nurses' help, intentions, and professional skills. Her hostility spoke through every move, sniff, and cutting remark. Jeanie couldn't blame the nurses for giving Estelle the privacy she so vehemently defended.

Estelle looked into the silver-gray ruffles of cotton wool that clouded the skies in one of Oregon's more subtle beauties. Wisps of silver played through a break in the clouds. She registered Jeanie's presence with only the flicker of a dismissing eye. She had not spoken a word in the ten minutes since Jeanie's arrival.

Rita wandered onto Jeanie's lap, and considered exploratory moves onto the wheelchair. Jeanie placed her on Estelle's lap, lifted one of the lifeless hands, and moved it on top. Rita readily settled into a purring ball, content to take a nap. Jeanie drew Estelle's hand over the bright fur.

"Estelle, you didn't answer me. Do you miss going to work?"

Estelle's carved face stirred. Hoarse words emerged from the frozen lips. "Is that all you can find to say, Mrs. McCoy? Is your imagination really so lacking?"

"What would you have me say?" Damn her anyway. Jeanie was so sick of walking on eggs. Estelle wouldn't want pity, even if she offered it. "Gee, Estelle, I'm sorry they had to cut your leg off below the knee? How are you going to manage with only one foot, and just half of that? Is that blunt enough for you?"

The chin quivered. Estelle was resolutely silent.

"How about this? It could have been worse. You could have been plastered into unrecognizable pieces on the pavement yesterday morning, like Vic Dunlap. His wife adored him. She called him her Pillsbury Doughboy. He was earning extra money to take her to Hawaii." There was no reaction. "It may not matter to you, but it mattered to Debbie, and Mackie Sandoval, and me, and Danny Rivera."

Estelle's head jerked. "Danny Rivera? Was he hurt?"

"Not Danny. Vic was the night guard." Jeanie watched the color come back into Estelle's face. "Why? Do you know Danny Rivera?" *Everybody* knew Danny Rivera. It was unreal. But then again, they all lived and worked in the same sector of society.

At Risk of Being a Fool

Estelle turned away. "I met him a time or two. In the course of business."

"A nice man," said Jeanie.

"He's twenty years my junior, Mrs. McCoy. Get your mind out of the gutter."

"Ah, that's nice. That's the Estelle I've learned to know and love."

The rigid face twitched and tightened again.

"I asked if you missed going to work. Are you planning a return in the near future? Or," she added, "in the distant future?"

"They did this to me." Estelle sat in profile, her face unforgiving.

"All of them?" Jeanie found a perverse pleasure in the rudeness. Talking with Estelle might be as tense as a Cold War, but it was a relief from the rules to which she'd bound herself for her entire life. "All twenty-odd girls hid in collusion, and built a pipe bomb in the Bright Futures' back shed, and then crept to your apartment across town in the dead of night to booby trap your car. Fluffy thinking, Estelle."

Estelle turned on her, with wolf-like ferocity. "Absolutely rational thinking, my naïve Mrs. McCoy. Criminals, all of them, not one with a decent background. Whom else would you accuse? The grocery clerk? One of my neighbors at the apartment complex? I don't even know their names, not one."

"I'll bet your neighbors know yours, though." Jeanie bit her lip on the acid tone.

"Violence is their nature!" Estelle screamed. "They're evil, disease-ridden drug addicts, thieves, and hookers."

"Who have no appreciation for the effort you've put into their rehabilitation."

"No!" The shout bounced off the walls, circled Jeanie's head, and fell.

A timid knock sounded on the door. A young nurse peered inside, hesitation written in every line of her face. "Er—?"

"We're just fine, thanks," caroled Jeanie with her most teacherly smile. "Close the door please. We don't want the cat to get out, now do we?"

"Er, no, of course not." After a moment, the nurse decided to put herself on the outside of the door instead of the inside.

Estelle pressed the backs of her hands to her cheeks, trying to push back the high color.

"But which one, Estelle? Which one do you think did this? And which twenty didn't? And why would she bother? She'd know every girl in the place would be suspected."

Estelle lowered her hands, and wiped them quickly on her gown. Dampness spotted the cloth, telling its own tale. Without thought, she dropped a hand on Rita.

"I don't know. I've been thinking, and thinking, all day, ever since—" She looked at the stump of her leg sticking out in front of her wheelchair, and flinched away. "Ever since they forced me out of bed into this wheelchair. I hadn't thought it through before then. They all—"

"Justice, Estelle. Remember the justice model. Not all of them. Maybe not any of them."

"I've gone over the infractions I recall. I just don't know. If I had their files, perhaps. I keep forgetting things."

"How could any of them find the time, Estelle?"

"Even you're not that silly, Jeanie. The searches turn up cell phones with a fair regularity," Estelle said. Her color had returned to normal.

"How often do you actually run a full search?" The

danger was past for the moment. Estelle was thinking again.

"Weekly, at least. On different days, different times. I know most of the favorite hiding spots." She snorted. "I've been there longer than any of them, since the place was built."

"They're not too happy under Dolores right now."

"Nonsense. They should be as happy as pigs in a dumpster."

"They say she's unpredictable, and the food's bad." She shifted into Brynna's cadence. " 'Torrez was a bitch, but she didn't pull nothing. It was all there in the fuckin' rule book, God, she knew it by heart.' "

A shoulder muscle twitched. Estelle's mouth pulled down on one side as she covered her face with her hands again. After a moment, Rita rose on her hind legs, and nudged one hand impatiently. Estelle let her hand fall into the cat's fur and Rita subsided. Estelle turned her wheelchair to face Jeanie. Her eyes were wet.

"Which one said that?"

"It could have been any of them."

"I could take a guess."

"But you won't." There was a moment's silence. "They didn't love you, Estelle, but in a backhanded way some of them, at least, appreciated your more positive qualities." *She'll never forgive me if she starts crying in earnest.* "At least the few you allowed to show on occasion."

"Humph."

"Estelle, I need your help."

Estelle shot her a disbelieving glance.

"I do, Estelle. They've closed my school. Too many coincidences they said, too many connections between the kids and the recent violence."

"Sensible."

"They're my kids, Estelle. I'm fond of them." She overrode Estelle's snort. "They need to earn their GEDs. If they lose this chance, some of them will never try again."

"Corrections has its own GED program."

"Two of my kids are not in Corrections or transition facilities. Another is a voluntary, and without the program, I don't think she'll make it. It's good for all of them, to learn in a classroom situation, to have to get along with other people. I've made home visits to three of them, and left a message for the fourth. But Dolores has cut me off. She won't let me visit the girls, and she refuses to let them come to class tomorrow. It's testing day. Brynna has to take the Science test, and Sorrel's been doing community service, but Dolores won't let them come."

"It's a non-issue. Brynna and Sorrel will join classes with the others. The only reason they're in your program is for the work experience portion."

"Blast it, Estelle, quit trying to stab me and open your mind. Sorrel needs this opportunity. She's growing as a person. We can rehabilitate her. It's not *justice,* yanking her out of a situation where she's succeeding."

"Tell me the rest of it." The flat statement lay there, inert, a challenge.

"Brynna's finally improving her attitude—"

"Tell me the rest of it. There's more to this than GED. Isn't there?"

Jeanie opened her mouth and closed it. "Yes, there is. But it's confidential. You'll have to trust me."

"Trust you? You barge into my life, badger me, and tell me I must do this, or mustn't do that? And I'm supposed to trust you? Turn it around, Jeanie McCoy. Do it, I dare you. Trust me."

"It's not my story to tell."

At Risk of Being a Fool

"It's got to be either Brynna or Sorrel. I could find out in half an hour on the phone if I wanted to. If I cared."

"But you don't. I care for them."

"You *think* I don't. You quoted one of them to me. Was that a true quote? All right, then. I create a wall of safety around those girls. They don't appreciate it, and they don't need to. I am a barrier between them and temptation. If, for the rest of their lives, they're living so as not to wind up in my care again, that's exactly what I want. What do you think the justice model is, Jeanie? You saw my article. Did you actually read it?"

"Yes."

"And you agreed with none of it."

"With parts of it, Estelle, but not the rigidity, the power-play stuff you pull on them."

"Are you always the perfect teacher? Nor am I the perfect correction supervisor. Nonetheless, I am reasonably good at what I do, and that is to provide a bridge for juvenile offenders back into mainstream society, with a clear understanding of consequences for their actions."

"All right. You're right. It's a difficult job, and it's one I couldn't do."

"As I could never teach. You want my help and you want me to do things your way. I cannot. We can, however, collaborate for the best interests of our mutual charges. To do that, you must trust me."

"You could throw them both back into Corrections for another two years."

"I will agree not to do so based on any information you give me in this conversation. Further than that, I am not prepared to go."

Jeanie spun her wedding ring on her finger. If she gave Estelle more power over Sorrel's life, the results could be horrific. Not only that, but she'd be breaking her promise of confidentiality. She could ruin Sorrel's confidence in her.

"It was good of you to come by," Estelle said with difficulty. "To keep me company. Thank you."

Jeanie heard every one of the multiple layers. Estelle offered closure to the hospital visits, with more grace than Jeanie thought she had possessed. She'd also sacrificed a piece of her own pride. Perhaps, after all, Estelle did understand what she was asking.

"Sorrel's pregnant."

"When?" Estelle snapped, instantly tense.

"Not on your watch. I figure it happened when she was sneaking out of Esperanza."

"Does Randy know?"

"Randy knows that something's going on, and has chosen not to look too closely. Dolores doesn't have a clue, and we're keeping it that way. Sorrel wants to hide the pregnancy until she can get out of Bright Futures. I arranged the community service to keep her out of Dolores' eyesight. And before you ask, I doubt very much she had anything to do with the bomb that took off your foot, but I can't prove it, and I could be wrong. If she goes back to Corrections," Jeanie concluded, "the baby might wind up with her mother."

"Foster care is more likely, at least to begin with."

"She doesn't want an abortion. She wants to get out, have her baby, and help her mother raise both children."

"Abortions are preferable in dysfunctional families. In my opinion."

"Have you seen Tiffany? With Sorrel?"

"Yes." An exasperated sigh. "Yes, I've seen them together. But the family is dysfunctional. You can't deny that."

"Sorrel can learn."

At Risk of Being a Fool

Estelle pursed her lips. "Here, take your cat."

"Where are you going?"

"To find a phone."

"Estelle!" By the time Jeanie got Rita in her carrier, Estelle was halfway down the hall to the nurses' station.

"I need a phone with an outside line," she demanded.

"There's a phone in your room," Jeanie interjected. "Let's—"

"A phone, young woman." Estelle slapped the countertop.

The nurse puffed up, affronted. Jeanie caught her eye, shrugged, mouthing "Sorry." The nurse softened, lifted the handset, punched two numbers, and rotated the phone towards Estelle.

"You'll need to make it fast."

Estelle and the nurse traded frosty glances as Estelle dialed a number. "Mrs. Torrez here," she announced. "Please connect me with Mrs. Cuthbert immediately. Thank you."

"Estelle, if you say anything—"

"Dolores? Mrs. Torrez here. I have not received an RB-359 since I was hospitalized. Where is your progress report? Yes. Verbal will do for the moment, but please forward your notes as soon as we finish. Yes. I see. All seven of them? How can you justify that? Come now, Dolores, transportation woes are eternal. If you are unable to cope—"

Estelle's skill with the cut-and-jab interview technique had not dulled with her accident. Jeanie listened with guilty pleasure, sharing a rueful smile with the nurse. The nurse snapped her fingers, and a man in a blue lab coat moved up to join the fascinated eavesdroppers.

". . . matter of the work-release girls. There are two of them, I believe, in the program with Miss Sandoval. Their job performance reports were satisfactory, but I don't believe that teacher, McCoy-somebody, has submitted an L-23 on their studies. Have Mary Mahoney press for an official report when she drops the girls off for their classes today. No class. Why on earth not? Pitiful. I certainly hope that woman intends to continue on a home visit basis, or I'll have a few things to say about breach of contract. In fact, give me her phone number, and I'll call right now . . . Oh. You think so. Please be certain of it. Now, Randy Firman informs me that Sorrel Quintana is required to perform community service, and that he's lined something up. I had a few things to say to him, I can tell you. Imagine not clearing it with me first, incredible. However, be that as it may, we are required to comply. I gather he arranged transportation? Good, I would have insisted, in any case. Anything else? All right, I'll be expecting your RB-359 no later than tomorrow morning, nine a.m. And of course, you'll attach the explanatory addendums for your deviations from protocol. Each of them. Of course. Thank you, Dolores, and good day."

Estelle put down the phone, and bridled at the admiring looks of Jeanie, the nurse, and the lab technician. "Thank you," she said icily, "for the use of the telephone, if not for the privacy generally accorded to personal conversations."

"It was too good to miss," said Jeanie. "Beautifully done."

"Humph. Now, you," Estelle jabbed a finger at the nurse, "call my doctor immediately—"

"Estelle, hush."

"I *beg* your pardon."

"Hush. Thank you." Jeanie smiled at the nurse. "My friend would appreciate it if you could contact her attending physician so she can discuss prosthetics and occupational therapy with him, if you would be so kind. That

At Risk of Being a Fool

was what you were going to say, wasn't it, Estelle?"

"Roughly," said Estelle, grudgingly. She started to speak, but Jeanie distracted her by dropping the cat carrier into her lap. The nurse grinned back at her, and raised a thumb in the air as Jeanie wheeled her away.

"Jeanie, can't we take a day off for once?" said Brynna in disgust.

"You want a day off?" asked Sorrel. "Cuthbert's got Josie scrubbing all the paint off the inside of the shed. Josie was complaining about the roaches. Go ahead, give her a hand, why don't you?"

"God, no," Brynna said. She grabbed the science book off the top of the stack. "Looks better already."

Ordinarily, Bright Futures used its conference room for meetings with parole officers, social workers, and lawyers. Therefore, it had better furniture than the girls did. More importantly, Jeanie could lock the door. Rita was unaffected by the tension. She was busy pursuing a ball of paper across the floor.

Jeanie said, "How are things going these days?"

"Worse," said Sorrel. Brynna nodded. "Torrez had a million regs, but at least we knew what they were. Cuthbert comes up with new ones all the time."

"Like yesterday," Brynna said. "When all of a sudden we're separating the trash different. She told morning cooks, but not evening cooks, so then she's breathing down our necks, screaming at us, like we did it on purpose. Two fuckin' demerits each." She shot a glance towards the door, flushed red, and shut her mouth tightly.

"What I figure is," said Sorrel, "she's trying to prove she's as good as Torrez, get herself a promotion, so she's changing stuff. Kherra said something about new brooms yesterday, made a lot of sense."

"What about the brooms?" Brynna said apprehensively. "Are there new ones?"

Sorrel glanced at Brynna with more tolerance than usual. "No, Bryn. I mean Cuthbert's setting herself up as competition, so Torrez can't come back again."

Brynna looked at Sorrel in undisguised horror. "Oh, God. Jeanie, can she do that?"

"I wouldn't worry about it, Brynna, not yet. Mrs. Torrez isn't out of the hospital yet, and even when she is, she'll have physical therapy, and occupational therapy. It will probably be weeks before she'll know if she can come back. Of course, she may not want to."

"Torrez was a bitch," said Brynna, "but we knew what was going on when she was around."

"You should have seen breakfast today. You'd have puked," said Sorrel.

"It's probably easier to slip out now, isn't it?" said Jeanie, testing the waters.

Both girls turned on her with identical looks of suspicion.

Jeanie sighed. "I'm sorry, I'm not good at this. Look, I don't want to give you ammunition on each other, but there's something I'd like to ask."

Brynna and Sorrel exchanged glances. "Go ahead," said Sorrel.

"I was at Esperanza yesterday. Linda said they'd had problems sometimes, with residents sneaking out for drugs, or to meet friends."

Sorrel's lip quirked. "Like me, huh?"

"Yeah, like you. So you were bounced back to Corrections, and then got placed here, right?"

"Yeah."

"Same for you, Brynna?"

At Risk of Being a Fool

"I came here from Corrections. Didn't go anywhere else." She studied her fingernails, bitten to the quick as usual. "If I thought I could get away, I'd run. At least, sometimes I would."

"Where would you go?"

"I don't know. I don't care. I'm just sick of being locked up."

"So what I understand is, if either of you is slipping out, you're coming back right away, and no one knows it." Jeanie watched Rita instead of the girls. "But, I hear that Quinto's place is like a fortress. No way anyone could get out of there."

Sorrel laughed. Jeanie looked at her inquiringly.

"A guy I know says it's harder to get in than it is to get out." There was a mocking lilt to her voice.

"They thought Rita was a dangerous criminal," offered Jeanie. Rita played with Brynna's shoelaces, managing to choke herself.

"Anybody can get out of anywhere," Sorrel said, "if it matters enough, and you're smart enough. What matters to me now is my family, and I'd lose them. So I wouldn't run."

"I would," Brynna whispered. "But I'd get caught, I know it. They'd bump me back to Corrections. I get scared, so I don't risk it."

Brynna twisted her hands together, and looked at her knotted fingers. Sorrel rested her hand on Brynna's for a fleeting moment, unaware of having stunned both women.

"Running is dumb," Sorrel said. "At least, if you've got a chance to get out the legal way, it's dumb."

"So if someone wanted to get something," Jeanie pursued, "or to pass a message, slipping out of these places is possible."

"Phones are easier," said Brynna. "Call ahead, get something dropped to you at a bus stop or something." Brynna chuckled weakly. "I've thought about it some. Running, calling a friend to fly the Five, get me away. They'd catch me sure if I stuck around. I'd hop a bus, be long gone, that's what I'd do. Damn, I wish there was trains running back of this place, like you got, Jeanie. I'd be out one night, and on it like a flash."

"It would be a temptation," said Jeanie. "Sometimes, I look out, and want to jump on, myself." She heaved a sigh.

"What's 'flying the Five' mean?"

"Portland's so close," said Brynna, "when you drive down I-5 to Salem, that's what you call it, flying the Five."

"Ah, makes sense. Well, I brought your textbooks, Brynna. Sorrel's already got hers, but Mrs. Cuthbert didn't know that." She gave the girls a conspiratorial look. "Think you're up to studying today?"

The girls exchanged a glance, and chorused, "Roaches." Jeanie laughed, and left them the textbooks. The girls transferred to the study desks in the main room. After a while, Brynna felt Sorrel's gaze on her.

"What?" she said defensively.

"Just wondering."

Brynna edged away. "Wondering what?"

"Just wondering how you knew about the trains behind Jeanie's house."

He leaned against a tree, every sense alert. The girl slipped away, her shadow merging indistinguishably with the building. His glance roamed the side of the building and the street beyond. There was no traffic. There were no motorcycles cutting the air with their power; no cars cruising the street, with the drivers trapped by windows and doors into a false sense of safety.

Only because he was listening for it, he heard the tiny click of a thumbnail against the inside of the dining room

At Risk of Being a Fool

window. Once, twice, three times.

He slouched away, his hands in his jacket pockets. The ridges of the car keys were friendly to his hands, but their familiar texture was no comfort. One by one, he'd talked to most of them, by phone or straight out. He'd talked to another guy, too, one in a position to know stuff he couldn't. He had no choice, once he knew she was going from house to house, to police, to schools, to everybody in the phone book. In class, at least, he could watch her, so he knew what she was up to. The knowledge settled like a weight on his shoulders, permanently.

Well, shit.

The thing was, she made him laugh. Funny stuff on TV, even the jokes of his friends had a hard edge to them, like practical jokes, and humiliations. They were funny, you had to admit. It was normal to him, just the way life was.

But there she was, with her little phrases, words twisted around on themselves, the twinkle in her eye, waiting to see if anybody'd catch them. He'd asked her once, early on, why the hell she bothered with a dog anyway. And she'd said, he's cheaper than a tow truck. She'd been gone for several minutes before it hit him, what she'd meant. Like if she'd been walking and passed out, the dog would tow her home.

She'd die a lot quicker than the guard had. He had the touch now, could plan things better, to kill when he meant to, instead of just ripping off feet. It turned out that was enough with Torrez. He hadn't needed to kill her, just take her out of action. With Jeanie, it was the mouth he had to stop. Rip her feet off, and the mouth would just keep going, and going, and going, like the Energizer rabbit.

It wouldn't hurt her much. It would be fast; she'd never know.

But it bothered him somehow.

SEVENTEEN

Sorrel sat in the classroom, her books and papers spread in front of her, her eyes darting from Dillon, to Rosalie, Quinto, Brynna, and Tonio. They all looked strange to her, after a week away from class. They wouldn't even be together now if it weren't for testing day.

Sorrel had watched people all her life. She'd had to, or they'd get the edge on her. Look at all the shit Mama had to put up with, like those people trying to take Grandma away, and put her in a home. They'd tried to take Sorrel away a few times, when she was little. They said Mama drank too much, stayed out too late, and wasn't a good mother. What did they did they know about it? Mama loved her like nobody else, and she loved Mama. Mama'd stolen food to feed Sorrel. Mama'd kicked out a boyfriend once for touching her. The shit had limped off with his dick in his hands, cussing a blue streak. What the hell, Mama said. He was just a shit, nothing like as important as a daughter.

They'd stuck Sorrel in foster care several times, but she'd raised enough hell the fake "parents" shoved her out, and she'd gone back to Mama. That was how it was supposed to be, mother and daughter. It hurt like hell, being away from Tiffany, but at least Tiffany had Mama and Grandma.

Kherra watched people, too. At first, Sorrel figured Kherra was looking for angles, ways to get the edge on people, but it wasn't that at all. It was like Kherra looked for trouble spots and weaknesses, and fixed 'em up before people knew they were there.

At Risk of Being a Fool

Kherra would look at a mindless woman drooling in a corner, and say, *Betsy's fretting about her husband again.* Before you knew it, Betsy and Kherra were putting pictures together in a photo album, and Betsy was talking in her fragmented way about vacations she and her husband had been on. Looking at photos of a grinning young Betsy in Hawaii with a bald guy, seeing her fingers trace the man's homely features, Sorrel had felt— Well, she didn't know how she felt.

All those old folks, they weren't just hunks of garbage tossed into a can. They had lives, and stories to tell. Sorrel had watched Kherra closer after that. She'd tried her own first mind-reading stunt a few days ago.

"Leda wants to cook again," she'd told Kherra.

"How you goin' manage that, girl? You can't put her with no knives, or hot surfaces. It's not safe."

Sorrel raided Jeanie's cupboards, brought in tortillas, cheese, olives, pickles, and a little bag of those tiny carrots. She'd hauled in Leda, and put her with the plates, and wedges of food. Sorrel chopped and microwaved behind Leda's back, and stuck the results within reach. That old woman came alive, her fingers edging tiny snacks together, neat platefuls of appetizers, just like you saw on the cooking shows.

"Where's the parsley?" asked Leda, looking for all the world like those women in the commercials who lived in their kitchens. They seemed to get such pleasure out of it, and Sorrel had always scoffed at the idea. But here was Leda, insisting Sorrel cut the carrots into flowers with four sharp strokes of a knife. It was tricky keeping the knife out of Leda's hands, but the carrots had looked pretty.

Kherra ran off to the kitchen next door at the regular retirement home, and grabbed up parsley, radishes, and whatever she could swipe. Other ladies livened up, spreading tablecloths, napkins, trotting down the halls to invite their "good friends," and somehow the whole thing turned into a church social or something. Bill and Edward, the only men in the building, responded with pleasure to the extra attention lavished on them as the only available hosts. Leda, beaming with pride, acted as hostess.

Kherra, the extra pair of hands, with "yes, ma'ams" and earnest nods, spared a moment for a long, glowing look at Sorrel. God, it felt so good. Not ever, in her life, had she felt that good, except when Tiffany was born.

But Kherra wasn't blind, not like Jeanie was. She saw the bad stuff as easy as the good. Yesterday, that old lady Livia had been in a hell of a rage at Phyllis. Jeanie would have spent a lot of time in useless soft talk. Kherra hadn't wasted time. With strong arms and stern talk, she'd enveloped the screaming woman, and moved her to a different room, while Nadezda calmed Phyllis.

Talk and action both, sometimes soft, sometimes stern: bunny rabbit and bulldozer, that was Kherra. Come to think of it, Jeanie was a bit of a bulldozer too, sometimes. Know-it-all Kemmerich hadn't squeaked once since she told him off.

Now, when Sorrel looked around the classroom, it was like there was two of every person. There was the Quinto she knew, and there was the one that Kherra and Jeanie'd see. And the same with Brynna, Dillon, Rosalie, and Tonio. It was like looking out a window, and then somebody opened it and you felt the breeze, heard the kids playing, smelled the acrid scent of burning rubber, and whiff of lilac.

Sitting in her classroom chair, Sorrel felt a deep unease. They all seemed different from usual. Rosalie acted like she was stuck to her desk, eyes on her book, pencil moving steadily over the paper. Well, she would be different, Sorrel told herself; she was testing later today. Maybe that's all it was, with Rosalie. Dillon was wound up, but he was testing, too. Mackie would be here in a few minutes, to drive them to the testing center.

Brynna was edgy, like a pig in a slaughterhouse. Now, *that* was different. As she watched, Brynna raised her head and looked back at her. Brynna darted a quick look at the guys, and back to Sorrel. Brynna's fingers lifted to her lips for a nibble, and Sorrel scowled at her. She'd have to lay off those fingernails if she wanted to borrow Sorrel's nail polish again. It was a waste of good polish, if she was just going to chew it off.

Tonio cracked his knuckles, and crossed his legs the other direction. Restlessness swept through him in waves. He'd be quiet for a bit, and then shift around in a flurry of sudden moves. That was different, too. At least Sorrel thought it was. She wondered what Kherra would make of him.

Watching Jeanie zipping around the room, trailed by Corrigan, that was the weirdest feeling of all. She'd known Jeanie for weeks, but she'd never thought about her. Jeanie wasn't a threat, and that was all that mattered. But for all her jokes and smiles, Jeanie was hurting. Kherra said so. Watching the dog, Sorrel realized that even Corrigan knew it. Jeanie was fooling herself, waiting for Edward to get better again. He'd never get better, only worse. Everyone knew it. Jeanie said she knew it. But she didn't believe it, Kherra said. In Jeanie's heart, she didn't believe it.

"Well, shoot," Jeanie exploded. "I must have left your testing applications in the car. I'll go look. If Mackie shows up, stall her until I get the papers. Hang onto the cat for me." She bustled out the door.

Sorrel turned her considering gaze on Quinto, and frowned a bit. Quinto hunched over his desk like a scared dog, taking up as little space as he could. It was weird, thinking of Quinto like he was a real person, not just some clown who everybody made fun of, walked past, ignored. His claim to fame was his gang, and they were all miles away. His white knuckles clenched on the pencil as it drew disconnected doodles. Maybe she was wrong, and he wasn't scared. Maybe he was mad, and hiding it. He had a lot more muscle than she'd thought. He'd get really buff, working on a construction site. He was small, quick, and probably strong.

The phone rang. No one answered it. She waited for Jeanie to come back, but the door stayed closed. Sorrel met Brynna's glance, and then Rosalie's. Sorrel got up, and crossed into the office.

"Yeah, hi. GED School," she added belatedly.

"Hello? Jeanie, is that you?"

"Uh, no, she's gone outside. You want I should get her?"

"No, no. This is her sister, Michelle Connery. I'm calling from Germany."

"Germany? No shit? Really?"

Michelle laughed. "No shit. Which one are you? Brynna or Sorrel?"

"Sorrel. How'd you know?"

"I know all of you. I'll bet I could even describe what you're wearing. Jeanie writes to me through e-mail."

The idea jolted her. Descriptions of her floated halfway across the world. "Uh, let me get her. She just went to the car, to get the test apps."

"Well— No, I guess not. I feel kind of silly, calling. Look, can you just tell me, Sorrel? Is she doing okay?"

"I guess. She's maybe a little stressed about her husband, but he's doing good. At least," said Sorrel, remembering Kherra, "as good as you could expect."

There was a sigh. "Yes, I know. But that's all, as far as you know? There's nothing going on with the school?"

"No, not really, just usual stuff."

"Good. You see? It was silly of me to call. Thanks a lot, you've relieved my mind."

"Why? What were you thinking?"

"Oh. Well, I just got this e-mail from her. She wrote it last night, her time. I only just got in. It's eleven p.m. here."

Sorrel blinked. She checked a clock. Two p.m.

"And the more I read it, the more I thought she might be in danger."

"Why?"

"It's nothing, Sorrel. I'm sure if something's going on, you'd know about it. And while I know you have your secrets, I do know this. You wouldn't stand by and let my sister get hurt."

Sorrel bit her lip, heedless of the lipstick. Her uneasiness grew. "How'd you figure that?"

"Because Jeanie knows it. It's as clear as can be in her letters. I feel I know all of you as well as I know anyone here."

"What am I wearing?" said Sorrel tightly.

"How's that again?"

"My clothes. What am I wearing?" A pause. "It's important."

Michelle laughed. "Give me a clue. What's the color scheme?"

"Blue."

"Ah, let's see. Hmm. Start at the bottom. Open-toed sandals, black. Dark blue polish on the toes. Then dark blue stretch pants, and a T-shirt, lighter blue, a little baggy, no slogans. How am I doing?"

"What else?"

"Yes, that was the easy part, wasn't it? Bright blue nail polish, aqua, maybe, with glitter in it. Eye shadow the exact shade, with a shine to it. Dark mascara, startling black, I think Jeanie called it. Lipstick, glossy red, brighter than usual, more makeup than usual. Earrings, I think, big hoops, silver? Hair swept back, and up. In fact," said Michelle delicately, "the entire effect is to draw the eye upwards. Jeanie says you're astute. She's got an amazing eye for detail, considering how little she cares for her own appearance. Tell me, did I get the entire thing wrong? Completely off base?"

"No." There was a lump in her throat. "There's no glitter. I got that airbrushed kind of nails, put 'em on yesterday. But they're blue."

Michelle crowed. "Ha! The old girl guessed right! Well, thanks Sorrel, you've certainly brightened up my evening. I can sleep in peace. Though I bet Mackie Sandoval dashes in all worried. I left her a voice mail." The rich chortle, so much like Jeanie's, hung in the air as Sorrel put down the receiver.

Mechanically, she walked into the middle of the classroom. Her cheeks were fever-hot. They all stared at her, even Dillon.

"I just want to know one thing." Was that her voice? Cracked and strained. "Why does it matter that there's a train track behind Jeanie's house?"

Nobody said a word.

"Come on, guys. Nothing's happened yet. I just don't want her to get hurt. She's a friend of mine. Why does it matter about the fuckin' train?"

At Risk of Being a Fool

Into the silence came the rattling roar of a motorcycle. Fuckin' lawyer, she thought absently. Every time he saw her, he gave her that look, like she was crap. She ought to stab his tires for him. He had it coming. His bike's rattle ebbed for a moment as he turned the corner. The motor gunned, and the bike roared past the building. The classroom windows rattled with the vibrations.

Dillon glanced at the window. She followed his look. The blinds swayed, knocked against the window, eased their movement, and were still.

"Oh my God," she said. "It's the rattling. The train would set off the damned bomb. Oh, crap! You motherfuckers, if she's hurt, I'm gonna kill you."

Sorrel ran, slamming the door behind her. Where did Jeanie park her fuckin' car? Sorrel careened out the side door. She paused a moment, letting the door fall into place. What if she was wrong? She forced herself to slow down, approach Jeanie's car at a walk, as if nothing was happening.

Jeanie's butt was sticking out, while she rummaged through the jumbled contents of the back seat. Jeanie kept an orderly classroom, an organized desk, but the back seat of her car was a mess.

"Hey, Jeanie? You've got a phone call."

"I'll be there in a minute. I found Rosalie's papers, so Dillon's have to be here somewhere. Looks like Rita randomized them for me."

Sorrel strove for a casual tone. "It's your sister. On the phone."

Jeanie popped out the car. "Michelle? From Germany? Is she okay?"

"I think so. She's still on the line," Sorrel lied. "Come on."

"Oh, well, I guess I should, just for a minute."

Jeanie started to slam the car door, but Sorrel intercepted her, closing it with a small click. In the distance, she heard the motorcycle approaching again, this time on the street behind the building. Damned idiot, must of forgot his briefcase. The roar made her nervous, but that was stupid. The vibrations couldn't set off a bomb, if there was one in the car. Not vibrations from a motorcycle, anyway.

There's no bomb, there can't be a bomb. Strangeness descended on her, threatening her, shaking her, forcing her to listen. Michelle thought there was danger, because of things Jeanie wrote to her. Michelle could describe, to the tiniest detail, what a girl was wearing half a world away. There was danger somewhere, and it centered on Jeanie. But not here, not now. Wasn't that the whole point of the train behind the house? That he could leave a bomb there, to explode in the night, set off by the rumble of the train?

She had time to warn Jeanie. She'd get a security guard to check out that car, just to be sure. She'd talk to Randy and Kherra. Maybe they could talk Jeanie into moving for a few days, until it was safer. She could sleep at the Nest in a spare bed. It would be all right, she'd found out in time.

The relief was enormous.

Sorrel skipped up the steps to the back door and opened it. She looked back impatiently. Jeanie was still leafing through the papers in her hand, looking puzzled.

"Come on. She's waiting," said Sorrel, as irritated as though her lie were the truth. She'd have to get in there, and take the phone off the hook. She'd pretend they'd gotten disconnected. "Move it, Jeanie, it's long distance from Germany, for God's sake."

Jeanie trotted towards the door. Sorrel held it halfway open, tapping her foot.

At Risk of Being a Fool

The car exploded with wrenching shrieks of metal and a ball of fire.

"No!" screamed Sorrel. Waves of rolling heat enveloped her, blocked by the door. The car was in flames, spitting glass shards and metal chunks into the air. Jeanie fell forward onto the steps and stopped moving. Sorrel threw the door back, and jumped forward, the furnace that had been the car searing her flesh. She grabbed Jeanie's unresisting arm, dragged her inside, and yanked the door shut. The spreading explosions beat on the door with the hypnotic sound of a heavy metal rock band.

Frantically, Sorrel ran her hands over the still, bloodied form, fingers searching for injuries, as Kherra had insisted she'd learn. Tears streamed down her cheeks as she screamed into the empty air.

"You fuckin' son of a bitch, I'm gonna kill you!"

Rosalie stood transfixed as the reverberations shook the room.

Dillon shot out of his chair. "Holy shit!"

He tore through the door. To the right, a door closed to the sound of Sorrel's curses. Dillon bolted the other way. Sudden comprehension hit Rosalie, and she flew after him. She raced down the hallway, rounded the corner, passed him, and threw herself against the front door to the building, blocking his exit. She leaned there, quivering with fear.

"Get out of my way, you fuckin' bitch."

"No." She could scarcely hear herself over the pounding of her heart. "You did this, you hurt her, you killed her."

"Move, or I'm gonna kill *you*."

His huge hands approached her throat. She watched them, mesmerized, a deer caught in the headlights before certain death. She could see the callous ridges at the base of his fingers, the webbing spread between his fingers and thumb, the slicing scars across the palm of his right hand.

"No. You are a bad man," she whispered. In the midst of her fear, a sunburst flashed in her mind. *Daddy, I love you.* "My father would say so. *Un cabrón*," she said with soft certainty. She was going die; she knew it, even as his arm drew back sharply for the punch that would break her neck.

The fist came towards her, lightning fast, curved, and slammed into the wall next to the door. Unbelieving, Rosalie watched Dillon drop to the floor on his knees, head and neck bent, a coiled spring ready to free itself. For a long moment, nothing happened.

He sat back on his heels, dug into his pocket, and ripped out his cell phone. "Randy." The voice was harsh. "Get the fuck over here. Tell Grandma I didn't do it." A strangled breath. "Shit, Randy, move your ass. I need you."

He disconnected and held up the phone. Numbly, she touched it. He released it and let his hands fall.

From around the corner bolted a frantic ball of fur, mewing hysterically at the piercing pain in her eardrums. Rita skidded to a stop, scrambling up Dillon's knee. Automatically, he cupped the cat safely against his shirt. He half-turned in the direction she'd come.

"Who the fuck let the cat out?" he bellowed.

Rosalie's call was the third received by the 911 dispatchers.

Jeanie lay in the hallway. Sorrel crouched over her, her hair a curtain around Jeanie's face. One hand, slippery with blood, pressed Jeanie's throat gauging her pulse, as the other tossed folds of Dillon's trench coat over the still form. She avoided looking at Jeanie's right thigh where Mackie worked frantically, applying pressure to the gaping wound.

At Risk of Being a Fool

Blood spattered Dillon's trench coat. Dillon leaned against the wall, head down, thumbs hooked into the top of his belt. Randy stood next to him, shoulder to shoulder.

"I'm gonna kill you," said Sorrel. They were nearly the only words she'd spoken in the last ten minutes. She spoke solely to the dark-headed kid standing on Randy's other side. "Soon's she's safe, no matter how long it takes, I'm gonna kill you." Her chant grew ragged and rose to a shriek. "Don't you got no clue what she does for us? She plants acorns, for God's sake, so they'll turn into oak trees. You bastard!"

"Wasn't me," said Tonio. The words, repeated too many times, enraged her.

"You *knew* about the train. You cased her house, didn't you, fucker?"

"Why you figure that?" The words were even, unemotional.

"Because," Sorrel's words skidded to a halt. She studied Jeanie's face in her confusion. The freckles stood out like peppercorns on cottage cheese. She must be in shock, like Kherra talked about. Where was the damned ambulance? "Bastard," she muttered.

"She knows 'cause I told her," said Brynna. Sorrel's eyes flew up. "And I know, 'cause you told me so. You've been everywhere, Tonio, haven't you? Didn't tell me that, but I can guess. Out at the courthouse, over at Quinto's place." Brynna's eyes dropped to Jeanie's head. Her face hardened. "At Futures, too. And everywhere the damned bombs were, that's where you were. First."

Tonio moved, shoulders tensing. Brynna stepped back. Tonio's glance flickered from face to face: Randy, Dillon, Mackie, Quinto. He relaxed, and leaned back against the wall.

"Prove it."

243

"I don't have to prove it," Sorrel said viciously. "I know. And they won't be able to prove anything against me, dipshit, the day they find you in an alley, carved into little, tiny bits. They won't even be able to identify you, because you won't have a face left."

Their eyes locked, power and threat shooting from one set of eyes to the other.

"It wasn't Tonio," Jeanie whispered. Every gaze pinned itself to the battered form on the floor.

"You hush, Jeanie girl," said Sorrel, in an unconscious blend of Kherra and Jeanie herself. "You're gonna be all right. He didn't get you. The ambulance will be here real soon. You just don't understand mother-fuckers like him, blow up anybody gets in the way of his precious drug sales." Her gaze flicked to Brynna, and then away. "It's okay, Jeanie. It's good you're talking, you're going be all right, you hear? Mackie says so, she's got her First Aid card."

Jeanie stirred. Sorrel's hand loosened, and smoothed the hair out of Jeanie's eyes.

"It's not Tonio," Jeanie said. "It wasn't, was it? It didn't have anything to do with drugs, or the lawyer, or even that escaped convict. You know it, and I know it." Her eyes were closed, but she seemed to be talking to someone. "Come on. You know it wasn't Tonio. You can't let him do this. He's protecting his homey. Isn't he?"

The hallway was still for a long moment.

"Yeah," said Quinto.

EIGHTEEN

Sometimes at night, along about August, Tonio watched the shooting stars, bright and fierce, disrupting the pattern of the night sky. He tried to follow them, tried to see the pattern, where each one came from, and where it went, knowing all the time that the next flash would appear out of nowhere.

He was a shooting star, Ricardo was. He'd always been, from the beginning. Tonio had followed, with the rest of the homeboys, hypnotized by the flashing brilliance of a man with fire in his veins.

Tonio had been a kid, only fourteen, when they'd locked up Ricardo. He'd felt blinded, imprisoned, like he'd been cut off from the sky, living without Ricardo. He'd grieved for that brilliant grin, the wild look Ricardo threw as he ran, daring the rest of them to follow. Quinto was only twelve then. To him, his brother was a god. Ricardo laughed as he punched the kid on the shoulder. Some day, he'd promised, some day, you'll keep up with me. Go home now; take care of Mama.

A year or two passed without him. Tonio was the gang second, the organizer. Life was safer and tamer, but the thrill vanished with Ricardo. Quinto kept eager tabs on him, all agog over Ricky's exploits in D-Home, MacLaren, and the treatment centers. At first the fights, the stories, were legendary, a tiger ripping his way through the rabbits, the deer, and the small scavengers. Then, all of a sudden, everything changed. Ricardo turned a new leaf, they said, was cooperative and eager to learn. The early suspicion of the wardens, the counselors, faded as the change seemed permanent, covered with that magnetic smile of which Ricardo was master.

One time, some teacher hauled Tonio and a bunch of kids to the Portland zoo. Tonio, the quiet kid, memorized the animals, and matched them up with lessons he'd learned. The tiger had camouflage, black lines to dull the outline of the orange muscle-bound predator. *And if someone cages a tiger in a small box, with no room to run, he'll pace, and pace, and pace, and make a beautiful picture for others to see. Inside, he's crazy-mad, biding his time, waiting until the cage opens and he can kill his captors.*

Quinto's gang membership was only a matter of time. The homeys loved his artistry, despised his witlessness, but ultimately protected him, as their last connection to Ricardo. Quinto whispered the messages, of the ways Ricardo had found to sneak out, earn some money, get some drugs here, sell them there, acting as a middleman. The money wasn't the big thing. It was the thrill of escape, the secret laughter as he snuck back in, to play innocent for another day.

There were close calls, even for Ricardo. He'd snowed Bryce Wogan and Danny Rivera, but not that old buddy of his, Vic Dunlap. Dunlap stirred up trouble. Rivera was only half-convinced, but Ricardo saw the writing on the wall. He quit using Rivera's job sites as drug drops. Ricardo told Mackie he wasn't happy in construction, and she'd found him a different job. No reflection on Danny Rivera, of course. There were back slaps on all sides, and Ricardo's charming, self-deprecating grin allaying Danny's fears, even as he said good-bye. In the back of his mind, Ricardo had marked the name, Vic Dunlap, as a score to settle. Ricardo

At Risk of Being a Fool

sailed through his sentence and probation, and returned to Portland like a boomerang, to his white-collar job and connections on the legit side.

Around the same time, cops picked up Tonio for minor larceny. He felt guilty at his relief of being free of the gang, with their rough affection and smothering needs. Tonio put his time in D-Home to good use, observing successes and failures alike, judging his chances for a life worth living. He'd dropped a few words to a counselor, another few to a warden, and in no time at all they'd arranged his future, never suspecting that he'd arranged it for himself.

Uncle Carlos didn't give a damn. A little money came through Tonio's hands, as long as he was in school. Some of it paid for his uncle's beer and an address, a place to get mail and phone messages while he lived in his car, taking care of himself. Raising himself.

It shocked him, finding Quinto in the same class. The old relationship snapped into place. He had to take care of the kid. Ricardo was living good. He had a nice house, nice apartment, said Quinto, with mingled pride and disquiet. Monday night was visitation night at Quinto's House. Quinto set up a meet for Tonio afterwards at the park nearby.

At first, Ricardo's magic sucked in Tonio all over again. He admired the confident young guy on management track, with the nice motorcycle. Almost, he believed in the change. But once or twice, the façade slipped, and Tonio faced the caged tiger with the crazy-mad look. Love and fear wrenched at him, his loyalties split between his old life and the new. Portland, after all, was only forty miles away. Ricardo was free to roam any hours besides the forty he worked at the store. Flying the Five. Look at all the times Ricardo had led them down, right down I-5 to good old

Salem. Oregon's capital, he'd say, clearly relishing the thought of mayhem in the land where blind politicos made their laws.

When the pipe bomb took out Bryce Wogan, he'd thought of Ricardo. It made no sense. Ricardo never sparked against Wogan, and that was years before Wogan's daughter got rooked into selling drugs. Ricky liked Rivera just fine, even if he had set him down as an easy mark. Besides, no matter how he figured it, he couldn't see Ricky setting up a pipe bomb on a day Quinto was working the site.

Unsettled, Tonio asked Quinto a few things. Quinto was clueless, like always. Quinto didn't work afternoons or weekends either. He'd only worked on the Saturday of the bomb because the job was a bit behind. Ricardo could have set the bomb, certain his brother would be out of the way. The timing was bad, but Ricardo relished risk. He'd have loved slipping into a working site, probably in a hotwired supplier's truck, dropping off a box, and slipping out again, to hide in Portland less than an hour later.

The nights shrank, as Tonio made the rounds of anybody he could figure, anyone that Ricardo might have earmarked. Vic Dunlap worked days at the courthouse. Quinto knew it, because Vic and Danny were tight. Tonio took a chance. Ricky came to see Quinto on Monday evenings. Tuesday morning Tonio called in a bomb threat to the courthouse, and damned if he wasn't right. There really was a pipe bomb. Still he wondered, was Ricardo scaring people, or was he out to kill?

When Ricardo came to the school, he saw it for sure. Her ex-student's shining success even blinded Mackie. She couldn't see that Ricardo was a bomb ready to explode. Tonio set himself full time to figuring out his old buddy's

At Risk of Being a Fool

tricks, and planning how to stop them, being proactive. Narking on his old leader wasn't an option.

Logic said Ricardo would hook back up with Brynna. They'd worked together in Portland, their gang and the girl gang, hand-in-hand in a bunch of things, and drugs was one. The girl gang had drug connections all over the damned West Coast. Brynna swore to him, up and down, that that was all in the past. Yeah, right. The damned girl never could see past today.

So, Tonio put Bright Futures in his rounds, checking the perimeter, looking over the cars for signs of tampering. Ricardo would have to work at night, so as not to be "missing" from his regular apartment, his wonderful job, his new, brightly-patterned friends. Friends, with little habits that the "jobs" didn't know about.

He met up with Ricardo at Bright Futures. Ricardo was in a rage. Torrez was a major obstacle, getting in the way of business. Tonio knew that himself. He'd seen Torrez roaming outside Futures at night, even on days she was off work. Now, Brynna was scared to sneak out, and Ricardo had to get his messages through. The nursery was too good a spot to give up, way out of the normal traffic plans, partway to Portland. One person tossed a package out his window as he drove by, and Brynna snatched it later out of the ditch. On set days, she'd hide it at the edge of the grounds, and Ricardo would come pick it up again. From the fevered glint in his eyes, he was using it as well as selling it.

Tonio tried to calm things down. Torrez was a bitch, right enough, but if she got hurt at Bright Futures, all the girls would be grilled by the cops, and there was no knowing what plans would get messed up. The cops might turn up Brynna, and besides, Tonio had a girlfriend at Futures. Could Ricardo lay off Torrez a while, until Tonio's girl got out?

Ricardo nodded. It was something he understood. A guy had to protect his friends. Tonio hoped he'd solved the problem, but Ricardo just got Torrez at her apartment instead. God, that shook him. Even though he'd known she was a target, he hadn't been checking her apartment, and that poor bitch lost a leg out of it. He should've seen it coming. Ricky'd always had a short fuse. When he was high, he never thought twice before doing whatever the hell he wanted.

He'd been running scared since then, worrying about who Ricardo would go after next. And the moment he'd thought it through, he knew. Quinto was the key. It must have scraped Ricardo raw, seeing Quinto's hero worship for Danny Rivera, seeing him get so wild about building houses instead of trailing after Ricardo like he'd done all his life. Ricardo would get rid of Rivera. It was revenge on Rivera and on the company, for stealing his brother from him.

Tonio's fear escalated. Who else, he wondered. Who else did Quinto look up to? Was Mackie in danger, or Jeanie?

Sleep was only a memory for Tonio, as he tried to protect the world. He'd checked the damned construction site just before the guard got there. Stupid, he thought, idiot. But he'd just scaled in the back way, checked the trusses, and totally forgotten the gate. If Vic hadn't triggered the bomb, Danny would have. It was the sort of gambling Ricardo loved, not knowing which victim would fall first. Flip a coin, and death swoops in, heads or tails.

And here he was again, trailing around at night after Ricardo, hoping like hell he could catch him before the cops did. Ricardo was still a few steps up on him, like always, flashing on ahead, shouting, "Follow me." Tonio checked

At Risk of Being a Fool

the chain link fence. Still locked. If he was here, he hadn't taken his ride inside. He hadn't seen the motorcycle anywhere around here, but that didn't mean anything. Ricardo wouldn't have seen Tonio's car, either. He'd parked several blocks over and walked.

He should have realized Ricardo was watching the school. He'd blinded himself into thinking that Ricardo kept his tricks for nights or weekends. It hadn't even occurred to him that Ricardo had started playing around with remote controls. Ricardo had just watched Jeanie near the car this afternoon after planting his package. Then he punched his little button, and off he'd gone on his motorcycle, to the glorious sounds of lives wrecked behind him. And what had she done to him? Only encouraged Quinto to turn towards construction, and away from Ricky. Only been a part of the program that Ricardo had decided to close down, forever. Jeanie, Rivera, and Mackie.

Tonio studied the fence, both ways, looking for pipes, bags, and any little thing that might conceal a bomb. He grabbed the fence and ran up the side, dropping down the other. His steps slowed at the scuffling sound inside the nearly completed building. Ricardo was up in the rafters, just where Tonio had figured. A tearing sound made him jump. Ricardo, tearing off a hunk of duct tape.

"Ricardo," he called, in the thread of a voice that carried only to its intended destination. "Hey, homey, what's up?" Stupid, he told himself.

Ricardo flinched, turned, and poised to leap down. "Tonio? Hey, Flaco, how you doing? Come to join me on a job?"

"Came to tell you, I don't think that's just the best place. What if Quinto spots it? You know how he is. He'll blow himself to hell and back. Or does he already know about this?" The thought sickened him. Not Quinto, not everybody's little brother, excited about his blueprints and whatever Rivera'd taught him today.

"Naw. Trust Quinto with a secret?" Even now, with his hands on a pipe bomb, Ricardo's irrepressible humor reared its head. Tonio smiled weakly. "Naw, my bro won't touch this, not him. I worked with Rivera, remember. He always checks the beams and rafters himself. In case," he said caressingly, "of an accident. How 'bout that, huh? Little accident." He laid the pipe bomb along the wooden frame, and ripped free another length of duct tape.

"Ricardo."

"Hmm?" The eyes measured the bomb, tore the tape, attached it to a side beam, and let it dangle while he peeled off a third.

"Ricardo, they know."

The hands froze. "How's that again?" The words were soft, deadly.

"After you blew up the car, they figured it out, about the remote in the bomb."

"The car? Hmm, yeah. How's that fuckin' teacher of yours?"

"Dead," lied Tonio. He wet his dry lips.

"Good. She had too much, you know, influence on my little brother. Can't have that, now can we?" His words were a cruel mimicry of every counselor, every do-gooder who'd dared try to mold him into something he wasn't.

"So Ricky, it's too dangerous to try another one so soon. Right, bro? So leave it alone, for now. Come on, bring it on down with you. We'll put it in my car."

"Your car." Ricardo rose, crouching among the rafters like a giant spider. "You sure that's just how it happened, are you?" One of the spider legs moved and tested a strand.

At Risk of Being a Fool

"You didn't go and nark, did you, buddy? Homey? No, Flaco wouldn't do that, not to the big man, not to me."

" 'Course not, Ricky, I wouldn't nark on you."

"If you didn't nark, how come you're wandering around free? Seems like the cops'd hang onto you guys real tight, your teacher getting hurt and all." His voice deepened with menace. "Unless you narked, offered to set me up, right now!"

"No!" God, what would he believe? That some black lady he'd never seen before had come to the station? Fussed at the cops on his teacher's say-so? And then, after she got Tonio to her house, she'd fed him, gave him a bed, and never checked once to see if he was still in it. Weird woman, that Kherra. He couldn't say any of that, even if he *hadn't* said Jeanie was dead. "Hey, I can still pick a lock on handcuffs. You think I lost my touch? There was a street fight went down, real riot over on the east side. Station was so busy, they stuck me in a corner and forgot me. Gave me plenty of time to slip the cuffs, and slide on out. Get real, Ricky. Did I nark on you after you blew up Torrez? Dunlap?"

"No," said Ricardo, considering. "That's a fact." His look was speculative. "Look, just split, will you. Get out of the way. You don't gotta know nothing. Long as Rivera shows up tomorrow, nobody warns him off, we're in good shape."

"Ricardo—"

"Get the fuck out of here, Flaco. Move your ass."

Tonio took a step forward. "Ricky, come off it. Not tonight, okay? Leave it for now." He took another step, his eyes riveted upwards on the crouching figure above. "I told you, they know about you, they're looking for you. That's why I came to find you."

"And you came here? To find me?"

"Yeah. And if I can see it, you can bet the cops will. And so will Quinto. What you think he's going to do, if Rivera gets it? He can't take this stuff, Ricky. He's not like us. You know that. He's an artist."

"I know he's an artist. Ain't that what I've been saying?" The shout shook the rafters. Ricardo dropped his voice. "He's an artist, and he ain't gonna use his art with Rivera. I got a place for him, a job. He'd do great at that art school, I'm telling you. I'm going up in the world, Flaco, and I'm taking my homeys with me. Quinto, and you, and all the others."

"I don't want that. Quinto doesn't want that. Let us be."

"You! You don't know what the fuck you want. I'm *telling* you what you want, and it ain't any crackerjack job greasing machines, living in your damned car. You want a good job, lots of money, girls hanging on you."

"No."

"Don't tell me no! You hear me? You don't say no to me, you fuckass. I'm the *man*."

"Ricky, I love you, man. Won't you listen to me? Hear me? They're going to come get you, and lock you up for murder one, and you'll stay in that prison and rot until you're an old man. Bring it down. Come with me. Get away."

The faint sound of a car engine rolled up the street. Ricardo turned his head.

"See?" said Tonio fiercely. "That's the cops. What do you think? They're going to come with sirens blaring so you can hear them? You got to come with me. I know the way out."

"You *did* nark on me." Ricardo's bitterness cut through him. "Flaco, you piece of shit."

At Risk of Being a Fool

"No! They guessed, just like I did. Come on!"

For a moment, he thought Ricardo would do it. He shone with that daredevil grin and sparkling black eyes, glittering with excitement. "Okay, Flaco, your way. Come on, boy. Follow me!"

Ricardo threw the pipe bomb to the floor, and soared down onto it, arms outstretched, laughter spinning wild, a demon flying into hell. Tonio leaped through the open wall, rolled, and ducked behind the tool shed as the building tore itself apart.

In the street, the car came closer and screeched to a halt. "Mary, ohmigod, it's exploded! Call 911, call the cops!"

The shooting star burned out.

NINETEEN

The face went straight to Jeanie's heart, bypassing her mind. Husband, sister, sons, it was always that way. Recognition came first, a jolt to the heart, and then vision.

Brown hair lay close to his head, cropped short above Keith's long face, and the flyaway ears. It baffled her that he could sleep that way, sitting in the chair, collapsed forward on her hospital bed, twisted sideways, as though he'd gone to sleep looking at her face. Six-foot-one, and thin as a rail, Keith lived every moment of his life at a dead run. In the past, his passions had been Dungeons and Dragons, skiing, and fencing. Just now, it was the dehumanizing life of a would-be actor in Hollywood. In a few years, it might be mountain climbing, or deep-sea diving. Or, she thought fondly, it might not.

It was thirteen hours of driving from L.A., dead-heading it. He must have taken off instantly, when someone called him. It was so "Keith," instant decision, action, and then a crash into oblivion. She didn't touch him, didn't want to wake him up, poor thing. Geoff would be here soon, no doubt. He was stuck with plane schedules.

Memory settled around her, a shroud of regret and depression.

Poor Quinto. When push came to shove, she knew it had to be Ricardo. She knew, too, that if she'd said the name first, neither Tonio nor Quinto would forgive her. Tonio wouldn't budge, so she'd worked on Quinto. *Clumsy of me.* But she'd been hurting so badly. She hadn't been thinking straight.

At Risk of Being a Fool

From day one, she'd seen Quinto's hand sketching the two faces side by side, or facing each other across a sloppily written essay: Ricardo, his brother, and Danny Rivera, his mentor. There were two heroes, but only one Quinto. He was the prize in the engagement. Danny was winning, and Ricardo couldn't bear it.

Keith's eyes opened, blank and staring.

"Hello, angel," she said.

Keith blinked, and life returned to his face. In twenty seconds, he was alert and focused. She'd seen this miracle in him since the day he was born. Geoff, on the other hand, required ice cubes down the back, and a gallon of coffee poured into the unresisting mouth. The two boys were night and day, chalk and cheese.

"Can't keep you out of trouble for anything, can we?" said Keith, grinning.

Her own smile surfaced, irresistibly. "I've got to keep you boys alert."

"I've got about a zillion things to tell you, to catch you up on things. Don't talk, okay, or we'll get sidetracked." He waved a finger at her.

"Yes, sir," she said.

"Where's my notebook? Ah, here we go. I got in three hours ago. I checked your house to see about the pets. They weren't there. Turns out one of your girls called Kherra at the Nest. Rita and Corrigan are both there, they're fine, and they'll stay there until you're out of the hospital. Kherra says so. Got that? It was the first thing you were going to ask, wasn't it?"

"Almost."

"I can guess the next one, too. Geoff's on the plane. He's renting a car, and he'll be down as soon as he can. He'll get here this afternoon. He talked to Aunt Shell, and promised her we'd send a long e-mail with the entire situation. He also gave her the hospital phone number, and made her promise not to call you until this afternoon, our time. Oh yeah, while I was at the house, I found a package for you."

Jeanie flinched.

"It's not a bomb, I had the cops check it," Keith said. "It's from Julianne. She sent it a week ago. Funny, Julianne's box getting to you right after this fiasco and just before Geoff did. Almost like she's psychic, huh? Anyway, the box is right here."

"Probably bulbs again." Jeanie couldn't help smiling at the thought.

"Well, yeah. Don't fuss about your mail; the cops opened it, not me. I wasn't violating your privacy. Okay? Right. Looks like a bag of dirt, but there was a letter in there too. She's not supposed to put first class letters inside of a parcel post package, but the cops decided to overlook it this once. The letter's there by the phone. So, are we all set on family and pets? Okay to move on?"

"Keith, I love you," she said, her eyes tearing.

"I love you, too. Now, there's a phone message," he said, not missing a beat, "from Mackie Sandoval. It's long, you ready? First, Mrs. Otero took Dillon by the ear, and made him choose a kitten from the Humane Association." He frowned. "Does that make sense?"

"Yes."

"Good, I was afraid it was my handwriting. Sorrel says she called Kherra about Tonio, and Kherra says she'll take care of him. Something about Kherra chasing him off from the Nest one night. I don't know what that's about, but my money's on Kherra, whatever it is. Sorrel says she'll be by to see you later when," he frowned at his handwriting,

At Risk of Being a Fool

"she's finished blackmailing Cuthbert. Amazing. By the way, Aunt Shell says we're supposed to get Sorrel a dozen bottles of nail polish in rainbow shades, and a couple of sets of airbrushed fake fingernails. Ugh. Geoff's siccing Julianne on it. She's going nuts with nothing to do but worry."

Keith took a deep breath while turning the page. "More from Mackie: Rosalie's Dad heard about the explosion on the radio, and came dashing down hotfoot to take care of his baby. Brynna's still shaking in a corner, but Mackie's got her in tow. Randy got Quinto released to Danny Rivera, and the two of them have gone fishing for the weekend."

"Wow," said Jeanie. "When Mackie gets moving, she doesn't let up for anything. Randy's not even Quinto's parole officer. I wonder how he shifted Mr. Maldonado."

"Maldonado's the one that wanted to put Rita through a metal detector, isn't he?"

"Well, actually, I may have exaggerated that incident just a bit."

Keith grinned at her. "Don't tell me. I liked your first version just fine. I read it to some of my friends, and they about died laughing."

"How's your father? Did you go by to see him?"

Keith's face stilled. "I talked to Nadezda. She says he's fine. Same as usual." His face tensed, but Jeanie put a finger over his lips. She ruffled his hair, and ran her hand down his cheek.

"You need to shave, Mr. Movie Star."

"No, I don't. They're only interested in my body—well, my arm, to be precise." He raised an eyebrow and took on a haughty look. "Including my elbow in the most recent soap commercial, you might want to know."

"Be still, my heart!"

He grinned at her and touched her hand. "I do love you,

mother mine. You drive me utterly insane, but I love you."

"The feeling is mutual, every bit of it, silly one."

After an hour, she managed to chase him off to her house, where he could catch a nap. He'd probably stay up late writing to Shell. She was glad he'd talked to Nadezda, and that Edward wasn't worrying about her. She touched the thought delicately, like a sore tooth, and shied away from it.

"Mrs. McCoy?"

Estelle wheeled herself in, holding herself at her most formal. She wore a bronze tweed suit jacket. From the waist down, a matching throw blanket covered her. Jeanie's eyebrows rose, and then lowered. "Nice outfit," she said. "Pendleton wool?"

"Naturally."

"Naturally," mocked Jeanie. They looked at each other.

Estelle coughed behind her hand. "You were right," she said.

"About what?"

"About my girls, about Bright Futures. It wasn't all of them. It wasn't even one of them. It was Ricardo Cervantes." She smiled. "You're so easy to read, Jeanie McCoy. Yes, of course, Brynna was involved. I'll never know how much. But I rather doubt, all in all, that she was to blame for much besides slipping out, perhaps arranging a drug deal or two. I suspect," she said deliberately, "that she can be rehabilitated, though I doubt I could do it myself. We have no rapport."

Jeanie discovered her mouth had dropped open. She shut it.

"Not, mind you, Mrs. McCoy, that I am by any means discarding the justice model in the juvenile system. I want to make that perfectly clear. Supposedly, they rehabilitated

At Risk of Being a Fool

Ricardo Cervantes, didn't they? Consequences for actions are the only provable—" Estelle's gaze fell to the blanket over the stump of her leg, and her voice broke, "provable means of—"

"Of preventing recidivism," offered Jeanie.

"Precisely," said Estelle, recovering.

"Hey," came a voice from the doorway. Sorrel strode in, glancing from Estelle to Jeanie. She hesitated, set her chin, and moved to the other side of the bed. "Sorry to interrupt, when you got a visitor and all, but I had to take the chance when I could get it, you know?"

"I'm glad you came, Sorrel. Were you hurt at all?"

"Not at all." Sorrel looked rueful, and then philosophical. No miscarriage, she meant. "God, can you believe that shit Ricardo? All those bombs. He was making them in his apartment, did you hear that? He had a stockpile in there, seven or eight more, the cops said. They had to evacuate the building just so they could search the place. Crazy. When did he find the time, that's what I want to know! Working a forty-hour week, doing community service, then flying the Five to get down here and bomb the shit out of everybody." She looked at Estelle, and seemed to consider. "I'm sorry you got so busted up. I hated your guts, but nobody deserves that. Good thing the bastard's dead."

Jeanie remained speechless. Trust Sorrel to sum the whole thing up in a few sentences.

Estelle unbent just a trifle. "I appreciate the sentiment, Miss Quintana. However, er, crudely expressed."

Sorrel rolled her eyes. "Some people never change, no matter what you do to them," she remarked. "But me, I'm changing. My whole family's changing. That's what I wanted to tell you, Jeanie. I talked to Mama last night—"

"Mrs. Cuthbert agreed to this long distance call?" said

Estelle in tones of polite interest.

"Estelle," said Jeanie. "Hush."

Sorrel grinned. "Well, yeah, actually, she did. There's stuff going on there, at Futures, you know? Anyway, I talked to Mama, and she said she'd check it out."

"Check what out?" Jeanie asked.

"Kherra says the Circle K by Oriole's Nest has an opening for a clerk, and that's what Mama does. And, I happen to know, 'cause I called him, your landlord has a two-bedroom unit open in that complex down the street from you, the one with the little playground? Top floor, right-hand side. So, if Mama gets the job, she, Tiffy, and Grandma are all moving down at the end of the month. If I pass my test—oh, hey! You didn't hear. I passed the Writing Test, Mackie found out yesterday, just before the bomb went off. Isn't that great!"

"Wonderful."

"Damned right. So that just leaves the math, and I figured maybe two more weeks, and then I've done the whole damned enchilada."

"Sorrel, one thing. The court job ends when you finish your GED."

"And that's another thing." said Sorrel, a magician pulling a rabbit out of a hat, "Kherra says—"

Jeanie was inured to the phrase, "Kherra says."

"—they're always short-handed at the Nest, and she can get me on permanently."

Despite a felony conviction? Kherra was pulling major strings. "You don't mind that?"

"Mind it? I'd love it. It's the best thing, Jeanie, I love it there. At the courthouse, they were always trying to find work for me to do, but at the Nest, there's so much to do, and no one has the time. It's a real job, Jeanie, not a play one."

At Risk of Being a Fool

"Not just a lot of butt-wiping?"

Sorrel threw back her head and laughed, a long roll of glee. "I can't believe you said that, Jeanie. Well, so what if there's a few butts to wipe? Those old ladies are worth the trouble."

"I'm proud of you," said Jeanie.

"Yeah, well. You don't mind?" Suddenly, Sorrel looked young. "Us moving in, down the street from you?"

"I'll be delighted to have you and your family as neighbors. All of your family."

"Yeah, good. So, that's okay, then. Besides, this way I can stay with Randy, not have to transfer or nothing." She looked at her sandals for a moment, looked up with a shy and delighted smile, turned, and disappeared through the door.

A faint frown creased Estelle's forehead. "Jeanie? Did you ever find out about the baby's father?"

"No. Kherra believes Sorrel thought he was the bomber, and she's greatly relieved that he wasn't. Beyond that, she won't say. Randy's figured out the pregnancy, but he's keeping quiet."

Estelle's glance was speculative. "I hope Randy isn't the father?"

"Hardly. She likes Randy. She even goes so far as to say he's not a shit, and if that's not conclusive, I don't know what is."

"And it wasn't Cervantes, either?"

Ricardo Cervantes. Jeanie covered her eyes with her hands. She'd met him, and he was dead now. She'd met him, and liked him, but he'd hated her.

"Jeanie?" The wheelchair rolled closer. "Jeanie, are you all right?"

"I'm sorry, Estelle. My injuries are nothing compared to

Jeanette Cottrell

yours. Lacerations, contusions, that's all. I shouldn't be such a wimp."

"Not to mention fifty stitches on your hip," said Estelle. "And a broken bone or two. I had a little chat with your nurse."

"Oh heavens, Estelle, don't go scaring off my nurses."

"All right."

The unusually quiet voice brought Jeanie to tears. "It's not that anyway, not the pain or the stitches. I just, somehow, can't deal with the fact that someone hates me. All my life, I've bothered people, pestered people, meddled with their lives. Always for their own good, I told myself. But now, I wonder. I meddled in Quinto's life, and his brother hated me. He wasn't just angry with me. He *hated* me."

"The man was certifiably insane, Jeanie." Estelle touched Jeanie's arm. "No one alive now hates you." She pulled out Jeanie's hand and trapped it between her own. "No one hates you, Jeanie. It is not remotely possible to hate you. I can tell you that for certain. I tried."

Estelle handed her a Kleenex, and she blew her nose. Obviously, it was a three-Kleenex job. Estelle pushed the box into her hands, and sat back.

"About that book you lent me," said Estelle.

"Which one?"

"The last one. Unalloyed, unabashed sentimentalism."

"What?"

"You heard me. Over-emotional tripe."

"How can you say that?" Face flushed with indignation, Jeanie threw the Kleenex box across the room. "Just what parts of Alex Haley's *Roots* do you consider over-emotional tripe?"

The smile on Estelle's face began slowly, spread wider,

At Risk of Being a Fool

reluctantly displayed her perfect teeth, and finally reached her eyes, sparkling.

"Ha," she crowed. "Gotcha!"

Once Jeanie was alone again, she wondered how she'd wangled a private room. She tussled with the idea for a moment and gave it up. Her mind was a marshmallow. Lightly toasted.

A glimmer of blue touched the sky. As she watched, clouds drifted across, obliterating it with the multi-layered silvered clouds, Oregon beauty at its finest. Some people thought the rains were depressing, but she'd always loved them. Some people thought being a teacher was depressing.

Some people were fools.

Twelve months of the year contained two months of summer, four months of rain, and six months of a brisk, breezy world of life, growing, ebbing, climbing, and falling. Teaching was the same.

Life is a potato. Her smile was fleeting. *Edward.*

She reached for Julianne's letter.

Dear Mama Jean:

When Geoff and I got married, you gave me a clump of your mother's calla lily. You about broke my heart, saying you wanted me to have it because I was your daughter now. Every time we moved, I divided the lily, and took part of it with me. Funny to think all the places your mom's lily is still growing, isn't it? I thought I'd send you a start for your new house.

I'm not good with words, like you and Aunt Shell. I don't know how to put this. But Papa Edward's not going to get better, and Aunt Shell's so far away, and Annalisa died, and I keep thinking that you must get lonely. I know you don't want to move to Florida, and haul Papa Edward so far. Geoff understands it too, really.

But Mama Jean, in your letters, it's as if you're hiding from us. They're funny, and I laugh, but I know there's a lot going on you don't tell us. Well, look at last spring. If Aunt Shell hadn't called, we still wouldn't know about Papa Edward.

You don't have to hide from us. You don't have to protect us anymore. I love you and admire you, and I really want to be your friend, and not just your daughter-in-law. So, when you plant this lily, please think of me? And maybe let me get a little closer to you?

Love always and forever, Julianne

Jeanie retrieved the box of Kleenex from the spot Estelle had parked it for safekeeping. She blew her nose loudly. *Can't I do anything but cry?* she thought disgustedly. Cry, weep, whimper, and scream. How had Edward put up with her, all those years?

Papa Edward's not going to get better.

Her children had lives of their own. Her own mother and mother-in-law had never quite stopped trying to bring her up. She'd sworn not to make the same mistakes. For years she'd watched, supported from afar, offered hints when asked, kept her mouth shut when she wasn't, and tried to spark laughter in the midst of their crises. And she'd been proud of that.

Anger surged. *That's not enough for you?* she thought at Julianne, thousands of miles away. *I take care of myself, and I manage just fine, thank you much. I don't need some little girl pulling at my heartstrings, urging me to open up and bleed all over everybody.*

Papa Edward's not going to get better.

At Risk of Being a Fool

She let the loss of Edward sweep over her. Kherra had spent months trying to make her see it. But all her life, when she was sick, the focus was on getting better. She hadn't been able to get past that. With Edward, getting better would never happen. If she were lucky, he'd hit a plateau and stay there for a while. Then with a lurch of a train, gearing down for a hill, he'd move slower, and slower, and finally stop altogether.

Edward was *not* going to get better.

What did that leave for a woman who watched, prodded, observed, meddled, and most of all fitted her life around other people? When she erupted with needs of her own, Edward soothed her, catered to her, infuriated her, and made her want to hit him. Like a padded cell, where it was all right to be crazy, Edward absorbed all the frenzied emotion of her life. Marriage worked that way, and hers had, for forty years.

Julianne was right. Apart from Shelley, she had no one with whom she could collapse into a pool of grieving Jell-O. She found her mind grappling with the image, distracting itself. Green Jell-O, she decided. Or perhaps butterscotch pudding.

. . . Think about letting me get a little closer to you?

Maybe. A little closer. Perhaps.

There was Julianne's box, on the floor under the table, with its plastic bag of dirt, holding a living offshoot of her mother's hopes and dreams, and then her own, and now Julianne's. How many generations before? How many in the future?

At the bottom of the typed letter was Julianne's signature, in blue ink, looping letters, rounded, and generous. She traced the outline with her finger.

Maybe, Julianne, she whispered. *I'll try.*

About the Author

JEANETTE COTTRELL has been a public school teacher for fifteen years. She teaches in an Oregon high school. *At Risk of Being a Fool* is her fourth book. She has also written an adult fantasy novel, and two children's novels. She lives with her family near Salem, Oregon.